BORDER GHOSTS

BORDER GHOSTS

DEPUTY RICOS TALE 4

BY

ELIZABETH A. GARCIA

IRON MOUNTAIN PRESS

HOUSTON, TEXAS

Border Ghost
Deputy Ricos Tale 4

First Printing
10 9 8 7 6 5 4 3 2 1

ISBN 13: 978-0-9905259-9-8

Edited by Lee Porche

Cover Concept by
Margarita Garcia

Illustrations by
Judy Singleton Probst

Iron Mountain Press
Houston, Texas

Dedication

There is no group of people more tenacious or harder-working than the Mexican people. This novel is dedicated to them and to Efrain Garcia Zapata, one of the finest human beings ever to come to the United States from anywhere.

Gracias por todo el amor, las experiencias, y las lecciones. Gracias especialmente por nuestra hija, Margarita Garcia, y por traer el hijo de nuestros corazones, Manuel Galindo, dentro de nuestras vidas. Thank you for all the love, the experiences, and the lessons. Thank you especially for our daughter, Margarita Garcia, and for bringing the son of our hearts, Manuel Galindo, into our lives.

Acknowledgements

My daughter Margarita Garcia designed the cover of this novel and nailed it on the first try. "What are your ideas for the cover, Mom?" she asks every time. She never fails to come up with something better than what I suggest. Thank you, Mija. I know you spend a lot of time and effort on my covers and thanking you in the front of the book doesn't really cut it.

Margarita, Amber, and my other "first readers" have read and continue to read millions of words on my behalf. Thank you from the bottom of my heart. Your encouragement and support keep me going and your astute observations and suggestions help me get things right.

Thank you, Skip Cottrell, for your support and for bugging me—"Did you write today?" Thank you for letting me to use your home as my private writing retreat and for allowing me to bounce ideas off your smart head.

I'm proud to have permission to use the original art of Judith S. Probst in my Deputy Ricos series. Her beautiful pen and ink drawings enhance any story I tell. Thank you, Judy!

My generous and talented friend Tim McKenna allowed me to use his photograph as my author photo. Thank you, also, to Julie McKenna for her help and for putting up with Tim and me. We took a trip into Basin of the Chisos Mountains in Big Bend National Park especially to get this photo. I can't look at it and not remember that perfect day spent with wonderful people.

I'm indebted to Jean Hardy-Pittman of Front Street Books in Alpine, Texas for her belief in me, for her (and her staff's) tireless promotion of my work.

I'm grateful for my two wonderful, wise sisters who have always cheered me on. They've put up with my wild tales since their births. Maybe they thought all kids had a big sister who made things up.

My editor, Lee Porche, is nit-picky and complimentary at the same time. She's a fan of Deputy Ricos, but she also whips her into shape. Lee is easy to work with and makes tedious work fun. Thank you for that, Lee, and for the attention you give to my manuscripts.

Tony Franco created my website and continues to help me with it. He gives excellent advice on technical things that make me tear at my hair. He's also a staunch supporter of me and promoter of my work. For all the things, thank you, Tony.

Although certain events in this novel are true, it is written as fiction. All names and most descriptions are fictitious. Any resemblance to a person living or dead or to an existing or long-gone ranching operation is also a coincidence. These things came from my imagination.

The most heartfelt thank-you of all goes to my readers. If nobody read my writing, what would be the point? Your appreciation of the Deputy Tales series spurs me on to more adventures.

In gratitude,

Beth Garcia
West Texas
November, 2014

The Works of Elizabeth A. Garcia, award winning author

One Bloody Shirt at a Time (Deputy Ricos Tale 1)
The Beautful Bones (Deputy Ricos Tale 2)
Darker Than Black (Deputy Ricos Tale 3)
Border Ghosts (Deputy Ricos Tale 4)
Hard Falls (Deputy Ricos Tale 5

and

The Reluctant Cowboy

Texas Authors Association Award for Crime Novel of the Year:

2014 winner: One Bloody Shirt at a Time
2015 winner: Border Ghosts

Beth can be found online at her personal website www.elizabethagarciaauthor.com and always through her Facebook page: www.facebook.com/ ElizabethAGarciaAuthor

In social media search for Ms. Garcia with the hash tag **#GARCIABOOKS**.

Chapter 1

The fiesta was over, the guests gone. A silvery, lopsided grin of a moon hung low in the clear winter sky. Dawn was not far off, and the night was cold and growing colder. Max's big stallion was jumpy with impatience, but Max was not ready to go.

"Whoa, Paco. Whoa, boy." Max shifted in the saddle, unzipped his jacket, checked his shirt pocket for nothing in particular, and re-zipped the jacket.

Lucia watched every move he made with eyes as black and star-filled as the night. "Thank you for everything, Max."

He smiled at her. "It was my pleasure, Lucia." Max had served as a *chambelan* at her *quinceañera*—one of her "court."

Quinceañera means "one who is fifteen," but it also refers to the special birthday party that marks the transition from childhood to womanhood. Once she is fifteen, a young woman is allowed to dance, date, and even to marry.

Lucia grinned up at Max. "The party was more fun than I imagined."

He laughed and agreed.

"The best part was dancing with you, Max."

He felt the same way and was still reeling from holding her so close. "I want to dance with you for the rest of my life, Lucia, but I have to go. I'll see you tomorrow." Still he lingered, adjusting this and that.

Lucia was wearing a pink ball gown, hand-stitched for this special occasion by her grandmother. It was not the stunning type of evening dress wealthy girls wore for their quinceañeras, but when

1

a person looked at Lucia, Max thought, they wouldn't even notice her clothes. Anything or nothing would suit such a beautiful girl.

The flimsy gown provided no protection from the cold, but Lucia's thoughts kept her warm. Today she was acknowledged as a woman, but she'd had womanly thoughts about Max for—how long? She looked at the ground so he wouldn't see the hot flush her desire put on her face.

Max couldn't delay his departure any longer. Her father would come looking for her soon. His brothers had returned home half an hour ago, and that would cause his parents to worry.

He bent down to straighten a stirrup. "Good night, Lucia."

She surprised him when she placed her soft lips on his and gave him the kiss she had dreamed of, long and tender and hungry. One hand caressed the back of his neck and with the other she steadied herself against the flank of the horse.

Max jumped down and took her into his arms. He knew her father might see them, but he couldn't stop himself.

"Lucia, Lucia," he whispered.

She moved her hands to his back and pressed him closer.

"Oh, I adore you, Lucia."

"And I adore you, Max."

From somewhere nearby her father coughed as he approached. "Buenas noches, Max," he said as he stepped into view. "We'll see you tomorrow."

"Buenas noches, señor."

Señor Rodriguez put his arm around his daughter. When he did, she turned back to Max. "Don't ever forget, Max."

"I won't, Lucia. How would I?"

As her father led her to the house, Max heard him ask, "Don't forget what?"

"That's between Max and me, Papi."

Max stood rooted to the spot, watching with his heart pounding in his ears, until they disappeared into the house. What he was never to forget was a promise he made when they were children, to marry Lucia. Of course he wouldn't forget, and he knew she wasn't worried that he would. It was her secret way of saying she loved him with all her heart.

He didn't move for a long time. Even though it was January and freezing, the night seemed filled with the sweet scent of honeysuckle.

Chapter 2

Barney and I were huddled with Mitch on the shoulder of a road that had become, in my mind, Desolation Drive. Blood soaked our clothing, and I could feel its stickiness in my hair. A northerly wind howled and blew dust in our faces. I shivered and blinked back tears.

Mitch put his arm around me and drew me to his side. "We did everything humanly possible, Margarita. You understand that, right?"

"I know, Mitch."

My friend Mitch Dalton is the head paramedic of Terlingua Fire & Emergency Medical Services. He was used to tragedies in a way, but of course he never truly gets used to them. No one does.

Barney, my fellow deputy, stepped away from us to yell, "Keep it moving!" at a gawking motorist. The vehicle sped on. Few people will argue with *"El Grandote."* He hunched against the wind and trudged back to us.

Four broken bodies had broken our hearts. An entire family had died because of abject stupidity mixed with alcohol. Harry Bledsoe, the husband and father of the family, still smelled of bourbon, even over the pervasive odor of his blood.

Harry was known to treat our up-and-down, curving highways as a NASCAR speedway, but he lacked the skill and mental acuity of a professional driver. He'd been stopped, warned, and had even received citations for his speed. Citing speeders goes against my moral code because I love to speed, but I had given him two. There's speeding and there's speeding with small children in your vehicle.

4

Barney had summed him up in three words as we peeled his body from the pavement, "Poor dead dumbass." Harry had crashed through the windshield and skidded along the asphalt; the result wasn't something you want me to describe.

My big ol' partner had clawed his way barehanded into twisted wreckage and dragged out two of the victims. One was the mother, who had died as we laid her on the stretcher, and the other was a child of six who had died in Barney's arms. The other child, age two, had been thrown into a ditch and was dead when I found her. I only thought to search for her because I knew the family, and they wouldn't have left her at home.

"Let me look at you again," Mitch said to Barney, whose hands were torn and cut and bleeding through a temporary bandage. "Better yet, let's go back to the clinic and I'll fix 'em up right."

Everyone agreed because standing in a freezing wind feeling desolate wasn't helping anyone, alive or dead. As Barney put it, "If we freeze and fall over by the road, then *we'll* be poor dead dumbasses." He's eloquent like that. But he did have a point.

Mitch drove away in the ambulance with the bodies. Both the local J.P. and the hearse from Alpine would meet him at the Fire & EMS office.

I walked to my car and Barney followed. "Thanks for coming, Ricos."

"Of course I came, Barney. You call, I come. Isn't that how it works?"

"Yes, but technically I wasn't supposed to call you."

"Who cares about technicalities?'"

"Well…"

I was on a temporary leave of absence, forced on me by the boss. "Sheriff Ben doesn't have to know every little thing that goes on here."

He grinned and shivered with equal intensity. "Right, Pard."

"Go home, Barney. You look like you murdered someone with an axe."

"And it appears you helped me."

I smiled at him and pulled away.

I hadn't driven but a few miles when I had a flat. My papi had told me to get the tire changed but I ignored his warning. Maybe the sheriff was right; I didn't listen. I got out to change the blasted thing, but I stared at it because doesn't that come first when changing a flat? Step One: stare hatefully at the offending tire. I wanted to kick it to shreds.

I started sobbing and couldn't stop, even when a truck pulled in behind my Mustang. I didn't want to look up; I wanted it to go away. Then things worsened.

"What's goin' on here?" The voice belonged to Wynne Raymore, my sometimes adversary/sometimes ally who is aggravating at all times, no matter which thing he's being. Usually he's somewhere between the two. Even he doesn't know where we stand most of the time.

Wynne is a 30-something-year-old sometimes-misogynist and avid follower of the Rush Limbaugh scream-and-rant-and-blame-all-the-wrong-people philosophy. But Wynne's not stupid except when it serves him. One time when he was grabbing me and being a jerk, I had no choice but to defend myself. In the scuffle I damaged his knee and broke his nose. Since then we'd reached a détente.

He repeated his question about what was going on, even though it must have been obvious. A woman with a flat tire was losing it on the highway.

"Nothing," I claimed without looking up.

"Are you crying?"

"No."

He took a deep breath. "Okay, let me rephrase that. Are you crying?"

"I said no; I'm not." I wiped my eyes on the sleeve of my jacket and turned to face him because I remembered I'm an adult.

"Holy shit, girl," he gasped when he saw the blood. "Who'd you kill?"

"Oh, it was just some guy hassling me."

He didn't buy that, but he changed the tire. It was a favor I appreciated more than I was able to articulate at that moment, except for, "Thank you, Wynne."

"Let's get a cup of coffee," he suggested as he wiped his grimy hands with a rag. "You're trembling from the cold." He gave me a sideways look. "Or else I'm starting to get to you."

"I can't go anywhere like this," I said, indicating my goriness.

"Oh hell, let 'em wonder what we've been doing." Then he asked, "What have you been doing?"

"I was called to an accident."

"I assume people were injured?"

My mouth opened but nothing came out.

"Sorry," he said. "That was a stupid thing to say."

I got back in my car. Wynne followed and stood at the door. "Can you tell me who was involved in the accident?"

"The Bledsoe family was killed, Wynne."

"Oh, that's terrible. Was he drinking?"

"The sheriff will release the details later today. I can't tell you anything until after that."

"I heard you weren't working now. Some deputy from Alpine is coming down. Are you going up there to work?"

"I'm taking a leave of absence for a few weeks," I admitted, even though I was sure he knew that.

"That's good." He leaned against the door. "You've definitely earned one."

When I looked up at Wynne, I thought I'd see a smirk. What I saw on his face was kindness, pure and simple. It was so unexpected I nearly started crying again.

He put his hand on my shoulder. "I know people are talking, but not everybody is against you. I hope you know you have friends."

"Thank you, Wynne. I do know that."

He started to say something but instead said, "So. Coffee?"

"I have to get cleaned up. You could come to my house." Then I could not believe I had invited Wynne Raymore to my house. It had to be PTSD, or else I had lost my mind.

He wiggled his eyebrows.

"If you can behave like a friend and not a lecher, I'll make you coffee."

"You kill all the fun with your damn rules," he grumped.

"Yeah, well, take it or leave it."

"I'll be nice."

"Want to follow me?"

"Sure, but I know where you live. Everybody knows where you live."

Great.

I showered and went back into the kitchen.

"You look pretty damn wonderful when you're not blood-spattered and crying your eyes out," Wynne commented.

"Thanks." I fixed myself a cup of tea and sat beside him at the table.

"Are you all right?"

"Yes. Thank you for asking. I'm still kind of shell-shocked."

"Do you want to talk about the accident? Your feelings about it, I mean."

"No. It was awful. I'd like to forget it for a while. Why don't you tell me about your week?"

"Nah." He stirred more cream into his mug. "It was boring."

"Just tell me anything. I need to think about something not gruesome. How is your kitty?"

Wynne brightened at the mention of his cat. "Oh, Fluffy is fat and happy, probably fatter than the last time you saw him."

I laughed at that. "What else is going on?"

"Okay, you're bound to hear about it sooner or later." He fidgeted and turned bright red. "I got a job."

"Why is that embarrassing to you?"

"I hate it when people mess with me about it."

"Why are they messing with you?"

"Well duh. I got a job."

"Congratulations. I think it's great."

"Don't you wanna hear what I'm doing first?"

"Sure. What are you doing?"

"I'm stocking product at the grocery store."

"That's not shameful, you know. It's honorable and you should be proud to be doing something useful."

"As opposed to—"

"Drinking beer all day and holding belching contests and hassling people."

"Yeah, I knew you'd think that, you bein' the law and all."

"It has nothing to do with the law. I'm a woman. I shop in that store, and I don't like to be hassled."

"Yes, I know. I have a crooked nose to prove it."

"Your nose is perfect."

"You think? You're just saying that because your mom set it." My mother is the local doctor.

"Ask anybody and they'll tell you your nose is as good as ever."

"That's easy for you to say, Karate Kid."

I shrugged. "Don't mess with a woman who knows self-defense."

"I gave up doing that." He paused, but not for long. "Let's just get to the point."

"And that is?"

"Some people say you're still affiliated with a cartel and you have no business staying in law enforcement."

I had fallen in love with the wrong man. I took his word that he was with the D.E.A. How would I have known he was a prominent member of the Martez Cartel?

"And I guess you're one of them," I said in response to Wynne's comment.

"Oh, hell no!" He shoved the mug so hard coffee sloshed onto the table. "I'm not that big of an asshole. Anybody with any sense knows you'd never get messed up in that cartel shit, even for the sake of a man. I should say especially not for a man."

"I didn't know who he was when I fell in love with him."

"I figured that."

I stared into my tea. "I thought he was with the D.E.A. until two government agencies came looking for me."

"I know. People here talk out their asses. You know that, right?"

"I wish people would talk to me instead of whispering behind my back about things they don't know. Who in this place doesn't know how I feel about drugs? I hate everything they stand for and, more than anything, what they've done to Mexico."

"We know it so well most of us could deliver that rant for you."

I smiled at him. "Good."

"So, what I think is you just have to keep going. Do what you know is right. When all is said and done, everyone knows who you are. You grew up here, for crying out loud. This shit storm will pass, like they always do."

"I believe that, but I want to say one more thing. If you tell this to people that'd be fine, in fact, I want you to."

"Okay."

"There are two things. I only saw the good side of Emilio Martez, and that was the man I fell in love with. The second thing is that he was gunned down by federal agencies from both sides of the river. In other words, the man is dead. Can't they let him rest?"

"I'm sorry he died, Margarita."

"Thank you, Wynne."

"When you feel better, I'd like to take you to dinner."

"When I feel better, I'll go."

"For real?"

"Yes. For real."

He fiddled with the coffee a while and then, "What I think is it's a lot of men whining because you went out with a stranger nobody knew and you won't go out with them."

"You're kidding. Really?"

"Yes. Really." He smiled and it was bright and from his heart. "Keep your pecker up, Deputy Ricos. You're gonna be fine. Truth is you're already fine."

Chapter 3

Max's father stepped into the bedroom shared by his three sons and saw that Max had returned from Lucia's party. His youngest boy was bent over a notebook of figures while the other two slept.

"You should be in bed, Hijo. It's so late."

Max shut the book, frustrated because he still didn't have enough money to get married. "Papa, let's go to the kitchen."

They sat at the table and his father looked at him, expecting something was coming.

Max took a deep breath. "I've decided I'm going to the United States to work."

"Oh Son, please not this again. I don't want you to go. Life is so hard there for Mexicans."

"I know, but it's hard here, too. If I go, it means my brothers can share the ranch with you. They can marry and have families. My share of our land and profit can go to them. You'll all be better off if I raise a family in the U.S. We just don't have enough here to support so many families. Times are hard."

"I know, son."

His father looked so sad it made Max's heart hurt. "I'll come back to visit."

"What about Lucia?"

"I'll definitely be back for her."

"So you would take her to the U.S.?"

"Yes, after I get settled."

"Your mother will take this hard, Max."

"I know, but you can help her understand."

"You know we want you to be happy and live your own life. If moving to the United States is your plan, we'll support you. But Max, it can be so dangerous."

"Yes, Papa, I've heard the stories. I promise I'll be careful."

"You say that, Son, but you don't even know all the dangers you'll face."

"I want to go; I need to go. Please support me in it."

"You'll have to protect Lucia."

"Yes sir. I know what I have to do."

"Just think about this before you decide anything."

"I have thought about it. It seems like the only way."

"Alfredo died trying to make a new life in the U.S." Alfredo was Max's cousin.

"I'm not going to use a coyote."

Alfredo had gone two years earlier, but he'd done it using the services of a coyote—a shadowy man who moved undocumented workers from one place to another after helping them cross the border. Alfredo paid what seemed a fortune to be transported from the Rio Grande to a ranch near Dallas where he had been offered work. Their cousin Augustín was already there with his family. The coyote had transported Alfredo eighty miles from the river before leaving the group locked in the back of an old bread van while he waited for a sign that the road was free of the Border Patrol agents who patrolled it.

There were no windows and no way to move air, and most had died from the heat and lack of water. The coyote had abandoned the van or else something had happened to him. They would never know.

"If you don't use a coyote, how will you get there?" asked his father.

"I'll walk."

"But Max, the ranch is near Dallas!"

"Stop worrying, Papa. I'll figure out a way."

"You're asking a lot of Lucia. She won't want to leave her family."

"She loves me and wants to make a life with me."

"I know, son. We'll talk more about it in the morning. Now you need to get some sleep, and so do I."

"I won't change my mind."

"No, I expect you won't. Did you have fun at the party?"

"Oh yes."

His father laughed and ruffled his hair. *"Buenas noches, Hijo. Te quiero."*

"Buenas noches, Papa. I love you, too."

Max crawled into bed, but he couldn't stop thinking of kissing Lucia.

Soon after the quinceañera, Max went to work for Lucia's father, Antonio Rodriguez. He was thinking about the party and about dancing with Lucia while he worked with a new colt in the Rodriguez barn.

Lucia crept in without making a sound, tiptoed to where he stood, and put her arms around his waist from behind. She pressed her body against him. "Don't speak," she whispered, as if he could have.

Max turned to face her, but her eyes darted up to the hay loft. She put her fingers against his lips and, with the other hand, pointed. Then she bolted up the wooden steps and lay on her stomach at the edge, grinning. He glanced around and then dashed up after her.

It was cold in the drafty barn, but she unzipped her jacket, unbuttoned her shirt, and put his hands against her warm breasts.

"Lucia—"

"Hush, Max. Don't you want to?"

It was practically all he thought about. "Yes," he croaked, "but I don't know what to do."

14

She whispered against his ear. "Don't you think we can figure it out?"

He hoped so and answered her with kisses. He couldn't believe he had his hands on Lucia's breasts. He had dreamed it, tried to imagine the feel of them, and made up various scenarios in which he not only touched them but ravished her.

As he caressed and fondled her, she whimpered and flattened herself against him. "Don't stop doing that, Max."

"I won't." He felt awkward and so aroused he couldn't think.

"I love you, Max." Lucia placed her small hand on his, giving him encouragement he didn't need.

"I love you, too, Mi Amor."

Lucia sat partway up. "Let's take off all our clothes," she suggested with a seductive smile. "You take off mine, and I'll help you take off yours."

That lasted ten seconds before they stripped off their own clothes and tossed them aside. They groped and felt and explored each other until they were sweating and breathless. Max was afraid he wouldn't be able to wait, but before long Lucia lay back against the straw and begged him to go ahead and do it.

It was over too soon for her, but after he got his breath, Lucia took his hand and showed him what to do. She cried, "Max, Max, Max," as if he would be lost to her. She moaned and writhed, and after a while, sighed and snuggled against him.

After they cuddled a few minutes, Max began to stroke her breasts. "Lucia," he whispered, "do you want to do it again?"

"Oh yes, Max. I never want to stop."

He grinned into her hair.

"Max, you won't stop loving me when I'm old, will you?"

"I can't imagine ever not loving you, Mi Amor. How would I be able to stop?"

"I don't want you to stop."

"I promise to love you until the day I die—and even after that."

Lucia giggled.

"Didn't it hurt you?" he asked a few minutes later.

"A little, but it felt so good I didn't want you to quit."

Max wanted to make love to her again and talk about marriage and going to the United States and making a plan for their lives, but the heavy door scraped open, and Lucia's father entered the barn.

Chapter 4

A week later the weather had warmed enough to spend time on my bluff. I laid out a sleeping bag and got lost in the scenery. From that height, Terlingua is a dot in a landscape as vast as the sky. In the grand scheme of things, petty gossip seems as insignificant as it is. My mountains trump a lot of bullshit.

I pulled my jacket tight, rolled onto my stomach, and rested my head on my hands. I was in that place between awake and asleep, when I felt more than heard someone else. I opened one eye, but all I saw at first were brown leather boots. They were too small to belong to Barney, the wrong style to be the sheriff's, a little larger than my papi's would be, and they weren't my friend Craig's. He wears combat boots most of the time.

"I don't guess anybody comes up here by accident." My out-of-breath father plopped down beside me. I don't know him well because he's not the man who raised me. Miguel Ricos, my papi, raised me. Zeke Pacheco fathered me, biologically speaking.

I tried to smile. It does take effort to visit my bluff if you don't have an ATV or a helicopter. The rough road is also steep, and its location is obscure.

"How did you find me?"

"I went by your office and talked to your partner. He thought you might be up here. Man, this is some kind of gorgeous. Is all of it yours?"

"Why are you here?"

"Some daughters would be happy to see their dad."

I didn't feel like being nice to him or anyone else.

"I'm happy to see you, Zeke." It didn't sound convincing, but it was the best I could do on short notice.

"The hell you are." He laughed. "I'm trying not to be offended."

17

"Why are you here really?"

"I want you to come to Dallas with me."

"Dallas?"

"You've heard of it, I presume?"

I gave him a look.

"I'll be there a week to teach a course on criminal investigations for the Dallas Police Department." My father is a Texas Ranger who lives in Austin. He heads up a UCIT (Unsolved Crimes Investigative Team) which takes him all over the state.

"And you want me to take your course?"

"No. I want to spend time with my daughter. Sheriff Ben told me he put you on a three-week leave."

"He thinks I have a bad attitude."

"What he thinks is that you've been through hell and you need to recuperate. He suspects you're wallowing in pain and self-pity."

"He sure thinks a lot."

Zeke sighed and looked away. I thought he was admiring Cimarron Mountain, a perfect and beautiful example of a wild, rugged, heart-of-the-desert mountain. It's mine, but nobody acknowledges that but me. My ownership is the heart-and-soul variety. It wouldn't stand up in court.

"Sheriff Duncan cares about you, Margarita."

"Please, Zeke. Spare me."

He lay down next to me, propped on one elbow, and looked right into my face. He took a breath and let it out slowly. "This is how I see it. You can stay up here all alone on your mountain and make yourself sick with your black thoughts. You can number and catalog all the reasons you hate everybody alive and wallow in self-pity until you jump right off this cliff. Or you can accompany me to Dallas where you might have fun. I know some nice places, and the trip will be my treat."

"What places?"

"So you're coming?"

"I guess so."

"Is that the best you can do?"

"Yippee."

"Maybe we should just forget it."

"I can't be excited right now."

"Are you still in pain?" He referred to my shoulder, which had taken a bullet three months before.

I shook my head no. "I'm back to running. It's the pain in my heart that won't..." My voice broke.

"Aw, Sweetheart, that takes longer, I know." He jumped up, pulled me to my feet, and hugged me. In spite of his lack of experience, Zeke Pacheco knew how to be a father when a daughter needed him.

"What is that one called?" Zeke asked.

I turned my head to see where he was pointing. "That's Maverick Mountain. Isn't it stunning?"

"Very, but everything I see is stunning."

That's true. My mesa is one-hundred percent out-of-this-world for magnificent views in all directions as far as the eye can see.

"When did you buy this land?"

"I didn't buy it, Zeke. A man gave it to me a while back for doing some detective work. He appreciated what I did."

"He sure knows how to show his gratitude."

"Yes, he's a generous man. It was a total surprise."

"Does he live here?"

"No. He lives in Wyoming."

"Is he wealthy?"

"Yes, and in a lot of ways. He's an incredible man."

"And he doesn't interest you?"

I laughed. "He would, but he's older than either of my fathers. Besides, he has a wife he adores."

"Okay. I'm just thinking of your best interests."

"Thanks, but I can take care of myself."

He looked doubtful and started to speak, but he wisely let it pass. Maybe it was more kind than wise, but my father seemed to be both.

After a few more minutes of taking in the Terlingua/Cimarron Mountain side, we moved the sleeping bag to the other side of the mesa. We let our legs dangle off the edge while we admired Big Bend National Park's skyline. Mountain after butte after cliff after mesa after mineral-painted hills and more mountains; it goes on and on. If you can watch the display for five minutes and not think or say, "Oh my God," I'll do your laundry for a month.

"Are you building a house?" Zeke indicated the bare beginnings of one large room and a porch.

"It belongs to my friend Craig."

"He's the older man you care for?"

"Yes, but we take care of each other."

"Where is he?"

"He's somewhere out in the desert."

"That narrows it down."

I laughed, but I had learned to live with the fact that Craig was always "somewhere out there."

"It's interesting that the porch is all but completed," Zeke observed, "but the house has been started and nothing more."

"That's because Craig likes to be outside. The only reason we're making an enclosed space is because I insisted. When it gets cold again, maybe he'll sleep inside. I want to know that he has a warm place to go. Sometimes the wind screams up here, and it can rain or snow. A sleeping bag under the stars won't cut it."

"He must be a tough old guy."

I laughed. "You have no idea." After a pause, I said, "Okay, Zeke. Why are we going to Dallas? You might not know this, but it's always better to tell the truth to your kid."

He laughed. "I chose Dallas because I have to go there. I invited you because you need a break from here, and I'd like to have you with me."

"Was this Sheriff Ben's idea?"

"No. It definitely was not his. He doesn't know anything about my schedule. I want to get to know my daughter better. Why is that a crime?"

"It's not a crime. It's a sweet idea. I guess I don't trust anybody."

"That's another reason to come with me. You can trust me, Margarita. I love you and want to know you better. I thought we could have some fun."

"Thank you, Zeke."

"It'll soon be February, and the weather might not be too bad."

I laughed. "That could go either way."

"There's one more thing."

"What's that?"

"I need your help, but only if you're interested."

"What is it?"

"I have a longtime friend named Edmundo Valentino whose son Francisco is in prison for killing his family. He swears the boy is innocent because he would never do such a heinous thing. I asked Ed to send me a copy of the trial transcript and told him I'd investigate if anything about the trial seemed suspicious."

"So something was wrong with the trial?"

"Several things were wrong. Francisco did not have solid legal representation. Whether his attorney was a public defender or appointed by the court, I'm not sure. Either way, the man was a poor excuse for a lawyer. The prosecution submitted their evidence, boom, boom, boom, and the defense never countered with much."

"Maybe he thought the evidence proved him guilty beyond a shadow of doubt."

"Since when does that stop an attorney from going all-out for his client?"

"It's not supposed to work like that, even if he is guilty," I said.

"Yes; I know. It all boiled down to money. The Valentino family doesn't have any, or not enough to pay a top-notch lawyer."

"You get what you pay for in attorneys too, I guess."

"That's exactly right."

"What else?"

"Francisco Valentino was tried for the rape of his wife, her murder, and the murders of his two small children."

"How horrible."

"He's been in the state prison three months, serving life without parole. But listen to this. His was not the only semen found in the wife. It never seemed to occur to the defense attorney or the police to question the full range of possible implications of that. The donor of the second sample might've been the perpetrator. I read through the transcript twice looking for a suggestion of that."

"You found nothing?"

Zeke nodded. "Because I'm not a trial attorney and have little experience with transcripts, I read it a third time. It seems like finding two samples of semen in the woman could've meant more than 'Mrs. Valentino had a lover, and her husband caught them and went berserk and killed his entire family.' If that's what happened, he murdered his sleeping babies."

"Why would a man kill his children because his wife cheated on him? It doesn't make any sense."

"The theory was that he went crazy when he found her with another man and killed everyone in a rage. It's hard to buy if you know his family background. I've known Kiko—Francisco— since he was a kid. And there are so many questions. Who was TOD?" TOD means The Other Donor. "What is his background?

Where was he when the murders occurred? Why wasn't he put on the stand?"

"What do you want me to do?"

"I want you to gather as much information as you can while I'm teaching. You could visit Kiko, interview his family members, and try to track down the unknown semen donor. Somebody has to know something, and that'll give us a place to start. I'll help as much as time allows."

"This isn't a Texas Rangers investigation?"

"No, it's not yet. This is me and you, if you'll agree, doing a personal favor for a friend. Depending on what we find, we might be able to turn it over to one of the law enforcement agencies. What do you think?"

"I'll do it, Zeke. I would love to go with you to Dallas."

My father had thrown me a lifeline, and even with a broken heart and a head full of dark thoughts, I knew enough to grab it.

Chapter 5

Max and Lucia froze. They went from heavy breathing to barely breathing.

"Max, are you in here?" Antonio Rodriguez called.

The lovers were naked and their clothes were strewn all over. Lucia's underwear was dangerously close to the edge of the loft. If her father looked up and saw his daughter's panties, Max was dead. No doubt.

"He isn't supposed to be here," Lucia whispered after her father had gone. "He was going to Chihuahua today."

"I'd better get dressed and find him. You get out when you can."

"I might be here all night."

"In that case, I'll come back later."

Lucia grinned and threw his shirt at him.

Max dressed quickly and scrambled down the ladder in record time. He found Sr. Rodriguez working in the yard at his house. Max felt sick with guilt and dread.

Lucia's father looked up at him. "Oh—there you are, Max."

"Yes sir. Were you looking for me?"

Lucia's father wheeled around. "You know damn well I was. I was in the barn, as were you and Lucia. What are your intentions with my daughter?"

"Well I—I want to marry her, sir. I love Lucia more than anything."

Max spoke so earnestly it was difficult for the older man to be hard on him. He knew that the only thing Lucia wanted was to make a life with her Max.

"Go get Lucia from the loft and bring her to the house."

Max flushed crimson. "Yes sir."

When Max headed back to the barn, Antonio Rodriguez smiled in spite of himself.

The two young people stood in front of Lucia's parents in their kitchen. Max was so nervous he felt like he was going to throw up.

"Lucia," her father barked, "this young man has asked for your hand in marriage. Do you intend to marry him?"

"Oh, yes. You know that, Papi. I told you a long time ago."

"You're too young."

"You married mama when she was fifteen."

"She was almost sixteen."

Lucia gave her father a look of exasperation. "Papi, you aren't going to tell Max no, are you?"

"No. Max is a good man, and it seems you've already committed to him."

"That's none of your business!"

"Then take your business out of my barn!"

Lucia's mom blushed. "Antonio…"

He ignored his wife and turned back to Max. "How will you support a family?"

Max didn't want to lay out his idea to go to the U.S. until he'd talked to Lucia and they made plans together. "I'll work hard. I've been saving money since I was twelve. I'll do whatever I have to do to support my family. You know me, sir. I'm a hard worker."

"Indeed you are, Max, but you're young to take on so much responsibility."

"Maybe so, but I am responsible. I'm seventeen, and I don't take marriage with Lucia lightly."

"Are you prepared to be a father?"

"Yes sir. I want to be a father."

"Max, you don't know how weighty a responsibility being a father is."

"I have a pretty good idea, sir."

Lucia had had enough. "Papi, we're already married by Mexican custom."

"Lucia!" her mother gasped.

Max couldn't believe she would say such a thing to her father.

She shrugged. "Well? That's how most people around here get married."

"I want to marry you in a church," Max blurted. He took her hand. "I want a proper marriage. I want to live with you forever, and I want God to bless us."

"We are already blessed," she said softly.

It was not unusual for the poor country people of México to marry in their teens. They had to grow up at a young age and be responsible for their own lives.

Two weeks later, Max and Lucia were married in the small church in the nearby village with their families and best friends present. Lucia wore a soft, simple, white dress made for her by her mother.

When they met at the church that day, Max's heart nearly stopped when he saw his bride. He couldn't believe that such a kind, happy, beautiful woman would want to marry him. He was plain and not as handsome as many of the young men in the village. Yet Lucia had chosen him.

Lucia was so happy she thought her heart would burst. Of all the men in the world, she had fallen in love with the best. Max's heart was true and kind. He was happy and full of ideas and adventure. He was a hard worker. His body was lean and muscular. How could a woman do better than Max?

Chapter 6

My mother the doctor notices any little thing. If my eyes aren't bright enough to suit her, or I look pale or lose weight, or my hair's not shiny, or if I seem distant, she starts; her trained eyes miss nothing.

Mom had been bugging me to come by, so I thought I should go before I left town. I visited her that evening and went in the back door calling, "Mom!"

She was in the kitchen making a salad. When it comes to eating, my papi's house is the place to be, but I didn't care about food.

"Hi Mom." I gave her the biggest smile I could muster.

She knew that all was not well. She hugged me and it was amazing that she offered me a salad instead of advice.

"Is there something I can do to help you?"

"You could cut up some cucumber. Here's a knife and cutting board."

"I saw Zeke today."

"You did? How is he?"

"He's fine. He's taking me to Dallas. I'm meeting him in Alpine tomorrow."

"What's he doing in Alpine?"

"He's tying up loose ends on an unsolved case he's been working. Tomorrow he's going to Dallas to teach a class in investigative procedure to the Dallas Police. It'll start Monday and he wants me to go along."

"And attend the course?"

"No. He says he wants to get to know me, and we're going to have fun."

"Zeke is a lot of fun."

"Well, I guess so, but I'm talking about father-daughter fun, not Stephanie Ricos let's-take-our-clothes-off-and-go-crazy fun."

27

Mom smacked me with a dish towel. "You can make fun of me all you want, but you have to admit the man is a hunk."

"You're talkin' about my daddy."

Mom laughed, but ten seconds later she took a deep breath and said, "Don't you think you need to talk to somebody? You weren't doing well in the first place, and then you attended that horrible accident. What I think is—"

"Stop it, Mom. I'm fine."

"You're lying. I think it will be good for you to go with Zeke. You have to stop being so distant and sad, and you look like hell—"

"Gee, thanks, Mom."

"Do not interrupt me!"

I lifted my hands in surrender.

"You're beautiful, but you seldom bother to comb your hair these days. You spend all your time hiding up on that mountain of yours."

"I'm not hiding."

"What did I just say? Let me speak!"

I made a zipping motion on my mouth.

"This community needs you. Sure, people talk, but soon they'll move on to someone else. All this bullshit will pass. The truth is I don't think there's another person in Brewster County who could do the job you do as well as you do it and with flair that is yours alone."

"Spoken like a true mother."

"Yes, I'm your mother, but even if I wasn't, I would see who you are. You care about these folks even though they gossip about you."

"Mom, please, you're off the deep end."

Poor Mom; she looked exasperated. She continued, but on a different line. "I think it'll be good for you to get away with Zeke. You'll see things you haven't seen before. Zeke does know Dallas."

"That's what he said."

"If you're not hiding on your mesa, what are you doing up there?"

"I write, look at the scenery, and think. Sometimes I'm hiding."

"What are you writing?"

"I'm just scribbling down some thoughts about the last few months."

"That's good; it'll help you process your loss."

I shrugged.

"Will it be a novel?"

"I don't know. Do you think it'll be too dark if I tell the truth?"

"I think you should tell it like it happened, but that's just my opinion."

"Yeah; otherwise, what's the point? I just wish I could change the ending."

Mom brushed hair back from my face with her fingers. "I wish so too, Baby."

She had made that affectionate gesture for as long as I could remember.

A beat or two later, she said, "Maybe while you're in Dallas you could check in with an AA meeting, just to see what it's about. Nobody there will know you, and it might help to speak your mind to people who understand."

"But Mom, I'm not drinking."

"I know, but you want to, don't you?"

"Yes."

"Well, think about it. Try it once."

"Okay, Mom. I will."

"Do you promise?"

"Please don't make me promise something I can't promise. If I promise you and then I don't go, I'll be even more depressed, and that'll make me drink."

She sighed. "I just wish I could help you."

"I'm sorry, Mom. I have to help myself. I know you love me,

and that's enough. Keep on loving me no matter what, and I'll be okay. That, I can promise."

Later that evening, my papi was just as difficult to deal with as my mother, but he served better food.

The next morning, I went by the office to say good-bye to Barney. Mostly I wanted him to see that I was still alive and not crying, and that I had bathed and fixed my hair.

When I opened the front door, he came out of my office looking sheepish. I'd caught him at something.

"Why are you in my office?"

"It's county property. Officially, it doesn't belong to you."

"You'd better tell me what's going on."

He plopped down in his chair. "Oh, hell." My partner blushed.

Whoa. "You better not be looking up porn sites on my computer."

"You know, you're really pissing me off."

"What else is new?"

"The truth is I was looking out your window."

"Ah."

He held up his bandaged hands. "It's hard for me to use a computer right now."

"Are you in a lot of pain?"

"Not too bad. Better. Anyhow, real men don't whine."

I had a wisecrack but he stopped it by saying, "I don't like to admit you're right about something, but I can see why you like to sit by that window. Things are kind of sad and bare out there right now, yet there's a beauty about it that speaks to—" He stopped abruptly.

"Go on. I love it when you talk like a poet."

"You know what? I don't miss you, not at all."

"Thank you. I don't miss you, either."

"You look better than the last time I saw you."

"Thanks. I came to tell you I'm going to Dallas with Zeke. He's teaching a class for the Dallas Police, and he invited me to come along. He says we'll have fun."

"Well, I hope you do, Ricos."

"I hope things go well for you while you're stuck here not missing me."

He made a smart-mouthed comment, but I went into my office and sat in the old chair. Ancient is a better word for it. The chair is overstuffed and covered with a flowery print that was probably never popular anywhere at any time. Some would say my chair is past its prime, but it's as comfortable as an old pair of cutoffs. Anyway, it's not about the chair. It's about the view from the window next to it.

When I looked out I breathed a sigh of relief. Everything was perfect. I always think something will be wrong, as if the scene needs my help. It never needs a thing from me, which is one of the qualities that make it so wonderful.

Most of the trees were leafless and the grasses dry and brown; winter does that to growing things, but everything was still exactly right. Without all the greenery sticking up and out all over the place, the rocky slopes of the hill could be seen more clearly. Some of the broken-off boulders are rough, angular, and broken along their edges. Others are rounded and polished-looking. Brutal extremes of weather and the slow, determined passage of time are what polish them.

Cactus Hill is the name I gave it, and I don't know if it has another name. It's a cactus- and boulder-strewn mountain of the short, wide variety. A giant, ragged chunk of reddish-brown rock sits on top of it like a crown. In many ways, the scene out my window is like a naturally good-looking woman. It doesn't matter when you see her, what season it is, or time of day. Even if it's early morning and she just got out of bed, she is still beautiful.

Barney appeared in the doorway, his six-and-a-half-foot frame filling it. "Ricos, I do miss you."

"I know. I miss you, too."

"Have you met the new deputy the sheriff sent?"

"No. Is it someone I know?"

"He's new. His name is Richard Mayhew, but he's called Buster."

"Isn't that a dog's name?"

"I wish I could tell the sheriff to bite me for sending me a teenager."

"How old is he?"

"He claims to be twenty-one, but I think he's eighteen at the most. I bet he doesn't shave yet."

"Well, this is your chance to train somebody from the ground up. Maybe he won't be as annoying as I am."

"Ricos, only you could be as annoying as you are."

"Thank you."

A second went by and he blurted, "I still see those bloody bodies, but it's worse when I'm trying to fall asleep."

I didn't need to ask which bodies, although we had seen a few in our time of working together. "Yes. I know, Barney."

"Do you know how to make them go away?"

"I wish I did. Time will help. I hope."

"I might be insane first."

"I know what you mean."

He heaved a long sigh. "When will you be back?"

"Next week. I'll call you. What's going on here?"

"Nothing you want to know."

"Are you sure?"

"Oh, pure bullshit is what's for dinner 'round here, drenched in a light chicken shit sauce, and served with a side of mouse turds."

I cracked up at his dead-on metaphors for Terlingua gossip.

After a few minutes, he got serious. "When will you come back to work?"

"As soon as I convince Sheriff Ben that I'm rested and ready to take on any responsibility he gives me. I need a better attitude."

"How the hell will you do all that?"

"Easy. See this smile?" I gave him a great big fake one. "See how sincere it is? Check my great hair while you're at it."

"Ricos, while you're gone, will you work on toning down that smart-ass attitude of yours?"

"No. Not likely."

"Alrighty then. Just keep on being you."

There you have it. That, in essence, is why I love the guy.

Chapter 7

The young couple crouched on the bank of the Rio Grande. They were hidden by the dark of night and a dense thicket of mesquite and tamarisk growth. As near as Max could figure it, their journey was not even half over. He was bone-weary and worried about his wife. They had not eaten a real meal or slept in a bed for almost a week, and the most dangerous part of their journey was just beginning.

Max had tried to leave Lucia in México, but she was a stubborn woman and wouldn't agree to stay behind. "I didn't marry you to live lonely," she had chastised him. "How can we have children if you don't live with me? We can't make love if you're in Texas and I'm in México."

The thought of living without her paralyzed Max, and he gave up on the plan to go alone. So she was accompanying him on a perilous journey, making the danger greater but keeping loneliness away.

It was an adventure of sorts, and every day he loved Lucia more. She made him laugh and was never afraid of anything. She remained calm and reasoned through their minor setbacks. She never complained and didn't care if she ate nothing and slept on the hard ground, as long as she was with her Max.

Lucia and Max had traveled by bus from Cuidad Chihuahua to Ojinaga, a town on the México-Texas border. They lacked the documents they needed to enter legally at the international bridge there, so they were on foot, working their way downriver over grueling terrain.

He squeezed her small hand in his as they waited at the bank. The river had a damp, earthy odor and loud rushing water that ground over stones and pebbles as it moved them towards the sea. The sound of it was intimidating in the dark.

On the other bank was a new country, a different land that offered opportunity in spite of danger. Yes, there would be risk and hardship, but Augustín had assured Max it would be worth it. The United States was a place full of promise with many jobs for men willing to work.

From where he hunkered on the bank in the pitch black of a moonless night, Max couldn't see the land he hungered for.

A man from a nearby settlement had said he would come and row them across in a small boat kept for that purpose, but they had been waiting nearly two hours. He was evidently not coming. To try to swim across in the dark would be suicide. They would have to wait until daylight. That brought different dangers, but there was no use worrying until they knew what they faced.

"We'll have to find a place to sleep," Max whispered to Lucia. "I don't think the old man is going to come tonight."

"He said he would come at night, but he didn't say which night," she responded and made him laugh.

They cleared a space to lay out their bedroll.

"Are you hungry, Max?"

"I'm always hungry."

"We still have biscuits and cheese." She made a face without meaning to.

"I don't know if we should be eating that moldy old cheese."

"It hasn't hurt us yet." She dug around for it in her knapsack.

He limped towards her with his back hunched, dragging one foot. He held his mouth in a twisted grimace. "Oh yeah? Is that what you think?"

Lucia squealed and ran, pretending to be frightened. She let him catch her and pull her into his arms. When they began to kiss, their sad supper was forgotten.

When the sun came up, the newlyweds got into the Rio Grande. They clung to each other and let the current do most of the work carrying them downstream. They had noticed a protruding spit of land on the other side where the current would take them. With a destination in mind, the river didn't seem as terrifying. In less than two minutes they were swept onto the little peninsula and lay laughing and sputtering. They were soaked, along with everything they carried.

Max didn't care. "We're in the United States of America!" he announced to the sky. He stood and shook himself off. "Lucia and Max have arrived, people!"

Lucia was not impressed. "It looks the same as over there," she said.

"But it's not the same," insisted her husband.

Max pulled out a tattered and now wet map of Texas and spread it out to dry, weighing down the edges with stones. Then he stood again and peered around. Lucia was correct that it looked the same as the other side, except for a highway that ran near the river. Other than that, it was the same. The rugged, red-brown mountains had jagged peaks stretching up towards the sky and sheer rock faces that plunged down to the ground. Some of them towered above colorful clay hills or strange rock formations. In the distance were higher mountains that were hazy in the morning's brightness. It was spectacular. Max wondered where humans got the idea that a river should separate land that was meant to be together.

Lucia and Max sat in the warm April sun to let their clothes dry. They watched the river and listened for sounds from the road. There appeared to be no traffic in this part of Texas, which was south of Presidio and north of a tiny settlement called Lajitas.

After a while, Max stood and offered Lucia his hand. "We should get walking. We have to find food today. My stomach hurts from being empty all the time."

"I'm hungry too," she said as she put on her shoes. "Maybe we'll pass a house where we can buy something. How far do you think we are from Lajitas?"

"I think it's about thirty-five miles away."

They began walking and holding hands. They stayed on the river side of the highway so they could duck into the vegetation if a green and white Border Patrol vehicle approached. They'd been told they were scarce on this remote route, but they hadn't come all this way to be returned to México. Max already felt giddy from the glorious life he sensed was coming.

They'd been walking thirty minutes when they heard a motor approaching. In the distance, Max could see an old black pickup headed their way. His first instinct was to hide but his stomach demanded food, and he hoped for a ride to a place where they could purchase something to eat.

Max kept glancing over his shoulder until the truck stopped. He was relieved to see that the bed was full of Mexican children laughing and playing. An adult asked in Spanish if they needed a ride.

"Sí señor, we sure would like one."

"I can take you to Terlingua, but that's as far as I'm going."

Max accepted the offer with a smile, and he and Lucia climbed into the back with the children and a couple of dogs.

"Would you like an orange?" A little girl with dark pigtails held one out to him. "We have lots of them."

"Yes, thank you. We're very hungry."

She handed him four oranges. "We have burritos, too. Want one?"

"Oh yes. Thank you. We've come a long way with little to eat."

"Where did you come from?"

"We came from near Chihuahua."

The little girl's eyes were wide.

Max and Lucia shared a bean burrito and watched the passing scenery. He tried not to eat too fast, but he wanted to cram the whole thing into his mouth at once. He had never been so hungry. He reminded himself that they were in the United States, and whatever discomfort he suffered now would be worth it.

Max was deep in thought as the scenery rolled by. He and Lucia would have children and make a life together in this great country. He would find a job, work hard, and never feel hungry again. His children would never know what it felt like to not have enough to eat. They would never have to go without shoes. They would be educated and become good citizens and live successful lives. He knew he was getting ahead of himself; they hadn't even left the border yet.

Max took Lucia's hand as the truck wound along the twisting highway. She smiled at him and squeezed his hand. He wanted to assure her that everything would be all right, but he laughed at himself. His positive-thinking Lucia would already assume that.

Three days later, they were still trudging cross-country through a hostile desert, but every time they were almost out of water they would come upon a hidden spring or a remote ranch house where there would be an outside hose. They were able to wash off, drink, and fill their water containers. This was an amazing country!

Their biggest problem was food. They'd been shocked at the cost of things in the small convenience store in Terlingua, so their purchases had been limited. They bought crackers, tortillas, a few cans of meat, cheese, and apples. They longed for frijoles, rice, and homemade tortillas but had no way to cook them.

Lucia was quiet and that worried Max. "Are you all right, Mi Amor?"

"We've been walking three days and the terrain still looks like home."

The sadness in her voice hurt Max's heart. He brought her hand to his mouth and kissed it. "That's because we're in the Chihuahuan Desert just like at home, so it is the same. I miss home, too."

"It's that we've never been away before." Her voice cracked and her bottom lip trembled. "I need to see my family and my garden, Max."

"Please don't cry, Chiquita." Max put his arms around her and she buried her face against his chest. "We'll go back to visit before you know it. Besides, you can have a garden where we're going."

She wasn't convinced, but she stopped crying. They walked along in silence until they stopped in the shade of a low mountain to rest.

Max lay down with his hands behind his head. "Please tell me a story and make me laugh, Preciosa."

Instead of making up a story, Lucia began to cry. Before long, they were huddled together weeping like a couple of lost children.

Max wiped tears from his eyes and then hers. "We'll be okay, Chiquita." He didn't know if he was trying to convince her or himself. He smoothed her silky hair back from her face and kissed her nose.

"We're just hungry and homesick," she sobbed.

"Do you want to go back?" He couldn't stand to see her so miserable.

Tears made streaks in the dust on her cheeks. She tried to smile. "We can't go back, Max. Our dreams are here. Besides, we're not quitters. We have to keep going for our babies. They'll have a future here they can't have in México. Maybe one day it will be different, but not now."

She continued to cry but was trying not to. Max gathered a bunch of wildflowers and presented them to her with a courtly bow. "These are for you, Mi Amor, the queen of my heart."

She laughed and her tears began to dry. They left a salty-sweet taste on her cheeks that Max kissed away.

Then they walked on across the desert.

Chapter 8

PRESENT DAY, ALPINE TO DALLAS, TX

Zeke and I met in the Sheriff's Office parking lot in Alpine. He greeted me with a bright smile. I returned it and even gave him a hug. I felt hopeful about whatever adventure he had planned. If nothing else happened, I'd get to know the man whose genes I carried.

"Don't you want to go in and say adiós to Sheriff Duncan?" my father wondered as we put my things into his white Texas Rangers truck.

"No. He knows I'm going, right?"

"Well yes, but he—"

"That's all he needs to know."

"But he—"

"Zeke, please don't say anything else about my boss. He forced me to take time off. I'm doing it; that's that."

He left it alone.

We pulled away from the Sheriff's Office and Zeke said, "I like this little town."

I thought if a person looked at Alpine as it is and not as a place where they have to go to buy things if they live in Terlingua, or pay a ticket, or go to the hospital, or as a place where their boss is and they're forced to go as part of their job, and where the jail is, and where the lawmen are out of control when it comes to hassling lawwomen, then yes; it's a nice town.

"Alpine is full of trees and green places," Zeke continued, "except there's less of that right now, of course."

"Yes, and there are a lot of flowering trees and bushes at certain times and tons of cowboys at all times; and at other times there are even deer in the streets."

He laughed. "Are you making fun of me?"

"No, it was just an observation. I didn't mean to sound so sarcastic. Barney says I have a problem with that, only he calls it my smart-ass-ism."

"Something tells me he has a touch of that himself."

"Oh yeah; he has a terminal case."

Zeke laughed, and after a few seconds, he said, "Another great thing about Alpine is the train. That's been a sound I've always loved for some reason. They're so mournful and heart-tugging."

"Oh no; I have a hopeless romantic for a father."

He smiled. "Don't you think trains are romantic?"

"Yes, I sure do."

We lapsed into silence for a while, each with our own thoughts. Mine were on the mountains. Alpine is a small town surrounded by them. They make up for not being notably high by being beautiful, and if you get up close, you see how full of secrets they are. They have magical places and hidden treasures, as do the mountains in the south of the county. Like everything else in our area, if you want to experience it, you can't just whiz by in your car and say you saw it.

Zeke glanced over at me. "Didn't you marry an Alpine cowboy?"

"Yes."

"Would you rather talk about something else?"

"It's okay. I can talk about Kevin. Why do you ask about him?"

"I want to get to know you, remember?"

"Kevin died in a bull riding accident. Did you know that?"

"Yes. Your mother told me. I was curious how you met him, what attracted you to him, that kind of thing."

"Some friends dragged me to a rodeo, and I saw this tall, good-looking, blond cowboy riding bulls. I figured he was tough, but not that bright. That didn't stop me from staring, though. He was checking me out too, but acting like he wasn't. He got thrown so hard I didn't think he would walk again, but he just got up, knocked off the dust, and came over and introduced himself to me. We talked a little while, and he asked me out. How could I say no to a man that smooth?"

Zeke laughed and agreed.

"I never went out with anyone else after that. We had so much fun, no matter where we went or what we were doing. I adored him. He was smart and kind and he treated me as if I had set the moon and all the stars into the sky."

"I know your mom thought the world of him."

"Oh yes. He loved Mom, too."

"Does it make you sad to talk about Kevin?"

"Yes, but I'm okay. I don't want to forget him."

"I'm sure you won't."

"I'm already forgetting little things. Emilio Martez pushed Kevin farther back in my memory. What I mean to say is I will always love Kevin, but Emilio was here and now. A dead man can't compete with a real flesh and blood man who's helping to make new memories. But now *he's* dead. Let's don't talk about Emilio, either. Let's talk about you, Zeke."

"What would you like to know about me?"

"What do you like to do for fun?"

"I like to play tennis and handball and soccer. And dancing should be on the list, but, to tell you the truth, I love to garden more than anything."

"Do you mean flowers or vegetables or what?"

"If it grows in dirt or water, it suits me. I like trees, fruit trees or any tree. Gardening doesn't fit with my professional path because I have to be gone from home so much."

"Well, I'm not a gardener, but I love to dance and play soccer."

For a while we talked about the things we like to do, things we like and don't like, and somehow the conversation came back around to my mother. Maybe that was because he was still trying to explain why he wasn't the man who raised me. I think he was trying to work it out in his own mind, because I got it.

"Zeke, were you in love with my mom?"

"No. Yes. I don't know. My feelings for your mom were confused. Does that upset you?"

"No."

"Life is complicated Margarita, and sometimes things don't go to the letter as they should or as you plan."

"I know that."

After a while, I drove and Zeke read me a letter he'd received from Francisco Valentino after he'd agreed to help. It was respectful and emotional and laid out the problems Zeke had already mentioned.

Then my father took a photograph out of the envelope and studied it. "It's heartbreaking to look at his family and know their fate. Even if Kiko didn't kill them, someone did. Either way, they're gone."

"If he's innocent, and he's doing time for killing them, it must make the loss even harder to bear."

"I can't imagine it. I'm a little afraid of what we might discover, though. What if Kiko is guilty and I have to tell his father that hard truth?"

"Why don't we find out first? Before you worry about it I mean."

Zeke flashed me a smile.

A few more miles passed, and I asked, "What were your parents like? Did you have a happy childhood?"

He stared out the window. "No, I didn't."

That was a surprise.

He looked over at me. "You see, I wasn't raised by my parents. They gave me up when I was a baby. I never knew them or even knew who they were."

"Then who raised you?"

"As a baby, I was in an orphanage in Dallas, and then I was put into foster care. I had seven different homes by the time I was eight. I don't remember most of them."

"I can't believe it. Someone must have loved you for you to turn out the way you did."

He chuckled. "I don't think anyone loved me. I guess I was a real handful when I was little, and by the time I went to the last foster home, they tried to beat the bad boy out of me. If you think I turned out well, that must be why."

"That's not what I meant, Zeke. I mean you're so loving and gentle. You learned that from someone."

"I don't think so, unless it happened before I was four years old. I don't remember anything before that."

"Do you know anything about your parents?"

"Well, I know what my foster parents told me, but I don't want to tell you."

"Why not?"

"These are your grandparents, Margarita. The implications are terrible. As far as genes go, I brought nothing good to the table."

"That's not true. I want you to tell me what you know, no matter how bad it is."

"My father died in prison, and my mother died on the Dallas streets. According to the foster parents, she was a crack whore."

"I don't believe it."

"Well believe it, please. It's the sad truth. Maybe you'll be sorry I ever came into your life."

"No, Zeke. You aren't your parents. You're my parent. I pictured you growing up more like I did, with a mom and dad who loved you. I feel so sad."

"Don't be sad, Sweetheart. I don't mean to make you sad."

"I don't care about your parents, Zeke. I only care about you. I think you would've been a great father, same as my papi. I guess

I should say you are a good father even if you didn't have one to learn from."

"Thank you, but I'm not as sure about that."

"I'm the daughter and I'm sure."

"It's sweet of you to say that. I'm doing my best."

I didn't mention it, but what he said about not having family made me feel adrift. My papi's relatives were not mine, except in my heart. I adored his parents, but we were never related, something I was still getting my head around. My mom's parents died long before I was born. She has two sisters I don't know well. I think they're great, and she adores them, but it's hard to be close to people you've seen four or five times in your life. Now I had nobody on Zeke's side, either. *What does it matter?* I thought, but it did. It did at least a little.

"I got over it a long time ago," Zeke claimed, but I thought he was saying that for my sake. "It's hard not to have any family, nobody to relate to in that way, I mean. I sometimes wish I could at least see a photo of them." The sadness in his voice was heart-wrenching. "That's one reason you're so important to me. I have family at last."

I glanced over and saw him wipe away a tear. That put me three seconds from bawling. "I'm proud you're my father, Zeke. You're smart and kind and successful. You kick ass for a living, and you know how I admire that. All the time I spent as a little girl playing G.I. Joe and Ninja Turtles and various Superheroes, who knew I was mimicking my real father?"

He laughed but didn't comment, and a few more miles went by.

Curiosity was killing me. "Who were your foster parents? Do you still have contact with them? Where do they live now?"

"They were not good people and you wouldn't want to know them. I left their house for good when I was thirteen, and I've never looked back. No, I don't contact them and where they live doesn't matter because you'll never have to meet them."

"I'm trying to understand this. How did you live on your own when you were thirteen? You were still a child."

"I was a child, but in another way I don't think I was ever a child."

"Where did you live? How did you get food and clothes? How could you have finished high school, let alone go to college and get a Master's degree?"

"That's too many questions at once."

"I'm sorry. Just answer the first question. How did you make it on your own when you were thirteen?"

"I went into Dallas because I figured I could get lost in a big city. I got a job washing dishes and lived in homeless shelters until some guy tried to crawl in bed with me. For a while I lived at the YMCA, but they had a limit on how long a person could stay there. I had to move around."

"And?"

"That's enough about me."

"No. Please go on. You haven't told me enough about you."

"I slept in abandoned buildings or garages. I favored garages attached to houses because they tended to be warm and sometimes had refrigerators or shelves of canned goods. Desperation caused me to be a thief."

"That's not hard to understand."

"Once I had saved enough money, I rented the crappiest little apartment you can imagine, but at least I didn't have to sleep with one eye open. I went to high school, but I tested out early. Then I went to the University of Texas on a football and academic scholarship. I also took out student loans. And I worked my ass off."

"You're amazing."

"I was raised to work hard. I think my foster parents took in kids rather than hire employees. We were a lot easier to shove around. They didn't have to pay us, and we needed to eat, and we didn't want to be beaten, so we worked. When I went to work for the Dallas P. D., I got their foster care certification removed permanently."

46

"Did they know it was you who did that?"

"I don't know. I don't care, either. They're listed on a national database of abusive foster adults, so they can't move to another state and get certification."

"Were you abused?"

"Yes. I had to get up at four in the morning to help with chores that were hard, particularly when I was small. I was just eight when I first lived with them. It was help out or be beaten, so I did what I could. I was considered a behavior problem if I spoke up for myself, so I got hit for that and sometimes not fed. Also, I used to run away a lot. I didn't want to live with those people."

"And who could blame you?"

"We had to pray before we could eat. What kind of god would people like that worship? I knew he was hateful. They tried to make us believe we were always standing on the precipice of hell. In their house, we thought we were already in it."

"I'm sorry you were treated like that, Zeke."

"For all their show of religion, my foster parents never took us to church. They went, but we had to stay home and do chores. Sundays were the best days because they'd be gone a long time. We'd do our chores as fast as we could and then play."

Every time I glanced at Zeke he was looking at me with sad eyes.

"I've said enough, Margarita. I didn't mean to tell you so much, but you asked."

"I want you to tell me everything."

"That will never happen, but I will tell you this. There was an old man who worked for them. Sometimes he would put me on his knee and tell me stories, so maybe I learned about love from him. I certainly did love him, and I believe he loved me, too."

"Did you ever look for your parents or try to find out about them?"

"No, I never did. They didn't want me. I faced up to that hard truth and stayed busy trying to make something of myself. I wanted to prove my foster parents wrong, I guess. They told me I was worthless, and that I'd die in a prison like my father did."

"But if you never looked for your parents, then you don't know if what your foster parents told you about them is true. Maybe they had to give you up for a reason. Maybe they didn't want to give you up, Zeke."

"Thank you for saying that, but I think what my foster parents told me is true. They had the records from the orphanage. I can live with it. I have lived with it." Zeke paused and, after a heavy sigh, continued. "What I mean to say is that I do live with it. Both of my parents were criminals and that's all I know about them."

I wanted to accept my father's story, but I couldn't.

"Please say something, Margarita."

"I don't know what to say. You could've become a bad guy, but instead you work to put the bad guys away. Somewhere in your history are good people. Maybe your parents went off track, but you were born with a lot of character. You had to be born with it if you didn't have a model for it."

Zeke chuckled. "I don't know if people are born with character or not."

"I don't know, either. If you weren't born with it, where did it come from?"

He shrugged. "I know that since I first found out I was going to be a father, I wanted to be a better man. It might not make sense to you since I wasn't the one who raised you, but just knowing about you gave me a feeling of family. That has steadied me. Do you understand what I mean?"

"Yes."

"I don't know if I would've been able to cope with a small child. Would I have beaten you and made you do difficult chores and pray to a vicious god? Those are the parenting skills I learned."

"Zeke, give yourself a break. You would probably have treated me the way you wanted to be treated all those years instead of the way you were treated."

"But I don't know that."

"Does my mother know any of this?"

"No, and I think it'd be best if you didn't tell her. I don't want her to hold anything else against me."

"I don't think she holds anything against you. She's had a great life doing what she wants. I've never heard her say one unkind thing about you. Stop making problems that don't exist. Neither of my parents holds anything against you."

"That's good."

"Is your family name Pacheco, or is that the name of your foster parents?"

"It's my father's name as far as I know. I would never use the name of my foster parents; I'd make one up first. Let's talk about something else."

"It's not your fault you were abandoned as a baby."

"Who wants to admit they have no knowledge of their ancestry? Who wants to admit their father was a killer, or some other form of criminal, and that their mother died addicted on the streets?"

"But you don't even know the truth of that, Zeke."

"Well, regardless, that's all I know."

After that, we talked about other things, but I couldn't let go of the feeling that Zeke must have relatives somewhere, which meant I did too. Even if his parents were dead, he would have uncles, aunts, cousins, and maybe even brothers and sisters. I wanted to know about them even if he didn't.

Chapter 9

<u>PRESENT DAY, DALLAS, TX</u>

Zeke had made a reservation at a luxury hotel in downtown Dallas. When I wondered out loud why he chose such an expensive place, he explained that it was a special treat for his daughter.

"Can you handle something like this for a week?" he asked.

I promised to give it my best shot.

The hotel was so fancy the doormen/bellmen wore sharp black and red uniforms similar to tuxedos, and every one of the staff acted as if we were royalty. It didn't take a minute to get used to that.

Zeke went into a momentary panic at check-in when the clerk told him they were booked full, and he couldn't rent a separate room for me as he'd planned.

He smacked his hand against his forehead. "Why didn't I reserve another room in advance? I'm so sorry; it slipped my mind."

"It'll be okay, Zeke."

"Are you sure? Won't it be improper?"

I laughed. "No. It'll be fine. We can make it work."

Once we saw the room, he realized it was not such a big deal. It was so large it was almost like having separate rooms. There were two queen-sized beds so far apart I thought we'd have to yell if we sat on our beds to talk.

The best thing was that we were on the fifteenth floor and the room had a balcony. We sat out there for a while even though it was cold. From so high up, the lights of the city were impressive, but they made the sky a pale, dirty-yellow color and obscured the stars.

"If there was a fifteenth floor in Terlingua and we were sitting on the balcony," I pointed out, "the stars would be so bright we'd need sunglasses."

Zeke laughed. "You're not in Terlingua anymore, Dorothy."

Yeah; I had that much figured out already.

Sunday was a lazy day. We got dressed late and had brunch at the hotel. After that we walked around downtown. Zeke had chosen a hotel perfectly situated for enjoying the arts district. The air was crisp but the sun was warm, and we sat in it for a while talking. I thought I was getting a handle on the man who was my father.

On Monday, Zeke made arrangements with prison officials for me to visit Francisco Valentino in the afternoon, which meant I had the morning free.

As he was leaving, he handed me a silver star Texas Rangers badge. "This will make things easier at the prison. There'll be fewer questions and faster cooperation. I told them I was sending my investigator, which is not entirely untrue."

"I feel a power trip coming on."

"Don't even think about doing anything else with my spare badge."

"But Zeke, it's better than magic. Doors open, questions get answered, and people get out of the way."

"Don't misuse my badge. Got it?"

After he left, my thoughts went to his parents. I love the challenge of a mystery, and this one involved my ancestors. I went to the concierge in the lobby and asked about orphanages.

The guy sputtered and flipped through materials on his desk. I guessed nobody ever asked him about orphanages. "There used to be a large one over on Waxhaw Street but it was torn down a few years ago."

"Do you know where it moved?"

"No. I have no idea."

"So you've never heard of any other place?"

"No, but we could look online," he suggested.

We found twenty-six listings for "children's homes" in the Dallas area. None of them had the word "orphanage" in their name, so perhaps it was an outdated term. I thanked the man and went back to the room to repeat the search on my laptop. I was able to eliminate over half the listings because they didn't take babies. Several were raising funds for homeless children or pregnant women, a few more took only girls, and some were specific about the kind of kids they helped, such as blind kids or children with other challenges. After reading about them and, in some cases, calling them, I narrowed it down to three that accepted babies and had been around long enough to have housed my father.

How could it hurt to find out who had put him into an orphanage and for what reason? And I happened to be in Dallas. That seemed more like a call to action than a coincidence. I didn't buy that crack whore story. He was talking about my grandmother.

I took a taxi to Jason's House because it was the largest place listed. I realized as I got out of the vehicle that I didn't have a story to give them that would force them to give up information. All I had was the truth and a star in my pocket.

There was a big sign in front of the office that read, "Jason's House, since 1933." This could be the right one, I thought, keeping it positive.

I introduced myself to a receptionist.

"How may I help you, Ms. Ricos?"

"I need information about a child that may have been placed here about forty-four to forty-seven years ago." I gave her the name, date of birth, and social security number of the child in question.

"I don't know if I can give you that information. You'll have to see the director," she said. "I'll get her. Just have a seat over there."

A tall, middle-aged woman with graying hair and startling green eyes walked up to me and introduced herself as Claire Winsted. She led me back to her office where I gave her the same information I had given the receptionist, except I added that the baby in question was my father.

She looked up the name Ezekiél Pacheco on her computer. She found two Pacheco males, but neither of them were the right age. She suggested I check with Child Protective Services and gave me their contact information. If the child was taken away from his parents, she said, they would have all the information. Even if the parents voluntarily gave him up, they might still have that information.

I thanked her for her help and left. To get info from CPS, I would need a court order, an act of God, or to be a Texas Ranger. Each was equally unlikely.

I headed back to the hotel, got out my laptop, and got back online to look at the rest of the Dallas listings under "children's homes." I wondered if Zeke was afraid to know the truth. If he knew for certain his father was a serial killer or a child molester or murderer, it'd be hard for a straight-arrow like him to stomach.

Then I wondered if I was doing something wrong. Because I'd want to know about my parents, I assumed the same thing about Zeke. Maybe if I didn't know I wouldn't want to know, either. It's different when you already know who your parents are. Did I have the right to look for people he might not want me to find? I decided not to do more until I'd spoken to him about it. If he didn't want me to do it, I wouldn't.

I was staring at the door of the room's mini-bar arguing with my bossy inner bitch when my cell phone rang.

The caller was Sheriff Ben. I took a breath and forced a smile onto my face and into my voice. "Good morning, Sheriff."

"Good morning. How are things going up there in Dallas?"

"Fine, I guess."

"We need to have a talk," he said, which meant he had things to say to me.

"All right, Sheriff." Fire away.

"I don't understand your resistance to taking time off. You've been through hell and you need a break. I think it's because I said you had to. That's it, isn't it?"

I hate it when he slams me upside the head with my own obstinacy and resistance to authority. "You should have been a psychiatrist, Sheriff Ben."

There was a scary pause. "I don't have the patience." He took a breath and I wanted to take cover. "I'm responsible for your well-being and for your behavior on the job. You've shown increasing signs of stress, and you're too short on patience."

"Yes, you said that before."

"I know, but you didn't seem to be listening."

"I heard you."

"I think it'll do you good to spend time with your father away from here."

"Yes, I think so, too. I'm doing what you asked, Sheriff. I'm taking time off, and I'm also helping someone else."

"That's good, Margarita, but I want you to stop avoiding me and treating me like I caused all your problems."

Had I been doing that? "I'm sorry, Sheriff. I don't blame you for any of it."

"If we have a problem, let's deal with it now, because it will only get worse."

"We don't have a problem, Sheriff Ben."

"All right, I'm taking you at your word."

"Thank you."

"Carry on."

I opened the door of the mini-bar and stared, but there was no sanity in there. Zeke called as if he knew I was looking for something to hang on to. He said he and the class were taking a break.

"How's it going?" I asked.

"Oh fine, I was wondering how you're doing."

"Great. I've been looking around Dallas."

"I want to take you to lunch, and then you can bring me back here and take the truck. Why don't you meet me in front of the hotel at twelve-fifteen?"

During lunch I started to mention investigating his past, but Zeke was so happy I didn't want to bring him down. His course was going well, and he said several times that he was excited to have a whole week to spend with his daughter.

After lunch, I took my father back to the police headquarters building where the training was being held.

"Call me if you hit a snag or need anything." He touched the brim of his hat in a farewell gesture.

"Do you want me to come back for you afterwards?"

"No, I'll meet you at the hotel. I'll get a ride or walk. Don't worry about me. I shouldn't be much later than 5:30. Let's go dining and dancing later."

"I'd love that, but I don't have the appropriate clothes for any-place fancy."

"We'll talk about where to go later. Good luck at the prison. If you're wearing the badge, you can stay as long as you need to." He left me with a smile.

The Hamilton Unit was as foreboding and intimidating as any prison, but it looked newish and was made of brick. The grass surrounding it was brown more than green, but the real detractor was a chain link fence topped with coils of barbed wire. Above those was razor wire that glinted in the sunlight and dared a person to try it. Equally menacing were four towers containing guards armed with rifles. Talk about intimidating. I felt guilty for breathing there.

The visiting hours were posted at the door but, being law enforcement, I didn't have to observe them. Zeke had talked to the warden about my visit, so I hoped I wouldn't need to have a conversation with him where I'd be forced to lie about my fictitious investigative position with the Texas Rangers. I was ready with a lie, but I didn't want to have to use it.

When I went in and gave my name, I saw that I was on a list. I had to show my driver's license to prove my identity and was taken into a small room and told to give up my weapon. I wasn't carrying one. A female corrections officer patted me down and she was thorough. She said we could skip the strip search since I was law enforcement. What strip search? I tried to banish from my head the sick, sexist jokes I knew about corrections officers and strip searches, but of course they were stuck there.

I was taken to another drab little room and told the prisoner would be brought to me within fifteen minutes. About the time the walls started closing in, Francisco Valentino was herded in by a stone-faced guard whose only acknowledgement was a curt nod in my direction. The prisoner was cuffed with his hands behind him and was shackled with chains connected to the metal cuffs on his ankles. That forced him to move in tiny, shuffling steps. It hurt me to see someone treated that way.

While the guard fastened the shackles to bolts in the concrete floor, Francisco grinned at me. He was a dark-skinned, young, Latino man, twenty-four years old according to his file. He had black hair cut short, no facial hair, and dark brown eyes that reflected his excitement about our meeting. There was nothing remarkable about him. He didn't look away or act shy or furtive or leer at me as some convicts did. He didn't have any tattoos I could see, let alone the dark and threatening ones prisoners give each other. And he sure didn't look like my idea of a baby killer.

"Hola." He leaned towards me as he greeted me, and I returned his greeting.

The guard announced him without looking at either of us, "Valentino, Francisco, number 1456278. Call me when you're done or if you need something."

"Thank you," I said. "I will."

"I'll be outside the door."

I nodded and turned back to the prisoner. "I'm Margarita Ricos, Zeke Pacheco's daughter." I leaned across the metal table and offered my hand, which he took with both of his. It was awkward, but he didn't have a choice because of the cuffs. At least they'd been moved to the front.

"I'm Francisco Valentino, but my friends call me Kiko. Thank you for coming. I can't believe you're here." He swallowed back emotion. "How is Zeke?"

"He's fine. He'll be by to see you, but he asked me to come get started because he's teaching a class all day."

"He told me."

"Zeke read your transcript, and he sees what you mean about your trial, which is why he wants to help you."

"Ask me anything you want to know." He seemed eager to tell his story to someone who would listen.

"I think we should start at the beginning. Tell me about the night of the murders, and be as detailed as possible. I might interrupt you with questions."

"Are you a Texas Ranger?"

I said, "Yes" for the benefit of the guard in case he was listening. He could also watch us through a window.

Kiko grinned and began his story. "My family was murdered on a Thursday night around eleven o'clock, according to the Medical Examiner. I was at work. I had two jobs, one of them at night."

"What did you do?"

"I worked at a Jiffy Lube during the day, forty hours per week. I worked about fifteen hours per week with a janitorial service. Normally I would've been home from five to ten, but the janitorial service asked me to come early. I was asleep when they called. It was eight o'clock."

He cleared his throat. "When I think about it, I realize that working two jobs was stupid. I think that's how I lost my wife's interest, but I did it for her and our children. I wanted them to have more than I had."

"I understand."

He swallowed hard. "I got home a little after two in the morning. I went straight to the kitchen to eat something, and I noticed the light on. I thought maybe Evie, my wife, had left it on. She did that sometimes. When she did it on purpose, there would be a note for me. I looked around but didn't see one, so I figured she had overlooked the light when she went to bed.

"We had a butcher block knife holder that was kept way back on the counter so our kids couldn't reach it or even see it." He paused and swallowed hard again then cleared his throat. "They were little."

He stared at his hands and continued. "It had been moved to the table, and I thought that was odd. Evie was careful with the kids. It wasn't like her to leave dangerous things around, but I still didn't think much about it. I put it back where we usually kept it."

Kiko's body language said he was coming to the worst part. He took a deep breath and continued. "I ate two sandwiches. When I was slicing the tomato I cut myself on the thumb. It bled but it wasn't serious. I washed it off and put a band-aid on it. After I ate, I set everything I used in the sink and went back to the bathroom. I washed up and got blood on one of the towels, which I put into the dirty clothes hamper. I mention this because it'll be important later."

Kiko stared at his hands and rubbed them together as if they pained him. "So then I—then I—I went into the bedroom and took off my clothes and put them over a chair. There was no light

58

except from a clock by the bed on my side." His facial muscles began to twitch.

"At first, I didn't notice the blood. I was turning back the covers, and I realized everything looked wrong. There was a dark shadow—it was blood but it just looked dark—and Evie was covered with it. I called out to her and when she didn't move or answer, I went to the wall and turned on the light."

Kiko put his head in his hands. When he looked up at me tears were rolling down his face. "She was dead. Blood was everywhere, and she was naked." His lips trembled. "That bastard had stripped her and left her like that. She wore a nightgown or sleep pants with a t-shirt when she went to bed because the kids would cry out and she'd go to them."

He breathed a long, shuddering sigh. "I couldn't think because I was in such a panic and so sad. I was so upset it never occurred to me that everything I did would be judged so harshly by people who didn't even know me. I touched her. So what? My God, she was my wife. I held her to me and talked to her. I told her I was so sorry, 'cause see, I thought it was my fault. I made her break up with him." His voice broke.

"Would you like something to drink?" I had seen a cold drink machine in the larger visitors' room, and I thought it would be a diversion.

"No, thanks; I think I would choke. Just give me a sec."

"Take all the time you need, Kiko."

"My attorney told me everybody knows not to touch anything, but I wasn't thinking clearly."

"What he said is not true. A normal reaction is to touch the people we love. I would have done the same thing."

"You would?"

"I definitely would."

"It was three in the morning, and my wife was in our bed covered with her own blood. I got her blood on me, and I left bloody fingerprints all over the place. It never occurred to me I'd be charged with her murder, for the love of God. I hadn't killed her. I would never have killed her. I did everything wrong because I wasn't thinking about being blamed for it. I covered her because I didn't want strangers to look at her naked."

He began to cry. "I guess you're not supposed to cover people."

I handed him a tissue. "I'm going to ask the guard for some water. I'll be right back." It was not about thirst; I needed a break so I could keep my cool. How believable is a sobbing Texas Ranger?

When I opened the door, the guard put his hand on it. "If you come out, you can't go back in unless you're searched again."

Since I had escaped that little treat, I kept my boots in the room. "If I give you money, will you bring two bottles of water from the machine in there?"

He nodded. I handed him four one-dollar bills and he called another guard via a walkie-talkie. He couldn't leave his post without a replacement, I presumed.

When he brought the water, I said, "Thank you," and smiled at him.

He didn't smile, but he grunted, "Welcome."

Kiko had composed himself and accepted a bottle of water with thanks. For a few minutes we talked about normal things such as the books he was able to borrow from the prison library, although he said "library" and left off "prison." I told him my perceptions of Dallas, not great, while he spoke of his hometown with affection. He had been to Terlingua but thought there "wasn't much to it." That was fine; the last thing we wanted in Terlingua was for everyone from Dallas to move there.

He picked up his horror story again. "I thought about my kids after I held Evie for a few minutes. I just wanted to look at them, you know, to comfort myself. They shared a room, but S-Susie slept in a crib." That was as far as he got. He ducked his head and held the cold bottle against his face.

I thought I should say something comforting, but what?

"My baby was not quite a year old and Freddy, Freddy, he was three," Kiko continued. "He slept in a twin bed with a railing because he fell out otherwise." He wiped his face with a tissue I handed him. "I went over to the bed and put my bloody hands on the railing and looked down at my dead son. He'd been stabbed, too. I t-t-turned around and went to the crib and picked up my baby. She was already c-cold. Who in hell would stab a baby? Who could do that?" His voice was so full of misery I wanted to put my head in my hands and cry until people quit hurting children.

"Three days after my family died, I was arrested."

"Did they take a statement from you before that?"

"Yes. I told the police what I've just told you."

"If you were working, you should have had an alibi, no?"

"No. I was working alone, of all the nights to work alone. I couldn't believe it. Two guys called in sick so I had to do this one office building by myself. The detectives thought that was 'convenient.' They said I could've left and come back. I maybe could've pulled that off, but I couldn't have finished my work, and I did finish. Who goes home, stabs their whole family, and goes back to work?"

"The problem with that," I said, "is the police have seen that kind of thing. They get jaded and are sometimes over-zealous."

"Well I could never have done it. I hope you believe me. Nobody else did, not even my attorney."

"I plan on seeing your attorney, but we'll talk about that later. I have a few questions for you." The transcript was in front of me. It was marked all over and looked like a paper graded by a psycho English professor.

"It seems to me you were convicted on a lot of circumstantial evidence."

"Yes. That's true."

"The partial fingerprint on the knife was never matched to anyone. I don't know if there wasn't enough of a print to get a match or if the prints were not in AFIS. Do you know?"

"I don't know. My attorney just said nobody had been matched to the print."

"And two missing knives were never found."

Kiko got worked up over that. "I know, right? But the detectives thought I was lying and we never had the two other knives."

"I'm going to visit the detectives that worked your case, and I'll try to get a look at the evidence."

"Thank you so much for helping me." He leaned towards me. His eyes were red from crying, but they were bright with hope.

"Zeke and I will investigate. That's all I can promise right now."

"That's enough. I just need someone to try."

"We need something concrete to either prove you didn't do it or that proves who did. It has to be something that can't be refuted."

"Maybe when you see the evidence for yourself you'll see something to help us," he said in a voice full of hope.

"What happened to your house?"

"My brother lives there now with my parents. He took over the payments when I went to prison."

"Would he let me in? I'd like to look around and get a feel for how things are laid out."

"My brother knows I didn't kill anyone. He'll let you in. His name is Javier Valentino." He gave me the address and phone number of his brother and said, "Call him and tell him you're trying to help me. I already told him about you and Zeke coming to see me. He'll help you any way he can. My parents will, too. They never believed I killed anyone and especially not their grandchildren."

"Kiko, what do you think happened?"

"I think the man my wife was seeing killed them. One of the problems in my defense was that there was no forced entry. That's because Evie had let him in. I knew she was going to because she was breaking up with him. I had told her to choose between us. I wasn't willing to put up with that shit anymore."

"You said at the trial his name is Donny. Do you know the rest of it?"

"Donny is all I can tell you. I never heard a last name or even wanted to know it until the murders."

"Do you know where he lives or works?"

"No. If I knew any of that I would've found him myself. I know he killed my family." Kiko broke down at that point.

I went to his side in spite of the prying eyes of the stone-faced guard. I hugged Kiko a while, but I doubt if it helped.

After he quit crying I said, "I'll try to find Donny, but I need something to go on besides his first name. Think. Did Evie ever say anything about him that might be a clue about where he lived or worked?"

"We talked about him twice. The first time was when I found out about him. The second time was when I told her to choose between us."

"Tell me how you found out about him."

"It made me so furious. My little boy told me one day when we were at the park. He'd come down the slide and his pants had fallen down a little. I was teasing him about girls seeing his underwear. He blurted that he'd seen Donny's. I thought it was one of those silly things little kids say. He was baby-talking; he wasn't even three, and I didn't think anything about it. Then he said, 'Mommy saw him too,' and that got my attention. I asked him who was Donny and he couldn't explain it. Then I asked if Donny was a little boy or a big boy and he said 'big.' I asked if he was adult big or a big kid. He said, 'A man, Daddy.'

"I confronted Evie and we had a big fight. I hit her. I'd never hit her before. She called the police on me, and they made a report that hurt me at the trial. When they came we'd already gotten it straightened out. She said she wouldn't see him anymore. But she saw him after that, when the kids were sleeping and I was working. I know I should've left her but I loved her, and I wanted to make things right. She loved me too, I believe. And we had little bitty kids to think about."

"I assume you made love when you were home between jobs?"

"Yes."

"The other semen was a trace, so they assumed the killer used a condom that broke or was improperly handled."

"They were convinced I raped her. They said I'd come home and found her with him, and I raped her out of fury and killed all of them. Why didn't they assume he raped her? They said I killed her because I caught him making love to her. Even if that was true, I wouldn't have hurt my children! And why wouldn't I have killed him too if I was on a killing rampage?"

"That's because what people do in a rage doesn't necessarily make sense."

"If I'd come home and found that man with my wife I would've beat him up, you can bet on that, but I wouldn't have killed him."

"They believed he got away from you," I said. "And they made it stick. I don't think we have a chance unless I can locate Donny. If we can match him and the print and the semen, then we'll have something."

"Yes."

"Kiko, do you think she broke it off with him and he killed her and the children as revenge? What motive would he have to kill the kids? Lovers kill each other, but seldom children, and not such small ones who don't know anything."

"I don't know. I've gone over and over it in my head. I don't understand it either unless it was a way to hurt me because I'd won her back. Maybe he's a sick fuck that got off on it for all I know. Excuse my language. I don't mean disrespect."

"No problem. I've heard the word before."

He grinned.

"Look, I'm going to have a look at your house and talk to your brother and parents. Then I'll speak with the detectives who worked your case and with your attorney. After that I'll be back, probably the day after tomorrow."

"When will Zeke come?"

"Zeke might come with me. It depends on how busy he is. I want you to be thinking about Donny and how I can locate him."

"I'll think about it, but I don't have any idea."

"He's crucial, so please think of something."

"I'll try, but I don't think I know anything about him. My wife's family refused to admit she had a lover. Even when the other semen was found in Evie, they said it was a mistake made by the CSIs. It was a mistake all right, but not like they thought. Maybe you should talk to them, but don't tell them you're trying to help me. They wanted me to get the needle or be hung on the courthouse lawn."

"Kiko, why didn't you get the death penalty for killing three people?"

"My attorney suggested to the court that I'd sneaked home, not to kill them but to get a little. When I got there and found another man, I went into a murderous rage. He convinced the jury it was a crime of passion, not premeditated murder. It was the one good thing he did for me."

"I see."

"I never went home until two in the morning."

"Okay. Can you think of anything else I should know? Anything at all might help, no matter how insignificant it might seem."

"I didn't kill them, Margarita. Please keep that in your mind when you hear terrible things about me. I'm not a killer, and the man who did it is free."

"I'll keep that in mind. Will you write down your wife's family's names and phone numbers, their addresses, and anything else I need to know." At the top of the page of my notebook I wrote: "I'm not a Texas Ranger, but Zeke is. He got me in to see you. Don't say anything or I won't be able to come back." When I handed him the notebook, he read that and grinned and nodded. Then he wrote down the information I requested.

"I'm sure I'll have more questions when I come back. I can't think of anything else right now." I stood and held out my hand to him.

He couldn't stand because he was bolted to the floor, but he took my hand in both of his. "Thank you. Somehow, I'll pay you and Zeke back."

"That isn't necessary. We don't expect anything, and we're not doing it for pay. Keep your money because you're going to need it."

"But I have to do something for you," he protested. "You're saving my life."

"I haven't done anything yet. Let's see what happens and then we'll talk, okay? I'll be back soon."

I called to the guard to say I was ready to go. He let me out without saying a word while another uniformed man began to unbolt Kiko from the floor.

Chapter 10

1966, MAX AND LUCIA

Lucia had stopped crying, but Max knew she was still feeling down because she wasn't laughing and making up stories. It worried him. One thing that would help both of them would be to eat something substantial, so he decided to stop early to camp and see what he could do about that.

He put his arm around his wife to halt her. "Let's find a shady place to make a camp. I'll see what I can find for us to eat."

Lucia flung her arm at the vast desert before them. Waves of heat shimmered in the distance. "There's nothing! We can't eat creosote bushes and cacti! We might as well keep walking." She sounded angry and close to another crying fit, too close.

"Mi Amor, we need to rest and eat." Max spoke with tenderness but was also firm. "We don't have a schedule to keep. Please let's stop."

She relented. "Okay, Max. I wouldn't mind lying down a while."

"Do you feel unwell?"

"I'm just tired. I wish I could take a bath."

"I'll try to find water while you rest."

"You aren't going to leave me here while you go look for it?"

"I'm not going far. If resting a while doesn't suit you, you could make a spot for a campfire. I'll kill something so we can eat a real meal."

"But how will you do that?"

"With my slingshot."

She scoffed, but he ignored her. She had no idea what he could do with the simple weapon. His aim was deadly.

Max helped Lucia lay out the bedroll in the protective indention of a cliff face.

"I'm sorry I cried, Max."

"Lucia, Mi Reina, it's all right if you cry. I cried too. We miss our families and our ranches. Sometimes I think…" He stopped speaking.

"Sometimes you think what?"

"I think I shouldn't have taken you away. I shouldn't have married you, Lucia. Your father is so much more prosperous than mine and—"

"Stop it, Max! My people are poor, too. You're trying to take the blame for my crying and that isn't right. I miss my family and most of all, my mom, but I don't want to live with anyone but you. I love you, Max. I always knew I would leave home one day and make a life with you. That's the way I want it." She stomped her foot. "Don't make me say this again, Max. You'll make me angry, and I'll think you're not happy to be with me."

When he didn't speak, she placed her hands on either side of his head and looked into his eyes and saw the love there.

Max pulled her to him and she rested her head against his chest. "I adore you, Luce," he whispered into her hair.

"I know, Max."

After a few minutes of holding her, he said, "We need to eat. I'm so hungry all my thoughts have turned negative."

She shrugged. "We could roast a sotol heart."

"Is that good?"

"It tastes awful, but it's something. Or we could roast an agave stem."

"Those are huge. It would take all week." Max sighed. "We might as well whip up some tequila if we stick around that long."

Lucia laughed, and it lifted Max's heart and her own.

"I'm not kidding," she said. "I know how to roast sotol."

"I'll do better than that." Max kissed her and then headed for a multi-layered mountain a short distance away. It wasn't high, but it looked promising because of its many humps and ridges and the canyons that would be formed by them. Maybe there would be a spring or water trapped in a *tinaja*—a natural depression in rock that will hold water for a while after a rain.

When Max returned, Lucia sat up and smiled at him. "Oh Max, you're so clean and handsome!"

He blushed. "I brought all the water I could carry so you can clean up, too." He sank to his knees beside her, pushed the hair back from her face, and kissed her dirty neck. She began to unbutton her shirt, but Max laid his hand on her arm to stop her. "Wait. Would you like me to undress and bathe you? I want to."

"Oh, yes."

He undressed her, taking his time, kissing and teasing her and giving special attention to each part of her.

Lucia loved it but she grew impatient. "Max, you're going too slowly."

"Shh, Lucia, don't tell me how to do it. I'm taking my time, like they do when they make fine wine."

"This is not wine making, Max. I hope you don't make me wait that long."

He didn't.

Later, they walked back over to the spring so they could clean up again. They used their water containers like a shower to bathe and took care not to get their scent or dirt in the spring. It could have been the only source of water for miles, and animals and humans would depend on it.

On the way back, Max killed two jackrabbits and a couple of large lizards. They roasted them on a hot fire and ate them with the last of the packaged tortillas. They stuffed themselves until they couldn't eat any more. Having food in their bellies felt wonderful; it didn't matter that it had been tough and tasteless. They had eaten too fast to notice.

Max made another trek to the waterhole to refill everything he could carry. The sun had set and a full moon rose over the desert.

They slept a while, wrapped in each other, and then talked about walking through the rest of the night. It was April, but trekking all day in the unrelenting sun was still hot work and moving at night would be pleasant and there was plenty of light for it.

"We should go now and take advantage of the full moon." Lucia rose and tried to pull Max up from where he lay, naked and exhausted, covered with a blanket.

He groaned. "No, Luce, I can't move yet."

"On second thought…" She pulled the blanket away slowly, first revealing the throbbing pulse in his neck. It made her feel weak. She moved the blanket a few more inches to uncover his sculpted chest. Lucia sucked her bottom lip as she studied him, taking him in as if committing every detail to memory. He had never seen her do that before, and he felt embarrassed at first and then aroused.

Lucia licked her lips as her eyes moved back up his body. When their eyes met, her smoldering look took Max's breath.

"Take your clothes off, Mi Amor."

Instead, she smiled and dragged the blanket to just past Max's stomach. His skin looked creamy golden in the moonlight.

"I want you, Max."

"Take your clothes off, Baby."

"Hush, Max. I want to look at you. I almost never have a chance."

"I'm nothing special and anyway…" His words trailed off because she wasn't listening and he couldn't think.

She pulled the blanket again. Her grin was wicked. "Oh, Max."

"Baby, please."

Lucia removed her shirt and bra but she took so much time doing it Max wanted to tear them off. Then he couldn't take his eyes off her breasts. He reached to touch her, but she pulled away.

"Stop teasing, Luce. This isn't fair."

"It's not like you to whine, Max. Please stop talking. I can't concentrate." She yanked the blanket to Max's knees.

"You say I'm beautiful, Max, but you are the beautiful one."

"Please let me touch you, Lucia."

"We have all night, Mi Amor."

She snatched the blanket away from him. Max gasped with the surprise of it.

Lucia removed the rest of her clothes and threw them aside. She released her hair, and it tumbled over her shoulders and covered her breasts. She stood above him with her legs on either side of him. She looked like a golden statue with glowing tresses.

Max realized he was holding his breath.

"Max, I want to get on top of you."

"Come on, Luce. Just do it. I'm dying here."

When at last he could reach her, he moved her hair back over her shoulder. It fell forward again and covered his chest. "Oh, Luce..."

She kept him awake the rest of the night with her slow, sweet loving until they were too exhausted to move. They slept through most of the following day and didn't walk on until the moon rose again. Maximiliano Pacheco would always believe his son was conceived during that magical, moonlit night.

Chapter 11

Interviewing Kiko didn't take as long as I'd thought it would, so I had some afternoon left. I sat in the truck near the entrance to the prison. What a grim place. It was hard to shake the feeling of despondency that oozed from its walls. I looked to the mountains for comfort, but there are no mountains in Dallas.

I had calls to make, but I started with Barney. When he said, "Sheriff's Office, Deputy George speaking," I said, "Are you looking out my window?"

"Hey, Ricos!" There was a pause. "You know, technically that window is—"

"Don't whine to me about technicalities. If you're not looking out the window, would you go there for me?"

"Okay…"

"I need you to describe it for me."

"You're losing it up there in Dallas, aren't you?"

"Pretty much. There're no mountains, and I'm at a prison."

"Oh no…what did you do?"

That got a laugh out of me. "I'm here to interview someone. Are you standing at my window yet?"

"Yup. You know that bald, bodacious, reddish-brown hunk of stone that was on top of your hill?"

"Yeah?"

"It's still there."

"Barney, don't mess with me. Tell me what else you see."

"It's winter, Ricos. Nothing has changed since you left. Most everything is still brown or gold or gone underground. It's nap time around here."

"So nothing's happening there?"

72

"There's nothing worth repeating. Same ol', same ol'. Somebody saw you with Zeke, so the buzz is you've got a new mexicano."

"I guess they're saying he's an undercover drug lord posing as a Texas Ranger, since all the drug lords are so enamored of the Rangers."

He laughed. "The guys at the café say he's your 'type.' I started to mention that he's your father, but you know where that would go."

"He is my type. He's kind and gentle, and he thinks about somebody besides himself once in a while. Somehow, this call is not cheering me up."

"Sorry, Ricos; how 'bout if I describe the Chisos Mountains?"

"Please do."

"They're lookin' good for a weathered ol' bunch of rocks. It's one of those clear, cold days when things seem closer than usual. They're just standing there with their peaks all raggedy and their rugged outcroppings poking out. They look like ten million bucks shining in the sun. I wish you could see them."

"I just did. Thank you, Barney."

Next I called Kiko's former defense attorney, Aaron Franklin, who agreed to see me in the morning at ten o'clock, even though he didn't think he could help me. I wondered if he ever helped anyone.

Then I called the Dallas Police Department and asked to speak with a detective who had worked on the Francisco Valentino case; any detective who worked it would do. I gave the officer the trial date and the date of the murders.

"We remember that one," he said. How would they have forgotten it?

I had to wait a long time, but a man came to the phone and barked, "Detective Morrison."

I explained who I was and that I wanted to speak with him about the triple murder Valentino case. I introduced myself as "Deputy Ricos" since I am and so I wouldn't implicate Zeke or the Texas

Rangers. I didn't want him to connect us and hoped he wouldn't. Zeke had said to interview Kiko, not talk to detectives.

"What for?"

"Do you have a problem with talking about it?"

"Well no, but—"

"That's great. Then I'd like to meet you."

"It'll have to be early," he grumped. "I'm in a special class at nine."

I bet you ten bucks I know your instructor.

We agreed to meet at eight in the morning at Dino's, a restaurant across the street from police headquarters.

My last call was to Kiko's brother's house and I reached his mother. She agreed to see me as soon as I said I was trying to help her son. It didn't hurt when I told her I was Zeke's daughter. She explained how to get there from the prison, a trip she was bound to know well.

I found the house but didn't want to go in. I sat in front for a moment to calm myself. The place was small and attractive, with a neat, fenced yard. Kiko had been working two jobs so his family could live there.

The residence was located in an old section of Dallas. A few blocks over were huge houses that were worth a fortune at one time. The area was near downtown, and the properties were being bought by doctors, attorneys, and other professionals to be remodeled as offices. The lots were full of ancient trees that were being spared, it appeared. If I couldn't have mountains, I'd have to settle for trees.

I checked myself in the rearview mirror and removed the Ranger badge. These people already knew who I was and wanted to see me because I was trying to help. I didn't have to pretend to be somebody in authority.

A plump Latina woman answered the door smiling. She greeted me as if she'd always known me.

"I'm Angela Valentino," she told me in Spanish, "and you're

Zeke's baby girl." I'd never been called that before. I offered my hand, but she grabbed me and hugged me close.

For a while we talked about the murders. She was tearful and spoke with so much raw emotion I was tempted to cry more than once. She expressed her belief in her son; he would never have killed his wife and children. She was outraged that so many details were either ignored or overlooked by the detectives and the defense attorney, and of course she expressed her sincere hope that I would be able to free him.

All I could do was promise her I was working on it. Whether or not we could prove his innocence remained to be seen.

I asked her about her son's late wife's lover and she knew even less about him than Kiko did.

"I never knew about Evelyn's affair until the murder. Kiko kept that from us. I guess he was ashamed his wife was cheating on him."

"So you don't know anything about the man?"

"I only know that Kiko told Evie to let him go or move out of the house. I was amazed for my son to have such a forgiving attitude about it. He loved that woman in spite of their problems. He said they were just getting it together again when she was murdered."

"Would it be convenient if I looked around the house? I'd like to get a feel for things, where the rooms are, and try to picture how it was. If now is inconvenient, I could come back some other time."

"You can do it right now if you want to. Everything has been changed since the murders. We couldn't live here otherwise. If you like, I could give you a quick tour then leave you alone with it. I need to go to the grocery store, so you can have the place to yourself to look around on your own."

"That would be perfect."

I followed her into the kitchen, which she said had been repainted, and a new floor was laid a year ago. Still, I could see how things would've been. The counters, sink, and table were in the same place. The knife holder and knives were now part of the evidence in storage at Dallas Police Headquarters.

"Kiko came in here first for something to eat. Then he went from here to the bathroom. Just follow me."

We went down a short hallway and Angela stepped aside so I could enter. Then she led me to the master bedroom, pointing to where the bed used to be and where the chair was that Kiko used when he removed his clothes. She showed me the position of the light switch and retraced his steps based on what he'd told her.

I braced myself for the children's room. She said her son Javier lived in the room now and every reminder of the children had been removed. It had been painted, re-carpeted, and decorated to suit Javier. Still, the room gave me the creeps. I have a merciless imagination, and it was easy to picture the way things were the night of the murders.

Angela showed me where the boy's bed was and then pointed out where the crib had been. "They're little angels now," she said in Spanish with tears in her voice. "I hope they look in on us from time to time and know how much we loved them."

There was nothing at all I could say. I hoped it, too.

"I'll run along now. Make yourself at home." She studied my face. "My, but you look like Zeke. He must be so proud you're working with him."

"Thank you. I hope he is. I won't be here long." I handed her my card. "Please call me if you think of anything important. Or you could call Zeke."

"I'll do that. Thank you so much for what you're doing for my son. He needs to come home where he can grieve in peace and pick up the pieces of his life. He's been so busy trying to defend himself I don't think the reality of his loss has hit him. I feel so sad for him. He's alone in that awful place where he's been reduced to a number."

"We're going to do everything we can. I need to know about Donny more than anything. If you think of a way to find him or run into anyone who knows about him, please call me. I believe finding him will be crucial to freeing Kiko."

She left me to wander around alone. I tried to keep my imagination from going off the deep end. Even if I deleted the blood-and-gore scenes, the place still seemed sad. I didn't see a way to glean information from it now that it had been cleaned of all crime evidence.

I meandered from one room to the next. Zeke and I would have to depend on evidence collected by Detective Morrison, and I hoped we could figure out something from that. Since that was the evidence that convicted Kiko, I felt little hope about it. If the physical findings convicted him, then maybe he was guilty. That possibility lurked in the back of my mind.

As I was leaving the Valentino residence, I spotted a shed in the backyard. The minute I pulled the metal door open I regretted it. These were the things from Kiko's previous life. Boxes were stacked and marked: 'Evelyn, clothes'; or 'Susie, clothes.' Baby toys, a folded up playpen, and a stroller were gathering cobwebs and dust. Some boxes held papers and books.

I perused the sad collection of things, looking for something, anything. I jumped when a man barked, "What are you doing here?"

I whirled around, startled. The man had to be Kiko's brother. He looked just like him. I introduced myself and explained what I was doing.

He shook my hand warmly. "You're Zeke's daughter. I knew he would help us."

"I can't make any promises. There's so much evidence against him."

"But it's circumstantial!"

"I'll look at it tomorrow. I had hoped to find something in the house, but of course everything has changed since the murders."

"We kept these things because Kiko should be the one to say what to do with it. We couldn't bear to get rid of his stuff. His whole life, or what was his life, is in these boxes. The only things missing are what the police took or things that were too bloody and ruined to be retrievable."

"Let's step outside, Javier. I want to ask you a few questions."

We sat at a picnic table in the backyard beneath an oak tree. A lonely swing set was a grim reminder of what had been lost.

"What did you think of Evelyn?" I asked.

"I liked her a lot until she started cheating on my brother. He was working his ass off to give her and their kids the best life he could. I thought it was bullshit when she took a boyfriend behind his back."

"Were you surprised?"

"Yes, very surprised. She and Kiko always seemed happy. I think she got bored doing the same stuff every day with the kids and keeping house and all. He was gone a lot, but he was working, for pity's sake."

"Do you know if Kiko ever cheated on her?"

"I don't think so. My brother was all about his family. He didn't have time for another woman. He spent every spare moment with his wife and kids."

"Are you older or younger than Kiko?"

"I'm two years older. We've always been close, and I think he would've said something if he was messing around with someone else. He's not one of those macho cheater types. He loved Evie; I know that, and he would've died for his children."

"If Kiko is innocent, then what do you think happened?"

"I think it was that guy Donny who Evie was fucking—sorry. Kiko told me she was breaking it off with him. Maybe he flipped out. It's extreme to kill a whole family, but since I don't know the man, who can say?"

"Any other thoughts?"

"They said someone raped Evie. Kiko would never do that. His semen was in her and the prosecution made a big deal of it. What is surprising about that? He lived with her and he loved her. What about the other semen? It didn't match anybody in their databases, but it was still there. The police tried to find Donny, but it wasn't much of an effort. It was probably Donny's semen."

"Do you know Donny's last name or where he lives or works? Or know someone who might know?"

"No, I don't know anything except what little I heard from my brother. He didn't know anything either."

"Do you have any idea how she might have met him? Did she work?"

"She did until Susie was born. She was planning to go back to work. My mom was going to take care of the kids for her."

"What did Evie do?"

"She worked as a waitress at Sonny's Diner. It's about six blocks from here, back towards downtown. She could have met him there or anywhere. She hadn't worked in over a year, so maybe she didn't meet him at Sonny's, come to think of it."

"Is that where she was going back to work?"

"I think so, but Kiko could tell you for sure. They liked her there and she used to do great in tips, so I assume she was going back. Plus, she could walk to work, which helped since they only had one car."

"If you think of anything, will you call me? Tomorrow I'm talking to one of the detectives who worked the case, and I'll try to get a look at the evidence. I don't know what else to tell you."

"Thank you for what you're doing."

"You're welcome, Javier."

"Will we get to see Zeke?"

"I'm sure you will. He's teaching a class during the day, or he'd be with me."

"Tell him I said 'hey.'"

"I will."

On the way back to the hotel, I decided to stop at the family home of Evelyn Valentino since it was nearby. Her parents' name was Mendoza.

The house was larger than the Valentino home but was in the same area. It appeared well-cared-for and the yard was full of dormant rosebushes. They made me think of the conversation with Barney, and that made me smile. Then I realized this would be just as sad as the last place I visited. Murder hurts a lot of innocent people, not just the ones who die.

Evie was the daughter of the people who lived there and her children were their grandchildren, too. I'd been thinking of them as hostile witnesses, and that wasn't fair. Surely they would have no objection to us finding out who had killed their daughter and her children.

A slender, middle-aged woman with jet black hair opened the door and regarded at me with curiosity. "Yes?" She looked me up and down, probably wondering who I was and what I wanted.

I told her I was Deputy Margarita Ricos, a special investigator. Not a lie. I was a deputy on a special investigation.

"How can I help you?" She had an "I don't care who you are" attitude.

"I'd like to talk to you about your daughter's murder. I apologize for dropping by, but I happened to be in the area."

"Would you like to come in?"

I followed her into a neat and comfortable-looking living room and sat when she invited me to. I noticed a photo of the Valentino family hanging on the wall. Kiko had been cut away. That told me what I needed to know about their feelings towards their son-in-law.

"What is this about?" She sat on the edge of the sofa, watching me in a nervous way. On the side table was a picture of Evie and her children.

"I'm reinvestigating the murder of your daughter."

"But why?"

"It's possible that Francisco Valentino didn't kill her."

Her eyes went wide. "How can that be? They proved Kiko killed her."

"Evidence has come to light that bears investigation." Not only was I lying, I spoke with authority when I had none. "There was another man involved with your daughter."

"That's a lie!" She swallowed hard. "There was talk of another man at the trial, and even before the trial." Her words were tightly controlled and measured. "It was a bullshit story Kiko made up. He was jealous of Evelyn and was always accusing her of cheating on him with somebody."

"You don't believe she had a lover?"

"Of course not! My daughter was a good woman and a good mother. She treated Kiko like a king. It's disgusting he would say such a thing about her. That man is exactly where he belongs."

"How would you explain the second semen deposit?"

"According to the crime lab, it was a very small amount, like a drop. I think they got their samples confused or something. Most of the semen found was Kiko's, and the D.A. seemed to think that was incriminating enough to put him away."

Mistakes of that type are rare, but I didn't argue with her, poor woman. If we had been talking about my daughter, I would most likely have been just as blind to her shortcomings.

Since I hesitated, she continued. "Kiko hit her once and accused her of cheating on him and God knows what else. She called the police so there was a record of it, and of course this came out in the trial."

"Did he hit her often?"

"No, I don't think so. Evie wouldn't have put up with it. She loved him, but she would never have let a man beat on her. I raised her to have self-respect and to defend herself when necessary. That's why she went straight to the phone and reported his abuse."

"Was there a time when you liked Kiko?"

"Yes, I liked him very much—before. He was responsible and worked hard to provide for his family. He grew up poor, in falling-down apartments, and he wanted his children to have a house and a yard. I respected that about him.

"When he asked us for Evie's hand, he told her father and me that he would do whatever it took to provide a good life for her." She sobbed. "We trusted that would be true and never imagined he'd kill her."

"Does Evie have sisters and brothers?" In close Hispanic families, and in fact in most families, sisters tell each other everything. They would know things their parents never knew.

"Yes, she had two sisters and one brother."

"Do they all live here in Dallas?"

"Yes. Her brother, Jaime, lives next door to us. Both of her sisters live together in an apartment downtown. I'll write down their address and phone number for you. Georgina works as a paralegal and Myrna is attending college at night and works during the day as a secretary at an investment firm."

"Do you think Jaime is at home now?"

"No; he and his wife are at work. I'll write down his number, too. His wife is named Gloria. She's expecting and won't be working much longer." Her bottom lip trembled. "We're excited to have more grandchildren, but we'll never forget Evie or her precious babies."

Chapter 12

Max and Lucia walked on through the full-moon night. Their spirits were renewed by love, food, sleep, and communion with one another. Lucia entertained Max with made-up stories about their new home, his fame and fortune as the best cowboy in Texas, and how healthy and beautiful their children would be.

Max and Lucia were homesick, but they didn't want to go back, not yet. They daydreamed of visiting and taking money to help their parents. They would take their babies to meet the family. The people they loved were waiting for them and would wait as long as it took. They knew they would be in their families' prayers every day, and that their parents would always watch the road for signs of their return. The thought was comforting in the face of the fatigue, hunger, and all the dangers they faced, known and unknown.

On their fifth day in the United States, and after four days of walking, they came to a more mountainous area and the trek became more difficult. The land was lovely though, and with more vegetation than where they had been. That would mean more rabbits and other small game.

At dawn, Max spotted a fence line. It was a welcome sign of civilization.

"Look, Lucia, this must be a ranch. Maybe I can get work, and we can eat better before we move farther north." At least there would be frijoles and tortillas.

Ranches often hired men passing through to do short-term projects, and even hired them as cowboys. Their spirits rose at thoughts of hot food and a safe place to sleep. They continued the up-and-down climbing and hiking.

Lucia saw them before Max did, and she let out a cry that alarmed him. His eyes followed hers to two dead coyotes hanging on the fence a few yards away.

She started to run towards them, but Max grabbed her arm. "No, Lucia. Wait." He listened intently for any sound and heard nothing but the wind. He felt uneasy and wasn't sure why.

"Oh, Max, they're so beautiful." Lucia spoke in a hush and her voice was full of sadness. As they passed the dead animals, she became angry. "What is the point of hanging them there? So some guy is a great shot with a rifle. So what?"

Max was holding her hand, and he squeezed it. "I don't know, Luce. Do you think they do it to scare away other coyotes?"

They laughed, but their laughter caught in their throats. Ahead were two men hanging on the fence, two Mexican men. There was a crude cardboard sign pinned to the rear of one of them: PRO- HIBIDA LA ENTRADA, Spanish for NO TRESPASSING. The message was clear enough without the sign.

Max glanced at Lucia. Her mouth was open, and the look on her face was one he had never seen. He would have given anything to spare her this sight.

"We have to take them down," Lucia cried. "This is so disrespectful."

"Yes. Let me think. What'll we do with them? We have no way to bury them, and we can't carry them." Max moved closer to the men, but motioned to Lucia to stay back. He looked at their faces and returned to her quickly. "If you'll keep a lookout, I'll get them off the fence."

"What am I looking out for?" Lucia had noticed him looking around, and it made her nervous.

"We don't want to end up on this fence!" Max wished he could take back the panic in his voice. He didn't want Lucia to be afraid, but they had to be wary. He continued to speak, but with forced calm. "We can't get caught taking these men down. Someone around here shot them just for being here. We're here too, Luce."

She nodded grimly.

"On this ranch, being Mexican is a crime." Then Max added, "We need to get out of here."

"We can't leave them like this."

"That's why I'm going to move them, and you're going to keep watch, okay?"

"Okay, Max. I understand."

Max's task was difficult. He had to lift each body from the fence without getting them caught on it. He carried them to the base of the largest tree he saw, a juniper. He worked up a sweat, even though the early morning hour was cool. Whatever pain the strain caused his body, his heart hurt worse. The dead men were young, not much older than he was, and they looked like brothers.

Once the bodies were laid side-by-side on the ground, Max removed their identification so he could send notice to their relatives. He removed everything personal, including the small amount of money they carried. All of it would be returned to México, but it made the young couple sad that the bodies would never be buried in their homeland, or be buried at all.

Lucia gathered a few wildflowers and some greenery and put a bouquet on the chest of each man while Max straightened their clothing and attempted to give them dignity. Then they bowed their heads over the dead men, and each said their own silent prayer. Max hoped their spirits had already returned to México. Lucia's thoughts were with their family and what incredible sadness they faced.

Max thought of taking the water containers, but they already had too much weight to carry. The men had food, the same type of homemade hard tack they'd brought from home. He stuffed it into his pack with gratitude. He didn't know how long it would be before he and Lucia found a place where they would be safe. They would need something to eat.

Max held out his hand to Lucia. "Let's go, Mi Amor. We shouldn't follow this fence line after all."

She grabbed his hand and forced herself to smile at him. With sad hearts, the couple headed away from where they had thought they'd be welcome. Max constantly checked over his shoulder, his ears perked for the sound of humans, horses, or gunshots.

When they came to the foothills of a sloping mountain, they ducked into the cool labyrinth of canyons formed by its arroyos. They didn't dare make a fire, which meant next to nothing to eat, but neither of them felt hungry. There they slept until the next rise of the moon.

Chapter 13

As I was about to put my key card in the hotel room's door, it opened. There stood Zeke in a black tuxedo with a purple shirt. Wow.

"Who's getting married?" I asked when he stepped up to hug me.

"I'm taking my best girl out on the town."

"Is that so, Tuxedo Man?"

"Do you like the way it looks?" He modeled it, turning around.

"You look amazing. Who's the lucky girl?"

"Who do you think? Come see what I bought you. I hope you'll like it. I know it's risky buying clothes for a woman."

On the bed was spread a gorgeous dress that was the same rich purple color as his shirt. It had long sleeves that ended in points at the hand. It was long and slinky and soft and silky. It was feminine without being frilly. I couldn't have picked a better dress myself.

"It's beautiful, Zeke. I love it!"

"I guess I know you better than you think I do."

"How did you know the right size?"

"Well, I held up my hands to the saleswoman and told her 'her hips are about this big' and 'she is this tall.' When she gaped at me, I called your mother."

I laughed. "Wow."

"I got the number out of your shoes. I hope you like them, too."

Next to the dress were shiny black pumps with criss-crossing straps and three-inch heels. They were beautiful.

"Stephanie says you like sexy shoes, but I thought those were about as sexy as a father should go."

"These are perfect, Zeke. Thank you."

"You're welcome. While you get dressed, I'm going to wait for you in the lobby. Just come down there when you're ready, okay?"

"Don't let some woman pick you up, Zeke."

"I already have a date."

"Right, but if you go to the lobby looking like that…"

"Put a move on it then."

Zeke took my hand and squeezed it. "This is the best restaurant in all of Dallas."

I had no doubt of it.

"Do you know why I brought you here?"

"To dine and dance?"

"Yes, those are reasons, but I have a history here. This is where I washed dishes and bussed tables and scrubbed bathrooms and cleaned up other peoples' messes when I was a kid. I told myself I'd come back here someday with a beautiful woman. I had no idea she'd be my daughter."

Tears sprang to my eyes. "Thank you, Zeke. I feel honored to have you as a father. You made it against practically all the odds there are."

"Don't give me too much credit, Margarita."

"Should I give the credit to your foster parents?"

"You know better than that."

That was a perfect intro to ask him for permission to do research into his background, but he was in a great mood, and I didn't want to ruin such a lovely evening. We danced until it was hard to stand then took a taxi back to the hotel.

We changed our clothes and sat on the balcony. I told him about my day and what I had discovered and pointed out what we still didn't know. Before long, we decided we should go to bed. Both of us had to get up early.

Zeke went in to the bathroom to brush his teeth and I made my surprise attack. "Will you be mad if I ask about your parents?"

"No." He came to the door, his toothbrush stuck in his mouth. "What?"

"Well, I was wondering if you'd be angry if I tried to find your records from the orphanage."

He went back into the bathroom without saying anything, and I thought I'd blown it. He finished brushing his teeth and came back into the room.

"It's okay with me. I can't imagine why you want to waste your time with it, but knock yourself out." He sat down on the edge of my bed. "You were going to do it anyway, weren't you?"

"No. I won't do it if you tell me not to, Zeke. I mean it. It's your past and you have a right to privacy."

"They're your grandparents, so you have rights, too. I just don't want you to get hurt or for me to get hurt. I guess that's why I never looked up my past. I've certainly had every mechanism to do that at my disposal."

"But weren't you curious? You're an investigator on the most elite team in Texas. It seems like you'd investigate your roots."

"Margarita, what you don't seem to understand is that I grew up hurting. I was convinced in my heart I had parents who loved me and would come for me if I waited. That's every orphan's dream. It hurt when I realized that was never going to happen. I got over it, and I don't want to hurt anymore."

"I'm sorry, but I keep thinking maybe they didn't give you up. Maybe something bad happened to them."

"Stop right there. I've wished that for as long as I can remember, and wishing just doesn't make it so. I know you want to do a good thing for me, and I appreciate it, but I can't get my hopes up again. If you want to find out for yourself, go ahead; I won't be angry. Just leave me out of it, okay?"

"If I find out something good, can I tell you?"

"Of course, but don't count on that. I've been passed around to various people. I've felt unwanted and unloved for most of my life. I went through hell in a hundred ways, and that was before I was sixteen. Now I have contentment and a daughter I'm proud of, and I don't want my parents to screw that up, too. I hope you can understand."

"I won't mention this again unless I find out something good."

"It won't work like you think. You're so full of hope. I don't want you to get hurt, Sweetheart. These people are your grandparents. I appreciate that you want to know about them, but I don't want either of us to be hurt."

"Okay, Zeke."

"I hate that I sound so whiny, but you haven't lived my life."

"I'm sorry. Maybe I'll leave the whole thing alone."

"That would be best. Besides, don't you have enough to investigate already, my little chip-off-the-old-block?"

We laughed, hugged, and went to bed. As I lay there, I thought I was going to have to accept my crack whore grandmother, my died-in-prison convict grandfather, and work hard to find out the truth about Kiko Valentino.

Yeah, right.

Day was dawning when I awakened with a start. Zeke was a few inches from my face staring at me. He stood up straight when my eyes opened.

"Good morning," he greeted. "I guess you wonder what I was doing."

"That question crossed my mind."

"I was looking at you."

"Yeah, I saw that. What for?"

He sat on the side of my bed, and I moved over a little to make room. "You'll think I'm weird, but I never went through the parenting stage of watching your baby in wonder, and I never even understood what that was about. I was coming back from the bathroom, and the light hit your face in a certain way, and I just thought how miraculous it is that I have a kid. I said to myself, 'Zeke, this face belongs to your daughter!' And I started studying it."

"What do you think?"

"You have a wonderful face, yet you look a little bit like me."

I laughed. "Look again. I look a lot like you."

"It makes me crazy with pride. I want to go out on the balcony and scream to the world that I have a kid! And she looks like me!"

"That's sweet. Maybe you should wait until the sun gets a bit higher in the sky. Someone might shoot you. Why are we talking about my face so early?"

"I didn't mean to wake you."

"So you were sneaky-peeking me?"

"Yes. I admit it."

"I like to look at your face, too. It's weird to see you after all this time. What I mean is I've been looking at your face every day since I can remember, but I didn't know it was yours. That thing parents do with their babies, I think the babies do it back. They bond. Maybe we're bonding."

"That's good, isn't it?"

"Yes, Zeke."

"You don't think I'm weird or creepy?"

"No. I think you're great."

He smacked me on the leg. "Get up! Let's get some breakfast and talk about what we're doing today. Kiko is not getting any younger or saner sitting over there in that prison."

Chapter 14

1966, MAX AND LUCIA

Max rolled over and pulled Lucia to him. "The moon is rising, Amor."

"That's not my fault," she murmured.

He laughed and buried his face in her hair. "We have to go."

As her mind cleared, the events of the previous day came back to Lucia in a rush. She held onto Max. "For the first time, I feel afraid of this country."

"Don't be afraid. It's some people, not the whole country. We'll be careful and get out of this area tonight. Then we'll be fine." He hoped.

The young couple had been walking less than an hour when fast-approaching hoof beats paralyzed them in their tracks. Max's eyes swept the area, but he saw no place to hide. All they could do was wait and see.

He pulled Lucia to a tall yucca and they sat against it, shaded from the bright light of the moon. Max held his wife's hand and prayed they wouldn't be noticed.

"Max," Lucia whispered as the sound came closer, "if they kill us, I hope they hang us together on the fence. I always want to be with you."

He squeezed her hand. "I love you, Lucia. Never forget it."

Within moments, three men on horseback galloped up in a cloud of dust and stopped at the yucca.

One of the men jumped down from his horse. "What are you doing here?" he demanded, using gringo Spanish.

"We're passing through, looking for work. We mean no harm." Max stood. Then he moved protectively in front of his wife, who was still seated.

"You're on the Wilson-McClintock Ranch," the cowboy growled, "without permission."

"Do you have work for me? I'm a good cowboy."

"You look young and strong," the man said as he looked Max over.

"Yes, I am."

"Who are you hiding in the shadows there?" He was trying hard to see Lucia, and it filled Max with dread.

"This is Lucia, my wife." He still didn't move from in front of her.

"Can she cook?"

"Yes sir, quite well. She can also ride and rope as well as any man I ever knew."

The three men exchanged looks and started laughing. One of them said, "On our ranch women do women's work, not cowboys' work." The leader translated that into Spanish, more or less.

"She can do whatever you need to have done." Max was sorry he'd said it that way.

The leader translated, and the men looked at each other and laughed. It was not good laughter but full of underlying meaning, and their looks were lecherous. They stared at Lucia and, although Max didn't understand their words, he felt great fear for his beautiful wife.

"We were looking for a good place to camp, and we saw your tracks." The one who appeared to be the leader answered a question Max hadn't had to ask. "In the morning we'll take you to headquarters to talk to the foreman. I'm sure there's work. How long have you been walking?"

"This is the beginning of the sixth day in Texas."

The men dismounted and tied the horses to the yucca. Max helped them unload saddlebags and then build a fire. He hoped they would cook something or offer food of any kind. He was so hungry he didn't care what it was.

Meanwhile, they watched his wife with hungry eyes. He told himself over and over that the men were just looking. They meant no harm. Men look at women. If a man didn't notice Lucia, he was blind.

The cowboys brought out biscuits, dried beef, fruit, cheese, and cookies. Max accepted with thanks everything he was offered and shared it with Lucia. He smiled and tried to reassure her wordlessly that all would be well.

After a while, a bottle of bourbon was brought out and passed around. Max had never had bourbon, only tequila and sotol, but he took a swig from the bottle when it was offered. Lucia passed it on without trying it. It smelled foul to her.

The men spoke of life on the ranch and told Max it was a good place to work. Everyone was treated with fairness and there was always plenty to eat. A married couple would be assigned a private room, they said. Max raised his eyes to the sky and hoped it was true.

When he glanced over at her, he saw the firelight reflected in Lucia's black eyes and the happiness, too. She was pleased at that news, her look plainly said.

Max looked back at the men. He tried to be serious but he was suppressing a smile. They talked about cattle and broncos, the pastures, the wells, and rodeos. Max was thinking of his naked wife and the way she had glowed in the light of the moon. He hoped the men would not want to stay awake talking and drinking much longer.

The next morning, the cowboys offered coffee, frijoles, bacon, and biscuits. It was more food than Max and Lucia had eaten in the entire previous week. There was plenty to go around, and when Max was full, they still offered more.

For a short time, they sat around drinking coffee and then began packing up the horses. It was decided that Max would ride behind Sam, the lightweight of the cowboys, and Lucia would ride behind Billy Joe, the one who seemed to be in charge. Max didn't like it, but they were tired of walking and might never find the headquarters unless they went with the cowboys. Besides, he needed to work and, once they got to the ranch, they would have food and even a real bed.

As Sam took off with Max, Lucia called, "Don't forget, Max."

"I never will, Lucia."

She held onto Billy Joe's belt and didn't put her arms around him until they began to gallop and she had no choice. It was that or be bounced off the back of the horse. He said something to her in English, but she had no idea what he meant and didn't answer.

They galloped along with the cool morning air in their faces. Mountains shone in the sunlight and quail scurried out of their way. The brightly colored wildflowers, stirred by a gentle breeze, seemed to bow to the passing riders in salute.

Everything will be okay, Max thought, willing it so. The Wilson-McClintock Ranch was beautiful, and he would work there until they could afford to move on to the Triple-Bar near Dallas.

Chapter 15

Detective Peter Morrison was a short, stocky man at least fifty years old. His hair was dark brown but graying. A thick Charlie Chaplin-style moustache and bushy eyebrows made him look more like an escapee from a comedy sketch than a serious detective, but I tried to maintain a grip on my imagination. His dark suit and coordinating tie, along with a name plate that read "DETECTIVE MORRISON," made him not funny.

When I walked in the door at Dino's, he was sitting by a window that looked out onto the street. He seemed lost in thought but saw me and quickly rose as if he knew who I was.

"Deputy Ricos?" He bowed slightly and stepped away from the table, ready to pull out the chair for me.

I took his hand and smiled at him. "How did you know me?"

"I don't know you yet. I guessed. I'm good at putting voices with faces. I guess it's something I've developed over years of talking to people."

He pulled out the chair for me and motioned to the waitress for coffee.

"Thank you for meeting with me, Detective Morrison. I'm sure you're busy, and I'll try not to take much of your time."

"How can I help you?"

"I was contacted by Francisco Valentino. He says he's been wrongfully imprisoned and asked for my help."

The detective rolled his eyes. "They all say that; I'm sure you know it."

"Yes. I know, but I promised him I would look into his case. He insists another man raped and murdered his wife. If you'll recall, there was a second deposit of semen found in Evelyn Valentino."

"Yes, but—" He tried to interrupt me but I didn't let him.

96

"It was never determined who it belonged to. Francisco believes it was a man his wife had been seeing. She was planning to break up with him and had let him into the house that night."

"And he went berserk with rage and killed all of them. Yes, I've heard this theory before, Deputy." Morrison was jerky with impatience.

"I'd like to hear your take on the case. You worked it, so I know you have a view of it that no one else could have." I gave him a radiant smile. *Take that.*

"I brought a copy of my notes because I knew you were going to ask that. You may keep them if you like. I was sent to the scene as one of the first responders." He lifted papers from the table but set them back on it. "Let me back up. The first thing to happen was a call to the 911 dispatcher at about 10:45 PM. A hysterical woman screamed, 'Help me; he's trying to get in. It's Del. I know it's Del trying to get in. He's going to kill me.'

"Then a few seconds later, she said, 'No, it's a mistake. I'm so sorry.' The dispatcher asked if she was sure all was well and she insisted it was. All this is recorded if you'd like to hear it. You don't have to take my word on it. Normally our protocol is to go to the scene anyway because often the call is legit and the caller loses their nerve for whatever reason. That night was so busy they had to call in off-duty officers. It was like a zoo at headquarters. I was working another murder when I got the call to go to the Valentino home."

He paused and stared at his coffee. "Honestly, I've never gone to a scene like that one. Remembering it kept me up nights."

"Please tell me about it."

"There was blood everywhere. It was tracked all over the house, back and forth from the master bedroom to the kids' room. It was the most gruesome sight you can imagine. The only footprints were those of Francisco Valentino, back and forth, back and forth. Our CSIs went nuts.

"Bloody fingerprints were in the kitchen, in the master bedroom, on the railing of the little boy's bed, and all over the crib. He was holding the baby girl when we got there, and he wouldn't let anyone take her for a long time. It was as if he'd gone insane. The poor little child had bled out in her crib, and what blood was on her and her clothes transferred to the front of her father on top of the mother's blood and the son's blood. He was soaked to the skin with their blood."

Morrison paused while the waitress poured more coffee in his mug. She gave me a disapproving look because I hadn't touched mine.

"It appeared he'd cut himself when trying to clean up the knife in the kitchen. There was a droplet of his blood on the counter and one on the floor and some of his blood in the sink. He tried to clean up in the bathroom. There was a smear there and a bloody towel in the dirty clothes hamper.

"What we thought happened was that Valentino suspected his wife was stepping out. He left work to spy on her and caught her with the guy. He went into a rage, scared the man away, and then raped his wife in his rage. After that, he killed her by stabbing her repeatedly."

"How do you explain the murder of the children?"

"It's hard to explain why a man would kill his innocent children, but the only thing I could figure out was that the smell of blood, the rage, and his violent actions against his wife sent him over the edge. He went on a murdering rampage. He might have killed anyone who got in his way at that point."

"Why wouldn't he have killed the other man?"

"I assume he got away, if there was another man."

"If you don't believe there was another man, how do explain two different deposits of semen?"

"She could have gotten that earlier in the day for all we know."

"Sure, but that still means there was another man."

"Say there was a man there. Valentino may have injured him but we couldn't be sure. There was a speck of blood on the butcher knife that didn't match any of the other parties involved. We assume it was the lover's blood."

"Did you try to find him?"

"Of course we did, but we hit one wall after another. All we had to go on was 'Del' from the phone call, and 'Donny,' which we got from the accused. He claimed his wife's lover's name was Donny. No one in the wife's family knew of him. I thought Del could be a shortened last name or maybe it was Dell or maybe there were two men. We searched both names, but we got nowhere."

"You tried Donny Dell I suppose?"

"Yes, but we got nothing. We asked neighbors, friends, and family if they knew a Donny or a Del or any version of those names. The wife's family swears she wasn't having an affair."

"Yes, I know."

"They say Francisco was jealous and made up a lover. But we did have that call about 'Del' in the wife's own voice, so there had to be something to that."

That was the first I'd heard about Del and wondered if Kiko had ever heard that name. "The phone call was never brought up at the trial, was it?"

"No, I don't believe it was. I guess the prosecutor thought he had enough without bringing that into it."

"So you never felt there was any evidence that pointed away from him?"

"No. I never did. The evidence supported my first impressions of that case."

"Would you let me look at it? I'd like to be able to tell Francisco that I saw it. I told him if the evidence says he did it, I'd have to go with that."

"I feel sorry for the guy," Morrison said. "He was eaten up with remorse, but that won't bring back those poor little children of his."

He paused to drink coffee. "Yes, to answer your question. I'll have the evidence brought from our storage facility. You can use one of the interview rooms to study it. I think you will agree with me when you see it."

"I'm sure I will, but I want to see it for myself."

"I can have it in the room and ready for you by three this afternoon. You'll just have to sign to get in and show your I.D."

I thanked Detective Morrison for his help.

"Let me know if you have any questions. I'll be out of class around four. You could leave me a message or wait for me at headquarters."

"Thanks, I will."

"You know, you remind me of our instructor. Do you know Zeke Pacheco?"

"He's my father."

"Well, I'll be."

Aaron Franklin's office was located in the Federal Building downtown, not far from our hotel. It was a short cab ride, so I decided to run. I needed to. Drink or run; there are days when I have to pick one.

I jogged out of the elevator and headed for the hotel doors. Before I reached them, one of the doormen opened the door as wide as it would go and held it like that. He was a wiry man of medium height with curly, close-cropped, white hair. His skin was the color of dark chocolate and looked just as smooth. So happy and energetic, I thought he could make the sun come out during a dark desert thunderstorm. He brought to mind a jazz musician but I have no idea why.

I laughed and stopped at the door. "Is this your subtle way of saying I'm wide?"

"Oh no, Baby Girl, I would never call you wide."

I was still suspicious. "You're trying to say something."

His dark eyes sparkled. "If you keep running, you'll never be wide."

"That's the general idea."

He laughed. "Not nobody chasin' you, I hope, unless you want him to."

I grinned and took off. His laughter faded as the door closed.

Running felt good to mind, body, and soul, and although I missed my usual scenery, running in a city is at least interesting. Some people glared at me as if I had stolen something. Others, usually in business attire, would smile, and I had the impression they wished they were running with me. Dodging traffic, pedestrians, and sidewalk obstructions was a constant challenge. I couldn't build up any speed or even settle into a steady jog. But hey, I was moving my body and clearing my mind and at the same time, not drinking. Touchdown for Team Ricos!

I changed my clothes in the lobby restroom of the building then found Aaron Franklin's office. After a secretary called him to the front, he greeted me and led me down a corridor to the inner domain. He was in a firm with two other attorneys. They didn't seem to be doing all that well, which was no big surprise if Kiko's case was an example of the quality of their work.

Aaron Franklin was a pudgy redhead with freckles. He was cute in a little-boy, Opie Taylor sort of way. Guessing, I thought late thirties, too old to have the little boy thing working for him.

"What can I do for you, Ms. Ricos?"

"I want to talk about your defense of Francisco Valentino. I'd like to record our conversation so I can refer to it later if that's okay."

"No." He waved his hand. "I don't agree to a recording."

That was no surprise. Attorneys never agree to that, but it's fun to ask. I got out a pen and notepad. "Either way, I have a few questions."

"Let's hear them." He was cold in addition to incompetent. "I assume you think he's innocent?"

"Don't you? You were his attorney."

He sighed as if I'd been there all day bothering him. "Yes, I was his attorney. No, I don't think he's innocent."

"I read the transcript of the trial, and it seems to me you went along with the prosecution on most things. It was rare for you to object to anything, and you didn't bring in many witnesses on behalf of Mr. Valentino."

"You're saying I didn't do my job." He shoved away from the desk and stood glaring down at me. If he meant to be intimidating, it worked.

"Please calm down, Mr. Franklin. I'm not here to criticize you."

"I don't need you to come in here and tell me how I should do my job. You're not an attorney, are you?"

"I'm not; I'm a deputy sheriff. I don't mean to insult your professional abilities. I'm trying to understand the things that happened."

He sat and tried to get his temper under control. "What is your purpose here?"

"Mr. Valentino contacted me proclaiming his innocence. He says he wasn't defended properly and that some of the evidence was ignored." I held up my hands to stop the tirade I knew was coming. "I know, I know. Don't get angry. I'm taking all of it with a grain at this point, but one thing does bother me."

"What's that?" His body language said *Bite me*.

"There was semen from two men in Mrs. Valentino. It was assumed her husband raped her and then killed her. Why wouldn't you, his defense attorney, try to make something out of that other semen? Maybe the other man was the rapist and killer. It seems like that would have put reasonable doubt in the minds of the jurors. It sure puts plenty of doubt in my mind."

"You only know what Valentino tells you."

"I read the trial transcript. But go ahead, enlighten me, please." I gave him a little *Bite me* attitude right back.

"All the evidence pointed to Francisco Valentino. You should look at it. You'll see what I mean." He was trying to dismiss me, but I wasn't having it.

"You haven't answered my question."

If looks could kill, I wouldn't be writing this. "The police tried to find the unknown man and couldn't track him down," he continued when I didn't offer to leave. "They also had unknown blood on the knife that killed Mrs. Valentino, so they thought her husband attacked her lover and he had somehow gotten away. Valentino is guilty as hell. He was covered in the blood of his family members."

"He admits he touched his wife," I said. "He was horrified and acted out of love and shock. He held her, and then he stumbled through the house and touched his kids, the walls, and their beds. He mixed the blood up all over the place. That doesn't make him guilty. If I came home and found my entire family stabbed to death, I might do the same thing. I can't imagine the horror of it and especially the kids. That would send me over the edge."

"He was over it," said Franklin. "He was holding the dead baby when the police got there."

"That doesn't make him guilty. He loved his child and picked her up. Wouldn't you pick up your dead baby?"

"I don't know. I wouldn't stab my baby."

"What makes you so sure he stabbed his?"

"Go look at the evidence; you'll see. Also, he was a wife-beater. That should tell you something."

"He hit her one time."

"So you think it's all right for men to hit women?"

"Of course not, but I wouldn't make the jump from hitting once to raping and killing her and the kids."

"Spousal abuse often escalates to killing."

"But it was one time."

"You don't know that. It was *reported* one time. He could have hit her hundreds of times."

"Even the wife's mother says he didn't abuse her."

"You've spoken with her?"

"Yes."

"You should have been his defense attorney."

"Look, I'm not saying he's innocent, just that the possibility is there. It seems like you would've glommed onto any little thing. Isn't that what defense attorneys do? I just can't believe you didn't bring up the unknown semen donor and the idea that he might have been the killer instead of Kiko."

"I did bring him up! The prosecutor used that against us, saying the semen proved the existence of the lover, which explained the rage and jealousy, which explained the murders. I didn't have anything that said something different."

"It's one thing to lose it with your spouse, but another to kill innocent babies. What father would do that?"

"Some macho Latino wife-beater is who," he spit.

"Oh, so it's about him being Latino. I can't believe I didn't get that at first."

"Look, I didn't mean it that way. I didn't think he was guilty only because he's Latino."

I stood. "Thanks for your time."

"I don't want you to leave with the wrong impression. I gave Valentino the best defense I could. I'm sorry I said what I did just now."

He was just sorry he'd let his racism show.

Chapter 16

1966, MAX AND LUCIA AND THE
WILSON- McCLINTOCK RANCH

Max told the ranch foreman he was a good cowboy and that was true, but even so, he was first assigned to build a rock wall separating two pastures. He worked with a crew of other mexicanos, so there was plenty of camaraderie in addition to the backbreaking work. The men joked, sang, and talked about their families and the land. It was beautiful, and that helped. The ranch was in the foothills of mountains and the vistas, even from where they were working, were magnificent.

Max understood that he was new and would have to prove himself, but he wondered when they would give him a chance to do that.

Lucia was put to work in the ranch kitchen. It was hard, constant work, but the other women welcomed her and made her feel at home. They spoke of family members working in the U.S. and of their families in Mexico. They made up stories and songs, an activity at which Lucia excelled.

In spite of long hours and grueling work, Max and Lucia were happy and looked forward to the day's end when they would be alone in their tiny room. There was scarcely space to turn around, but it had a bed with a mattress and a door that locked.

At the end of two weeks, Billy Joe, the cowboy Max had originally mistrusted and disliked, came to the living quarters of the Mexican workers at dark, as people were beginning to settle down for the night.

He took Max aside. "There's something you need to know, and then you can tell the other men for me. Today the ranch manager called the Border Patrol to come for you guys tomorrow."

"But tomorrow is payday."

"He isn't going to pay you."

"But we've worked so hard—"

"I know, Max, and I'm sorry, but listen to me." His tone was urgent. "You need to take all the food and water you can carry, and get out of here right now. Go as far away as you can go before daylight, and don't walk near any roads." Billy Joe took a crumpled paper from his pocket. "I made you a map that shows the highway, dirt roads, pastures, and ranches you should avoid. The Dagger Mountain Ranch is twenty miles from here, maybe less going cross-country. They're hiring, and they'll pay you for work done. I'm sorry I brought you here."

Max was too stunned and angry to speak.

"I didn't know this would happen. Please believe me."

"I'm not blaming you. Thank you for warning me." It made Max sick to think of all the damned hard work in the sun—for nothing. He would be leaving with his pockets as empty as when he'd arrived.

"You'll warn the others?"

"Yes."

"If you get caught, don't mention that I spoke with you."

"Of course I won't."

"Adiós, Max." They shook hands.

"Adiós, amigo."

An hour later, a group of seven men and one woman left behind the once-promising Wilson-McClintock Ranch.

Chapter 17

Back in the lobby bathroom, I stripped down to running clothes again and took off towards the hotel. It was a good thing I was preoccupied with thoughts of that poor-excuse-for-a-human-being attorney because I passed about a hundred bars. Every one of them looked like a dark, worry-free place to lose an afternoon. Flashing neon signs in windows taunted me. Miller. Heineken. Budweiser. Tecate. Who cared? Pick one and go for it.

I was so agitated by my interview with Aaron Franklin I ran the route twice to calm myself. When I headed for the hotel doors, the doorman held it as wide as it would go and made me laugh.

He tried to look serious, but his eyes gave him away. He started to speak but began to laugh instead. The sound was musical; maybe that was why I thought of a jazz musician when I saw him.

After I cleaned up, I went to my appointment with Georgina Mendoza, the sister of Evelyn Valentino. She had agreed to meet me at a coffee shop near her office but could only give me fifteen minutes because it was her afternoon break.

Georgina looked much like Evelyn. Her hair was shorter and she wore more make-up, but the resemblance was strong. We didn't need fifteen minutes to establish that if she knew anything about her sister's affair, she wasn't going to tell me about it.

She was quiet and resentful of someone trying to "drag up dirt" about her beloved murdered sister.

"She's dead," she spit. "Isn't that enough for you people?"

"I'm sorry for your loss," I said with feeling because I did feel sadness at the scope of the tragedy for all involved, "but what if an innocent man spends the rest of his life in prison?"

She gave a snorting laugh of derision. "That bastard is where he belongs."

"Have you always disliked him?"

"Of course not, but I hate him now. He stabbed Evie and her babies to death. Can't you understand that?"

"Sure, I can, but what if he didn't do it?"

"How did you get into this mess? What are you to Kiko? Are you a lover of his or what? What's it to you?"

She knew I was not a lover or even a personal friend. I supposed she wanted to insult me because she was angry and thought I was sullying her sister's reputation. I understood her feelings, but I needed to know what she knew.

"No, nothing like that," I assured her. "I've been assigned the investigation of his case because he may not have gotten a fair trial."

"Why? Because he went to prison?"

"No, it's because—"

"Who assigned you?"

"I'm assisting a Texas Ranger who is reopening the investigation. A question has been raised because there was semen found in your sister that did not belong to your brother-in-law."

"That's old news."

"Maybe so, but the case is being reopened."

She rubbed her temples. "That is such bullshit. It was probably a crime lab error. Isn't that possible?"

"It's not likely it was an error."

"Of course you're on the side of those people."

"I'm not on anyone's side. I'm investigating. I'm not here to drag up dirt about your sister. People have affairs. I'm not trying to say anything bad about her. I'm not judging her."

"You don't think it could have been an error?" Her eyes were pleading. "I mean it was just a tiny bit." She looked like she was going to cry.

"No. I don't think it was an error. The crime lab here is excellent. The Medical Examiners are careful and know what they're doing.

I don't believe a mistake was made, Georgina. A tiny bit of semen tells the same story as a large amount. I'm sorry. I think your sister was having an affair, and I think he was the man who killed her and her babies. If you'll think about it, I think that idea fits."

She said nothing, so I ploughed ahead. "Your mother told me Kiko loved his family. He was working hard to provide a good life for them. It doesn't make sense that he'd kill his children. His wife, maybe, but why kill the children?"

Georgina began to cry. "They were so little," she sobbed.

"Please help me put the right man in prison," I said softly. "If you know anything about Del or Donny, please tell me. I'm not sure which name is correct or if Del is a nickname for a long last name.

"Your mom won't have to know you've spoken with me. She wouldn't want Kiko to spend his life in prison if he's not guilty. I see the pain it causes her. He was a son-in-law she was fond of. Do you have any idea who Del is? Or Donny?"

"Once," she began slowly, "once I heard her talking on her cell phone and she said 'Del' a few times. She seemed upset that I'd been listening to her conversation, and she never said anything to me about what I'd overheard."

Yes! I was starting to get somewhere. Maybe.

"I was thinking," said Zeke when I answered my cell phone, "that we should have Mexican food tonight and go to that dance hall over on the Latino side of town."

"There's a Latino side of town?"

"Of course. There are stores and bars and dance halls. There's this place called Poncho's I hear is great. *Pura música mexicana todo el tiempo,* if you believe their advertising."

"Nothing but Mexican music all the time, huh?"

"¡Sí señorita!"

"Well sure, I'd love to go."

"Bueno pues. Adiós." Well, good.

At three that afternoon, I went to Police Headquarters and asked to see the evidence Detective Franklin had brought out of storage for me. I had to show my photo identification to the officer on duty and sign a form, and then he led me to a small room used for interrogation.

"You may not leave the room without advising me," he said. "Nor may you remove any piece of evidence. It's a general rule and not aimed at you."

"I understand."

There were three envelopes of crime scene photos on the gray metal table, and stacked against one leg were several cardboard storage boxes.

For a moment I stood still, unable to decide which horrible thing to look at first. I chose the photos in order to get it over with. Besides, other things would make more sense if I'd seen them.

I started with a large brown envelope marked "Valentino, Evelyn." The scene was bloody and so gruesome it turned my stomach. There were many photographs of her various stab wounds, but the worst were the full body shots. They showed a butchered human. Of course blood was everywhere, soaked into the bedding and some pooled on the floor. It was so awful it had an unreal quality.

Bloody footprints went back and forth, back and forth. That envelope contained the footprints in the master bedroom. There were also several photos of the wall and light switch that showed the fingerprints later determined to be Kiko's.

The next envelope was marked "Valentino, Francisco." I pulled the photos out and laid them on the table. There were shots of Kiko in a t-shirt and boxers, covered in blood. The look on his face was vacant in some and like a murdering madman in others. In one, he was crying hysterically and wiping his face with a bloody hand. My heart went out to such misery, guilty or not.

There was a heartbreaking photo of Kiko carrying his dead daughter in his arms. They were both covered in blood. Kiko looked as grief-stricken as anyone I'd ever seen. Tears filled my eyes until I couldn't see.

I sat down and took deep breaths to calm myself. I decided to leave the other pictures until later. I could see why the people first on the scene had jumped to conclusions. The emotion must have been unbearably intense.

I opened the first storage box and found Kiko's clothing in plastic bags marked with various exhibit numbers. My first thought was that there was no blood spatter and that should have helped the defense. But I realized that even if there had been, it became obliterated by all the blood that came later, when Kiko held his wife, touched his son, wiped his hands on his shirt, and picked up and held his daughter. Every victim had bled profusely.

In the same evidence box was the light switch with bloody fingerprints. The knife was also there, and the son's clothing as well as the daughter's. Everything was marked with exhibit numbers.

Another box contained sheets from the various beds. There was so much blood I imagined I could smell it through the plastic. I called to the officer, and he stood guard while I made a quick trip to the bathroom to splash cold water on my face. That helped until I reentered the bleak room that now seemed to smell of death.

One box contained papers: a signed statement by Kiko and statements by others: his mother, father, brother, and different members of the Mendoza family. There were interview notes, and there was the final report signed by Detective Morrison and another by a Detective Williams. There was the M.E.'s report and the DNA test results on the semen. There were various blood work results from tests on Francisco and each of the victims.

There was also a report about the partial prints found; they didn't match anything in AFIS or anyone from the house or any of their relatives. It was the same case with the blood. There was blood on the knife that wasn't consistent with any of the people tested. My bet was on Del whoever.

I looked at the photos from the children's room as quickly as possible so I could say I did. I didn't see anything about them that gave a clue as to who stabbed them. The victims were pitiful in their tiny size and defenselessness.

The photos were taken by someone emotional about what he or she was seeing. They photographed heart-wrenching details like the thick curl of hair on the boy's forehead. I didn't blame them and mention it because it's proof of what a highly-charged scene it was. I could almost hear the sound of medics and detectives jumping to conclusions. At a scene like that one, it's hard not to want to blame someone immediately, whoever is handy. On the surface at least, Francisco Valentino looked the most likely, and he certainly was the handiest. He was nearly comatose with shock and grief and was not making much sense. Worst of all, he wasn't aware that everything he did and said was being scrutinized by men who already thought him guilty. Since he didn't kill his family, it never occurred to him to protect his rights or weigh the answers he gave.

Then, on top of everything else, the court assigned him a prejudiced attorney who didn't half-try to defend him. Macho Latino wife-beater, my butt; we'd see about that.

I yanked up the semen report and informed Officer Watch Dog that I was taking it to the crime lab down the hall. Someone named Michael Wingman had signed off on it, so I wanted to talk to him. The officer called and informed the lab's receptionist, but she still needed identification when I arrived. I showed her my Brewster County deputy I.D. and waited.

After a while, a man in a white lab coat came to the reception area looking for me. He was about ten years older than I was and a lot taller. He was blond with brown eyes, and he was pale, probably from spending so much time in a lab.

"I'm Michael Wingman. How can I help you?"

I introduced myself and we shook hands. Then I said, "I'd like to speak to you about a report you signed."

"What are you doing? I don't mean to be rude, but isn't Brewster County a long way from here?"

"Yes, it is. I've already been approved to see evidence by the officer back there by the interrogation rooms and also by Detective Morrison."

He frowned and I got the impression he didn't think much of Morrison.

"I'm working a case with a Texas Ranger, Sergeant Zeke Pacheco, and—"

"Why didn't you say so? I know Zeke. Come on back."

Jeez. Like magic.

We entered Wingman's work space, and he shut the door even though there were other workstations. His seemed to be the only one occupied.

"How can I help you, Deputy Ricos?"

"I want to talk to you about the report you did on the Francisco Valentino rape and triple murder case."

"Is that one of mine in your hand?"

"Yes. Do you need to see it?"

"Well yes; I remember the case, but I need to see which one it is." He took it from me.

"What do you mean 'which one it is'? This is the only one."

"No it's not. There's another one. Did you find a problem?"

"No, but I want to ask you a question."

"You should have more than one report."

"Wait. What are you saying?"

"What is your question?"

"I want to know if there's a way to tell which semen was there first. There must be, so I'm wondering if you ran those tests and if you know which was first, because I don't find a report about it in any of the paperwork in the evidence boxes."

"I know it's there. Where did you look?"

"Detective Morrison had all the evidence from the trial brought to one to the interrogation rooms. I only found one report."

"I'll go over there with you and help you find it, but to answer your question, yes. There is a way to tell which semen deposit is the oldest. That report should be with the other evidence."

We walked over to the room, and he went through all the papers twice and didn't find it.

"This is the damnedest thing," he said, scratching his head. "I'm really perturbed."

I was starting to feel a little prickle of excitement. "Do you remember the results of your report?" I asked.

"Let's go back over to my office and I'll look it up."

When he found it and read it he said, "I don't know if I can tell you without permission."

"Whose permission do you need? I can get any permission you need." Big talk from a little deputy, but I knew Magic Man could get it.

"Are you working with the Dallas police on this?"

"I'm not with any police. This is Zeke's investigation."

He mulled it over.

"I can call him if you need to speak to him."

He looked around and then spoke in a hushed voice. "I'm going to get the report and tell you the results, if you swear it's for Zeke."

My heart flew into my throat. "It is for Zeke."

He came back holding a paper he was reading. He looked up from it and then blew me away. "Valentino's semen was the older deposit. Semen keeps a long time, but the sperm begin to die. I would say, judging by the viability of the sperm in the semen belonging to Mr. Valentino, it had been there at least four to five hours before the second deposit. Does that help you?"

Holy crap! I felt like turning cartwheels. "It proves Valentino was not the rapist. If he didn't rape her then it's less likely he killed her."

"I think that's true," Wingman said.

I seriously wanted to hug the man. "You don't know how much this helps. It changes everything about Kiko's case. May I have a copy of it?"

"Please tell Zeke that what he needs is a court order for all lab reports relating to this case, including all the work done pretrial. If you get that, the report is yours."

"The results of your report weren't mentioned in the trial."

He shrugged. "You're right. I testified about the semen belonging to Valentino, but I was never questioned about this report. Sometimes that happens. It was either not useful or was an oversight."

Or was suppressed, I thought. "You won't let anything happen to it?"

"I swear I won't."

"I'm worried that someone will remove it."

"Stop worrying. That won't happen but, in case, I'll take this copy home."

When I left the lab, I did give Michael Wingman a big hug. His work was almost bound to set Kiko free. At least it would get the wheels in motion. I couldn't wait to talk to Kiko and Zeke.

While I was putting away evidence, Zeke called. He asked what I was doing.

"I'm looking at evidence from Kiko's trial. I feel like I'm up to my neck in blood and gore."

"You sound like my kind of woman." Zeke laughed. "Aren't you ready to get out of there?"

"Yes, but I have one more interview." I lowered my voice. "I have proof Kiko did not rape his wife. It's irrefutable, Zeke. Now I just have to find the man that did rape her because, most likely, he's the one who killed her."

"You must be kidding. You have proof already?"

"I never kid around about evidence."

"I can't wait to hear how you pulled this off."

"I can't wait to tell you, but not here. How are your classes going?"

"Okay, I guess. I let 'em out a little early today."

"What are you teaching those guys?"

"Today we talked about waiting for the evidence to speak, not jumping to conclusions, not getting stuck on the first impressions we have because sometimes they're wrong, things like that."

"At least one person at the Dallas P.D. screwed up big time. He let his first impressions sway everything. I think he suppressed evidence that was crucial to the defense. He seems to have been all about jumping to conclusions."

"Are you talking about Detective Morrison?"

"Yes."

"He's a revered detective."

"Maybe so, but I've caught him with his pants down, and it's not pretty."

"This happens with veteran detectives sometimes. They think they've seen everything; they jump to conclusions or try to make the evidence fit their beliefs about the crime. That's why I'm here. As investigators, it's imperative to keep an open mind. We have to do the work required even though sometimes it feels like drudgery. We can't be lazy."

"Aren't you preaching to the choir, Sergeant Pacheco, or are you showing off?"

"Both, I guess."

"I'm doing the work, in case you haven't noticed. Also, I'd like to add that I'm not being paid."

"True, but you're paying it forward. Your kindness will be repaid in other ways."

At first, Myrna Mendoza was in no mood to help. She was as resistant as her sister had been. I did one heck of a sales job on her, including cajoling. I hate that. Then I resorted to begging, which I hate even worse. I'd been flying around giving a pretty good argument for Kiko, and until less than an hour ago, I didn't know if he was innocent or guilty. By the time I saw Myrna, I was practically giddy with the new info I had. It was another touchdown for Team Ricos.

I was so convincing that before long, she caved. "I know for a fact she was cheating on Kiko. I made her admit it. Please don't tell my mother. It would kill her."

I thought her mother needed to grow up and accept the facts of life, but I kept my opinion quiet and asked, "Do you know the man's name or where they met? Where he works or lives? Do you know anything about him?"

"At first she said she'd met him in the park where she took the kids to play, but later she admitted she'd met him at work. I had the impression he lived near her house, but she never said. I don't know if she knew."

"Did she ever say a name?"

"She never told me his name, but her son said he was called Donny. I wanted to kick her ass for letting her little boy know anything about him."

"Thank you, Myrna." I handed her my card. "Will you call me if you remember something else or if you hear anything more about him?"

She promised she would.

It was nearly five o'clock, but I took a taxi from the meeting with Ms. Mendoza to the Waverley Home, another orphanage that had been in business long enough to have housed Zeke as a baby. The online research I'd done showed that the majority of homes for children in the Dallas area had been established for forty years or more. Zeke had just turned forty-seven on the first of January.

The employees at the Waverley Home seem accustomed to having people looking for records of loved ones. They asked a few questions and accepted the true story I gave them, which was that I was looking for my father's history.

I waited twenty minutes while a secretary looked at old records online. It turned out the year I gave her was wrong. Zeke had been brought there, not as a newborn, but when he was fourteen months old. My heart went into my throat. I had found the right place. I began asking so many questions the woman laughed.

"All I can see here," she said, "is that Baby Pacheco was left by Mr. and Mrs. Herman Winchester. I have a Ft. Worth address for them. There is nothing here to indicate this information is to be kept confidential. Usually it is, but since that's not mentioned I can give it to you. You're lucky. In most cases, I wouldn't be allowed to tell you without a court order."

She wrote down the names, their last known address, and gave me a short, well-meaning lecture about approaching people who'd left babies at orphanages. She said sometimes they don't want to be contacted. That made sense. I was already trying to think of what to tell them that would make them want to talk to me.

The secretary went on to say that the information she had showed that they'd said the baby had been left behind by a housekeeper they employed for a short time. They assumed she'd abandoned him since they never heard from her again. Or perhaps something had happened to her. Either way, her baby boy had been left homeless.

The secretary said there was more information in storage, meaning a birth certificate, photos, or some other relevant information associated with the child. Would I like to have access to it?

Yes! I tried to be calm as I signed forms explaining my relationship to the Pacheco baby.

She explained that I must allow forty-eight hours for the records to be located and brought to her office. If I'd give her my phone number, she'd call me when she had the information. I was excited.

Chapter 18

1966, MAX AND LUCIA AND THE DAGGER MOUNTAIN RANCH

Once again, Max was doing general labor around a ranch. At least this one was paying him every week. He worked on wells and the growing network of irrigation systems, helped build or repair fences, repainted buildings, and dug post holes. He worked hard, as was his custom, but was fed well, enjoyed the other men working alongside him, and had the nights with Lucia in their private room.

Sometimes they would crawl out their window and onto the roof of the bunkhouse and lie together on a blanket to watch the stars. On other nights, when the moon was full, they would climb to the crest of a nearby hill and lie together in the milky light. They made love and told each other stories about the small ranch they would someday own. Their stories always included their children.

Lucia worked in the kitchen, which provided all the meals to the cowboys and other workers. Sometimes she helped with cleaning or laundry. Because of her youth, she was often assigned work in the vegetable garden. She jumped at any chance to spend time outside and loved working with the lush plants. From the yard she could admire the wide-open vistas and tall rugged mountains at the distant end of the ranch. She felt freer outside and not like a servant. She pretended she was working in her own garden.

One night while lying on the roof, she said, "I'm going to have a baby, Max."

He was so excited he couldn't contain it. He danced her around until some of the other couples came outside to see what was happening on the roof.

"We're having a baby," he shouted, waking everyone, "an American citizen with a Mexican soul."

Everyone congratulated the young couple, and one by one their neighbors returned to their beds. It was a long time before Max could settle down. He fell asleep with his head against Lucia's flat stomach. "You'll grow big soon," he whispered to his child.

The next day Max was given a chance to prove his skill as a cowboy. He impressed the foreman so much that he was moved into the cowboy crew and received a raise in pay of five dollars per day. Now he would be doing work he enjoyed and at which he excelled.

The extra money he earned was an answer to a prayer. They would soon be able to travel to the Triple Bar Ranch and join his cousin Augustín and his family. How they'd do that, Max wasn't sure, but with money many things were possible.

The one drawback to Max's new position was that sometimes the cowboys were gone overnight and often more than one night. He couldn't bear to be separated from Lucia, and yet there was no way around it. If he was going to be a cowboy, then he had to go where the rest of them went and do the work he was asked to do. He worked hard and without complaining, but his heart hurt and all he could think about was getting back to his love.

On his first night away from Lucia, when he laid out his bedroll he found a note in her careful printing. "I love you, Max," it read. "Look at the sky when you lie down to sleep, and know that I'm looking at it, too, and thinking of you." That was a comfort and he kept the note in a pocket over his heart for months.

When the cowboys came back after a week of rounding up calves in the early fall, he could see the changes happening to Lucia's body. It was nearly October and her waist was beginning to expand and her breasts had grown fuller. She seemed to glow from within. He had never seen her look so beautiful.

The owner of the ranch had a twenty-one-year-old son, Earl, who still lived on the ranch but didn't work at anything in particular. He liked to ride around in his new pickup and "check on the Mezzcans so's they don't diddle the day away."

One day he passed Lucia hanging laundry. He thought she was the most stunning beauty he'd ever seen. He went to the ranch manager, Terrance Judd, to ask about her.

"Terrance, I just saw the most gorgeous girl hanging laundry."

"Is that right?"

"Who is she?"

"I don't know. What does she look like?"

"She has long black hair and the best tits I ever saw—"

"Earl. Stop right there."

He shrugged. "Well, you asked."

"If she has a beautiful face, you're talking about Pacheco's wife. She's married to Max Pacheco, one of the cowboys, Earl. You best stay away from her."

"But she's so young and beautiful." He was surprised. "Are you sure she married a cowboy?" Earl hadn't noticed Lucia's growing waistline, had seen only the fullness of her body, the womanly curves, and he was filled with lust.

"Leave her alone, Earl," the manager warned sternly. "You don't want her husband to come after you."

"Why's that? Is he big?"

"Not especially. But he works hard every day and he's in better shape than you, and he's strong. If you mess with his wife, Earl, you might wake up dead."

Earl laughed and blew him off.

One day he joined the Mexican workers for lunch so he could watch her serve them. Some of the older women noticed and were alarmed. Earl spoke good Spanish from growing up around Mexican workers and their children, so they were unable to warn Lucia in front of him.

One of the women followed her into the pantry and whispered, "That young gringo is the owner's son. He hasn't taken his eyes off you. You should be careful because he's used to getting his way. He'll know Max is away for a while. Don't let him get you alone."

"Thanks, Elsa. I'll be careful." Lucia wasn't worried. If he made advances, she would tell him she was married and pregnant; surely that would discourage him.

Later, she was walking and a truck pulled up and stopped. It was Earl. He smiled and removed his hat. "Would you like a ride? Where are you going this time of day?"

"I'm walking for exercise because I'm expecting a child."

"You don't look like it." He leaned against the truck and chewed on the end of a cigar. He looked her up and down.

"Well, I am, in January."

"My name is Earl Wilson." He held out his hand and beamed at her.

"I'm Lucia Pacheco." She took his hand, afraid to take it and afraid not to.

He grinned. "I'm glad to meet you."

After a moment he tipped his hat to her. "See you around."

Lucia decided the older women were being overprotective of her, as was their nature. Maybe Earl Wilson once had his eye on her, but now that he knew she was married and pregnant, that would change everything. Besides, he was from a wealthy, educated family. What would he want with a poor Mexican girl who could carry on her back every single thing she owned? Surely he wouldn't want a woman who couldn't speak English and was not even a legal resident of his country.

What Earl Wilson wanted, more than he'd ever wanted anything, was to seduce the beautiful girl he had now seen up close. Touching her hand had inflamed him. He had never seen a woman so seductive.

Watching her walk away was sweet torture. He would have her; it was a matter of patience. Waiting would make it all the sweeter.

A week later, on a Friday evening, there was a dance at the ranch, hosted by the cowboys and other workers as a joint effort in celebration of the fall round-up and the cool weather. Any excuse would do for a party.

Nobody invited the owner or any of his sons or any of the ranch management other than the cowboy foreman. They wouldn't expect to be invited, nor would they have come if they were. There were occasions when the owner would throw a party for the workers, but he seldom showed at one of those and when he did he would be there just long enough to show his generous good will.

Earl Wilson came to the party with two men his age. They brought coolers full of beer and a case of tequila. They listened to the music, watched the dancing, and began to drink heavily. Earl had come to look at Lucia and size up her husband.

He'd asked Terrance Judd to have the Border Patrol come for Max Pacheco, but Terrance had flatly refused. He said Pacheco was the best cowboy of the entire outfit. No way was he going to turn him over to Immigration. In fact, he had already started the process of getting him proper documentation.

That angered Earl but he did not argue with him. Instead, he decided to come see the man for himself. How could some illegal Mexican boy be the best cowboy on the ranch? And whether or not he was, how did he treat his wife? Did he appreciate what he had? Would he look at other women? He was probably an idiot.

Earl's heart sank the minute he saw the two together. There was so much chemistry between them no one could miss it. And worse, the man adored her. He never seemed to see anyone but his wife. He was young, yes, but he was well built. He looked strong and wouldn't be so easy to take down.

When the young couple danced, they moved together as one and laughed and whispered. There was love between them. That would make his quest more difficult than he assumed, but the greater the challenge the greater the reward. The fact that she was already pregnant made it sweeter. There was no way she would get pregnant with his baby. That was one less worry.

When he saw Lucia head towards the bathroom he followed. Earl was so aroused he had trouble walking. She wore a long, flowing skirt that twirled when she danced and a white cotton blouse that showed the fullness of her breasts. He noticed, for the first time, that she was beginning to show her pregnancy, but not much.

"Hola, Lucia." He surprised her when she came out of the bathroom.

"Hola." She kept walking.

"Will you dance with me?"

"I'm here with my husband. I'll dance with you if he says it's okay, but you'll have to ask him."

"I'm going to speak with him now." He turned back towards the dance.

Lucia watched Earl speak with Max, and both of them looked at her as she approached. She wanted him to say no, but it was too late to tell him, and Max had said yes; one dance would be all right. He smiled at her, thinking he was pleasing her by allowing her to dance with her friend.

While Lucia and Earl were dancing, several of the men came to Max and warned him about Earl. They said his intentions were not honorable and he should not let him touch his wife, even in dancing.

"It's one dance," Max said. He wasn't worried. The rest of the dances were his. He had told Earl that clearly.

Knowing that her husband was watching, Earl was a perfect gentleman. Just being near Lucia was enough for him, for now. Her hair smelled wonderful and he loved the feel of her small hand in his, and the weightless way she moved. She was easy to lead on the dance floor, but would she be easy to lead into bed? He began to sweat.

While he danced with Max's wife, he was planning a way to get her husband into the hands of the Border Patrol. There had to be a way to get him out of there.

The next week there was a Border Patrol raid on the Dagger Mountain Ranch, but Terrance Judd had called Max into the office to tell him about his plan to make him a legal resident. When he saw the trucks go by, he hid the young cowboy in a closet in the back of the office.

Max expressed fear for Lucia and the manager seemed to understand. *"No llevan mujeres,"* he assured him. It was rare for them to take women. It was the men they were after.

When Max was safely hidden, Judd picked up his phone and called Randolph Wilson, the majority shareholder of the ranch and Earl's father. "Randy, Earl called Border Patrol to our operation, and worse, he has them looking for our best Mexican cowboy. You must do something about this right away."

"Why would Earl do such a thing?"

"If I had to guess, I'd say he's after the young man's wife. He was in here asking about her. I don't care who Earl sleeps with, but I want him to leave this man's woman alone. And we don't need Border Patrol snooping around here."

"I'll take care of it," Randolph Wilson promised. "I'm going to put him to work. He won't have time for chasing the help."

Judd had little hope of that. In his younger days, Randy, too, had been wild for the dark-skinned beauties who came and went from his ranch. Never mind that he had a lovely wife from a wealthy, well-respected ranching family.

Through it all, Terrance Judd had kept his mouth shut and turned a blind eye to his boss' indiscretions. When necessary, he quietly sent couples away to the next ranch. Damned if he was going to go through that hell again for the next generation. No. He wasn't going to do it.

Chapter 19

I was nervous that Zeke would want to know why I was late, but when I slipped the key card into the slot on the door, no one opened it. I set down my things and saw Zeke on the balcony. For a moment I stood looking at him. It made my heart hurt to know his mother had abandoned him. Why would she keep him fourteen months and then leave him behind? If she was a housekeeper, then she wasn't a crack whore. That was good news, wasn't it?

I turned on my laptop, being quiet about it, and searched Herman Winchester online. He owned a shipping company and a big restaurant in Fort Worth. He was married to Greta Gibbons, formerly of Dallas. His home address was not given, but I found it in the Ft. Worth phone book. I wrote it down, along with the phone number. Only then did my mind go back to Zeke on the balcony. He was wearing jeans and his warmly-lined denim jacket and his brown, tooled, leather boots. His hands were jammed in the pockets. It was cold. There was nothing unusual about the scene, yet somehow it was sad.

When I opened the sliding door, Zeke looked up at me and smiled, but there were tears on his face. The sadness was so palpable they could probably feel it on the street fifteen floors below.

"Zeke? Has something happened?" I put my hand on his shoulder, and he put his hand on top of it.

"I'm all right."

"I don't mean to pry, but you're crying."

He took a handkerchief from his pocket and wiped his face and blew his nose. "I've been thinking about some things best left alone."

I sat down next to him. "I do that too sometimes."

He smiled a sad smile. "Do you mind skipping dinner in Little Mexico?"

"No. We can go later. Mexican food and dancing will still be around tomorrow. I think the Mexicans are here to stay."

He laughed, and we said nothing for a while. Dusk changed to dark. I tried to imagine tall buildings as mountains but lighting made it too clear what they were. My mind went to the giant sleeping hulks at home and the way the sky glittered just out of reach. I stayed there until Zeke brought me back.

"Margarita, I want to tell you the rest of it, but I don't know how."

"I'd like to hear it whenever you want to tell me."

"Let's go inside. It's cold out here. We can get comfortable. Then I'll tell you."

"I could order something for dinner if you like."

"I'd like some coffee. This hotel has great coffee."

"Okay, but we should eat something."

He looked at the room service menu. "I'll have the portabella-veggie sandwich on sprouted bread, toasted."

"That sounds healthy."

He grinned. "I'm trying to save my body from inevitable decline."

I laughed because he looked like the picture of health. Huh. Maybe the way he ate was why. "I'll have that too."

Zeke went to take a shower. While he did that I compulsively checked on Herman and Greta Winchester again, looking for something, anything. Something dirty and underhanded was what I half-expected, but I found charity works by Greta, a successful business record on Herman, and no scandal. There were no news articles about the disappearance of a Mexican housekeeper forty-six years ago. No hints about a sordid affair between Herman and my grandmother that ended with him strangling her and burying her in the basement. Jeez, my mind had gone criminal. I always suspected the worst.

I turned my computer off as Zeke walked out of the bathroom dressed in blue-checkered flannel sleep pants and a long-sleeve gray t-shirt. I showered and dressed much the same way. I felt ready, mostly, for whatever he had to tell.

First we ate and while we did, we talked about his love of gardening and seeing things grow and my love of running.

"I used to run when I was younger," Zeke said, "but it became hard on my knees. Now I walk and sometimes play tennis."

"You look like you work out."

"Thank you. I do."

He told me he was a vegetarian and I felt ashamed for not noticing that. But we had not eaten together more than a few times, so I gave myself a break. There is a limit to how many things I can beat myself up about, and I reached that limit a while back.

I told Zeke about my love of desert-mountain terrain and that it was as much in my blood as he was. Talking about Cimarron Mountain, the Rio Grande, and my bluff lifted my spirits.

Zeke never asked what had kept me late, so I didn't tell him about my visit to the orphanage. I'd have more to tell after I spoke with the Winchesters anyway.

After dinner, he drank coffee and I drank the house raspberry lemonade. They are known for it, a reputation they deserve.

"All during my growing-up years," Zeke said, apropos of nothing, "I was called worthless and a troublemaker. You can't tell a kid he's trash every day and expect him to function normally. He's going to rebel and act out."

"Yes, of course."

"I could have become a criminal or a derelict, but I had a voice in me, and it wasn't a tiny voice. It was loud, and it repeated daily that I was born to do something good. I wasn't trash just because my parents had messed up. That was their lives, but I had my own." He paused and looked at me, and his face was so sad. "But other than working, my life has been shit." A tear rolled down his cheek. "I sure would like to get drunk right now."

Me, too.

"I haven't pulled a drunk in twelve years, but I want to. I'm an alcoholic."

I don't know why that news surprised me so much, but it did.

I started to say something, but Zeke was on a roll. "Of course I'm an alcoholic. Isn't that what losers become?"

"Zeke, stop. I'm your daughter, and I don't want to hear you say you're a loser. If loser and alcoholic are one and the same, then I'm a loser, too."

"You are not a loser!"

"I'm an alcoholic, Zeke, just like you."

His head whipped around. "No."

"Yes. If I drink, I can't stop. I feel like crap the next day, but I'll do it again. I stopped drinking because I want to be present in my life and not skulking in the shadows. I need to feel proud of who I am. I want to run and explore beautiful places and become as good a person and lawperson as I can be. I can't do any of that if I drink, and I'm not drinking, but I still want to."

"Wanting to drink will make us just as crazy as drinking."

"Yes, I know."

"I'm sorry. I shouldn't be laying any of this on you. You've had your own problems and...anyhow, I'm proud of you for not drinking."

"Thank you. I'm proud of you, too. It's hard. It seems like everybody drinks. I think I'd like to have a beer or a glass of wine or a bottle of wine. Even in my head, I go from one beer, pass on the wine, and end up with a bottle of Añejo Gold."

Zeke laughed in a way that said he understood.

"What is it that has you so upset, Zeke?" I ventured to ask after a few minutes of silence. "Is there a way I can help?"

Just like that, he began to tell me the thing he wanted to tell me. "When I was six, I lived for ten months with a nice couple who treated me well. They acted like I was theirs, but she got cancer, and they felt they couldn't care for me. It was terribly sad to be taken from them."

Zeke took a sip of coffee and continued. "When I was put back in the system, I stayed a while in a state home with other kids more or less my age. When I was eight I was put into foster care once more."

He drank more coffee; I thought if I tried to swallow anything, I would choke to death from the lump in my throat.

"I ran away twice," Zeke continued, "but each time I didn't have a clue where I was going to go or how I'd live. I stole things from stores in order to eat—peanuts, fruit, and sweets, mostly.

"I was brought back each time I ran away. It must have been easy to spot an eight-year-old living on his own. I never bathed or changed clothes, and when I could find a place to sleep, I slept hard, the way small children do. Someone always noticed me and reported me to the police or sheriff or whatever, and back I'd go to the place I'd run away from.

"I was branded a troublemaker and hoodlum at age eight. I wasn't either one. I was just a little boy who didn't belong anywhere and didn't know what to do about it. Also, I had this insane idea that I would find my real parents."

"What little child wouldn't think that?"

He shrugged. "According to my new foster parents, I was full of the devil and hard work would take care of that, hard work and beatings. The work was bad enough, but the beatings were worse. Remember I was eight years old and small for the kind of work being asked of me."

How could he think I would've forgotten that?

"I was lost and like any kid, I didn't like getting dragged out of bed and beaten out of sleep. So I ran away again when I was nine. I stayed gone an entire month. I broke into peoples' houses and ate and bathed and sometimes slept in a bed when time allowed. I looked for homes with kids and exchanged my clothes for clean ones.

"Once I was caught sleeping in a bed but, because I was clean, the people thought I was the new kid from down the street. They had me call my mom, which I pretended to do, and then I stayed for dinner. It's one of my happiest memories.

"To make a long story short, I didn't run away again until I was ten and even then I was sent back. I ran away more times than I can count. I figured out how to live in a more invisible way. I was still breaking into homes and taking whatever I needed, and I would eventually be caught each time.

"The mistake I made was sticking around the small town near where my foster parents lived. Once I turned thirteen, I made a plan that worked. I got myself lost in the big city of Dallas. By then I was a scammer and a damn good thief. I knew how to lie my way in and out of things. The law never caught me after that."

"That's the saddest story I've ever heard."

"Something positive came out of all that stealing and troublemaking."

"What is that?"

"Once when I was sitting in a jail cell waiting to be taken back, I met a Texas Ranger. I was almost thirteen at the time. He was there to help the sheriff with a murder investigation. I could tell by the way the sheriff deferred to him that he was an important man. The sheriff went to get something, and the man came over and told me his name was Brett Davidson. He reached through the bars and shook my little juvenile offender hand."

Zeke got up to get more coffee. "You need anything?"

"No. Thanks."

"I asked about his badge, which I thought was so cool. He said it was made from a pure silver five-peso coin from Mexico. I was enthralled. I asked if he was a sheriff, and he said he was a Texas Ranger. He'd been one for thirty years and his father before him."

"I think I see where this tale is going."

He laughed. "Yep. I asked a lot of questions, and he gave me straight answers and even told me some stories about his work. I asked how a person gets to be a Texas Ranger. I wanted to be like him. And I wanted that badge on my chest.

"I can still hear his gruff voice say I sure couldn't do it if I kept getting into scrapes with the law. I had to be law-abiding and pay attention to my studies. He laid it out for me. He gave me his card with his office number. That made such an impression on me, and for the first time in my life I had a goal. It was empowering for a kid nobody wanted, a kid who never had anybody to look up to. I made a plan, and I stuck to it even during some tough times."

"Wow, Zeke."

"I haven't told you the bad part yet."

Say what?

"I don't know how to say this to my daughter."

"Just give it to me straight and get it over with."

"My foster mother abused me—sexually, I mean. It started when I was ten. I don't know if I can talk about this."

"Take your time."

Zeke's hands had started trembling. "I've had therapy, but the things she did... She fucked up my relationships with women. I have no trust, and I almost never feel safe, and I don't treat them well."

"Oh, Zeke, I don't know what to say."

"When I turned thirteen, she started—she started—wanting—more from me. She wanted to have full-on sex and—and—I ran away and never looked back."

I realized I'd been holding my breath.

Zeke looked like he'd been through physical torture. "I think it might've been improper to tell you that. See? I don't know what's right or wrong to tell a woman."

"Zeke, take it easy on yourself. It's okay. I'm twenty-six years old, not six."

"I'll be right back." He went into the bathroom. When he returned, he'd brushed his hair and washed his face, but he still had a haunted look.

He changed the subject back to his mentor. "I owe a lot to Brett Davidson. He never knew until I was in college that I'd run away from abusive foster parents. He helped me get them shut down when I worked as a policeman. He was retired by then, but he knew everybody in law enforcement all over Texas. He was an amazing man, and he's the main reason I became a Texas Ranger.

"I loved calling him and listening to his stories. He thought he was encouraging some young criminal to follow the straight and narrow. He didn't know he was my lifeline, my father figure, my mentor, all rolled into one fine human being. I wish you could have met him, but he died years ago."

"I knew there had to be somebody who loved you," I said, "somebody you could respect and who set a good example."

"I wouldn't say he loved me, but he was the closest thing to a father I ever had. I wish he could know I became a Ranger. It would make him proud."

"I'm sure he was already proud of you."

"I guess he was. He came to my college graduation and said he was."

"Does my mom know any of this, Zeke?"

"Are you kidding? I was nineteen and even more messed up than I am now. I didn't know why, either, or told myself I didn't. At least now I can admit it."

For a few moments, neither of us spoke. Zeke threw out cold coffee and refilled his cup. I didn't think he was drinking it; it was something to do. When he was ready, he sat down and began to speak again.

"Truthfully, I think I was in love with your mother. It might not have been love, but it was the closest thing to it I'd ever felt for a woman. I cheated on her though, and did her wrong. I questioned everything she did. You know your mom. She didn't put up with me very long." He laughed but it wasn't happy. "I blame my career for my lack of a wife, but my career is not the problem."

"You told me you were married once."

"It was a disaster."

"How so?"

"I married a blond-haired, blue eyed, beautiful woman who had social status, but not much in the way of heart. She was white and having felt racism, I thought having an Anglo wife would make it better. Don't get me wrong, I had feelings for her but not love. By the standards used to judge things, I had it made, though. It didn't take long to see I'd made things worse. She wasn't who I wanted or even close. She lost in the deal, too. Friends deserted her because she married a Mexican man. She was shut out of her country club and high society shindigs. I think she began to look at me as 'less than' after that."

"Maybe she was frustrated and didn't know what to do."

"I saw the differences even more starkly between white privilege and my lack of it. And always, under that smiling façade, there was a sad, lost, little Mexican boy." He sighed. "He didn't go away."

"He's part of you, Zeke. I don't think you can ever make him go away. You have to love him and give him what he needs."

"How do you know that?"

"I grew up with Dr. Stephanie Ricos."

He gave me a heart-wrenching smile and my eyes filled with tears.

"I think that's enough for one night," Zeke said. "I'm exhausted. Do you mind if I lie down and read?"

"No, of course not."

I tried to read, but nothing held my interest. Zeke was lying on his side, facing the wall and not reading. He didn't even have a book open. I could feel his sadness as if he were over there sobbing.

I brushed my teeth, washed my face, and climbed on his bed. Then I spooned myself against his back and put my arms around him. I didn't say anything and neither did he, but he covered my hands with his and held them against his heart. We fell asleep like that and slept all night.

Chapter 20

1966, MAX AND LUCIA

The next time the Border Patrol received an anonymous tip, they came at night to raid the sleeping quarters of the workers. Their presence in the dark was a terror. Nobody knew what they would do. One of the men managed to sneak away and go for the big boss.

Terrance Judd heard frantic pounding on his door. He pulled on his pants and went to see what the hell was going on.

"Señor." The man removed his hat.

"Adolpho."

"Por favor, La Chota—Border Patrol!" Adolpho was breathless and waved his arm in the direction of the workers' quarters. Judd knew he had to get to the bunkhouse right away. He told Adolpho it would be safe to wait in his living room, but the frantic man was worried about his wife. Judd drove them as fast as he could and desperately hoped Max Pacheco and a couple of his other best hands would somehow escape capture.

Pacheco had told him this was his first time to work in the U.S., so if they caught him, they would take him to the border and send him back to Mexico with no punishment. He could come back the same way he'd come, but then the next time he was picked up he'd be held longer. If he continued to use his real name, he would be formally deported. That meant it would be difficult to make him a legal resident. It would also mean prison time for Pacheco; all this because the boss' son couldn't keep his dick in his pants. Judd fumed.

He was seething by the time he reached the bunkhouse. He was told by one of the workers that Max and Lucia were nowhere to be found. Relief washed over him, then panic. Maybe they had already left to find other work. Who could blame them?

He needn't have worried. Max and Lucia were safe in each other's arms in the dark on a sloping hill above the bunkhouse. There was not much moonlight but the couple had gone there anyway, preferring the freedom of outdoors and the immense starry sky to the confines of their small room.

They were making plans for their baby and enjoying each other. For a while, they watched the frenzied activity going on below, hoping their friends would be safe. They had no way to know the search was for Max.

"I'm glad we missed that little party," whispered Max as he pulled Lucia on top of him.

A week later, Lucia was working in the vegetable garden when Earl Wilson approached her, running hard.

"Your husband has been hurt," he cried breathlessly. "Come with me."

Without thinking about anything but Max, she followed him to a seldom-used barn at the end of the complex of bunkhouses and other outbuildings. He ran in ahead of her and held the door. Once she was inside, he shut and bolted it and grabbed her into his arms, laughing.

"You're so beautiful." His Spanish was almost perfect, which somehow made it worse. "I can't quit thinking about you."

He tried to kiss her while Lucia struggled to get away from him. "No! This is wrong. I can't be here with you."

"You want me too, don't you?" He pressed her hand against his groin.

"No! I don't!" He was too strong. She was terrified and screamed for help.

Earl stepped back and slapped her hard across the face. "Shut up! If you make another sound, I'll cut your throat." He produced a knife from his shirt pocket and waved it at her.

"What do you want?" She knew what he wanted, but she thought if she could get him to talk he might see her as a person and not an object to be taken.

"Take your shirt off."

"No. I'm going to have a baby, and I have a husband I love."

"That's touching, very sweet. You can take your shirt off, baby or not, husband or not. What's the harm? Your husband is not here. I'm just going to look."

"Please don't do this to us."

"Take your goddamn shirt off or I will cut it off. Understand? Do it now!"

Lucia unbuttoned the top button on her blouse with hands trembling so hard it took her ten times longer than normal. She brought them together, trying to hold them still, and then unbuttoned the second button.

"Hurry it up! I don't have all day. Someone is going to miss one of us."

That was what she hoped, or maybe she'd been seen running towards the old barn with Earl. It was nearing time for lunch and she'd be needed in the kitchen. They would send somebody to look for her if she failed to come to work.

The older women fussed over her all the time now that they knew about the baby. They made sure she ate enough and didn't stand too long or lift heavy things. She thought they were being silly, but she appreciated their concern and it made her miss her mother a little less.

Earl was impatient and agitated. "Take your goddamned shirt off *now!*" He stepped towards her holding the knife up.

She began to unbutton the third button. Earl sat down and unzipped his jeans, a mistake he'd soon regret. Lucia ran hard for the door and smacked the bolt back before Earl could get his pants up. She sprang through and kept running until she realized Earl was not pursuing her. He stood by the door of the barn, exposing himself and laughing.

Lucia re-buttoned her blouse and entered the kitchen, forcing herself to be calm. She was safe among women who cared about her. Max would be in for lunch and the thought cheered her. Just to see him was always a comfort.

"What in the world happened to you?" Amelia, the supervisor of the kitchen, was suspicious. "What did you do to your face?"

"What's wrong with my face?"

"There's a large bruise forming on the left side and your eye is swelling shut. Who hit you, Lucia? It must hurt a lot."

She reached up and gingerly touched her face and then slowly, trying to be calm, told the women what happened with Earl in the barn.

"He's not going to leave you alone," one of them said. "He will keep on until he rapes you. He knows you have no rights here."

"Every woman has the right not to be raped. I'll kill him first."

"There'll be trouble when Max finds out," warned another woman.

"You'll have to leave," was a different woman's opinion.

The thought of leaving made Lucia sad, and yet that had been their plan all along, to go to the Triple Bar Ranch. They had sent money home twice and still had enough to make the move, she thought. They never spent a dime.

Amelia sat Lucia down at the long table and gave her a clean dishrag full of ice. "Hold this against your face," she instructed. "It will keep the swelling down and will help with the pain, too."

After a while Amelia sat down next to her. "I think you should go to your room and stay there. When the cowboys come to eat, we'll tell Max you have a headache and are in bed asleep."

"But he'll come to check on me. I'm never sick and he'll be worried."

"He'll be too busy eating to go to you."

"You don't know Max. He will come."

"Go to your room, and we'll try to keep him away until we figure out what to do. Lock your door and don't open it!"

Max entered the kitchen, his eyes searching for Lucia. He sat at the table with the other cowboys. Bowls of steaming food were passed around, and he served himself, thinking she was in the pantry or had been sent on an errand. It was unlike her not to be there when he came to eat. She was always as eager to see him as he was to see her. Everyone teased them but it was good-natured.

Amelia brought a plate of hot tortillas to the table and set it down near Max. She put her hand on his shoulder. "She had a headache, and I sent her to the room to rest."

"She's never had a headache." He stood.

"Please don't disturb her, Max. Let her rest. She'll be fine. I'll look in on her after lunch."

"But she'll think something is wrong if I don't go to her. And besides, she's never ill. She knows I would come."

He lifted his plate, added five hot tortillas to it, and left amidst guffawing and crude jokes.

Max was alarmed to find the door to their room locked.

"Lucia!" He pounded on it. "Open up, Mi Amor. It's me."

When she opened the door he saw the reason for her headache.

"What happened, Luce?"

He put the plate of food on top of the chest of drawers and put his arms around her. She began to cry. He led her to the bed and sat on the edge with her.

"Please tell me everything." He hugged her to him.

"Promise me you won't go after him." She knew her comment told him what he needed to know.

"I won't promise that; I can't promise it."

Lucia told him everything while he held her, rage boiling inside him. When she finished the story he said, "I'll find him and he'll never bother you again."

"No, you can't do anything to him. You'll go to jail and then where will I be? Please think about it, Max. I need you. Let's go to the Triple Bar now, tonight. Augustín says it's a safe place to make a home."

"But I can't let this go. He has insulted us."

"Yes, you can let it go. You must."

"He was going to rape you. What kind of man would I be if I said nothing? You will lose respect for me. How would I ever face our son?"

"Max, don't be foolish. I'll never lose respect for you, and our son doesn't know anything about this. I feel him move now, but he doesn't know what's going on in the outside world yet. I don't think his eyes are even open." She had her hands on the small swell of her abdomen.

"Well, he can hear. I know he can. He'll know, Luce. Besides, I'll know. I have to be able to live with myself. No man can hit you or hurt you and get away with it while I live."

"But what if he kills you?"

"Have faith in your husband, Luce. I'm not an idiot. He's a coward. What kind of man seduces a woman with a knife?"

"A dangerous one," Lucia answered. "He has no conscience and no heart. You'll be no match for that. You're much more of a man, Max, but you're a good man. I think we should go now and not look back."

"Pack our things and be ready to go. I'll be back soon."

He left her standing there with her mouth open and dread in her heart.

Earl found Max before Max had a chance to find Earl. "We need to talk." He held up his hands in a position of surrender.

"Yes," replied Max.

"It's not like you think."

"How is it Earl? It sounds bad to me."

"Let's take a ride and talk about it." Earl indicated two saddled horses standing ready. Max knew better than to ride somewhere with him. Earl would be armed, and Max had nothing but his wits.

"No. We'll talk here."

They were alone in the barn. All of the cowboys except Max had gone back to work.

"Your wife invited me to the old barn, the one we almost never use now and she showed me her breasts."

That was all he got to say and Max was on him. "You're a liar!" He pummeled Earl with his fists.

"Those are some great tits she has. I never saw anything more beautiful." Earl ducked away from him. "She begged me to suck them."

Max was wild with anger. He jumped on Earl again and dragged him into the dirt. While they rolled around, Earl pulled out his knife and cut Max on the face. Both men staggered to their feet and Max retreated a few steps, wiping the blood from his face with his hand. He was so angry the pain didn't register.

"I have no weapon." He felt like a fool for saying it. Earl was not a man who would fight fair.

Earl was also a man who couldn't control his mouth. "I'm going to fuck her, whether you like it or not." He held the knife out in front of him.

"You will never touch her," Max spat.

"When you're gone, I'll fuck her blind."

"I'm not going anywhere." Max yanked up a heavy piece of wood from the floor. He swung it around his head a couple of times to get the feel of it.

"Come on, asshole," taunted Earl. "I'm going to kill you before this night is over, unless Border Patrol comes for you first. Either way, I'll be fucking Lucia."

"You never will." Max spoke through gritted teeth. "Never. Come closer with your knife."

"You think an old piece of wood is a match for my knife, wetback?"

Max knew it would be if he had half a chance to use it. He could take this soft, spoiled boy who'd never worked a full day in his life.

Earl stood still, holding the knife out. "I could give her a real life. She wouldn't have to work. If she stays with you, she'll be ugly in fifteen years, old before her time and so wrinkled you won't know her."

"Lucia doesn't want a life with you."

"Did you ask her? Did you give her a choice? Of course you didn't. You don't want to hear her answer, do you? All you stupid wetbacks are the same. You never give your women a choice about anything important."

"You don't know anything."

"Stupid! Ignorant! Wetback!"

"Come and get me," said Max. "Come on."

When Earl stepped forward, Max made a run for him and swung the wood as hard as he could. It crashed into Earl's shoulder and knocked the knife out of his hand. It flew through the air and landed near one of the stalls, too far away for Earl to reach it.

Earl was still coming at him, blinded by pain and rage. Max swung again and caught him on the side of the head. The larger man crumpled to the floor and stayed there, quiet at last. Max threw the wood to the floor and ran from the barn.

He burst into their room and grabbed Lucia's hand. "We have to go right now."

"What have you done? Look at your face!"

"I've knocked him unconscious. He started it, but that won't mean anything. Let's go, Luce. Right now. Come on."

He lifted both their packs, one over each shoulder.

"I can carry one. I'm pregnant, not weak and definitely not sick."

"You talk too much. Let's go. I've got the packs. Humor me one time."

She gave him a look but didn't say anything more about carrying a pack. As they approached the barn, she drew back in fear. "We're not taking horses? They could shoot us for that!"

"No, we're going to take the asshole's truck. We'll go as far as we can and then leave it somewhere where it can be found."

Lucia started to protest but thought better of it. They went through the barn to check on Earl. Max wanted to be sure he was still unconscious and not dead. Then they crawled up into his new Ford truck and got the hell out of there. Max had never driven anything newer than a 1960 model, but he figured it out quickly. The thing that threw him at first was that it was an automatic. He had only driven a stick-shift before. This was so easy it was ridiculous.

"No wonder he's so soft," he commented. "He didn't even have to change gears."

Lucia laughed in spite of being angry. "Where are we going in this stolen truck?" She knew Max was thinking of her health and safety and that of the baby.

"We're going to Dallas. And the truck is not stolen; it's borrowed for a few hours."

"Okay, when we get stopped, you tell that to the sheriff."

"Stop worrying."

"It is nice not to be walking."

After a moment Max turned to her. "Would you rather be married to a rich man, Luce?"

"Sure, if you were rich."

"No. I mean some other man, but a rich man, a man who could give you everything you want."

"You're the only man who can give me everything I want, Max."

Tears filled his eyes. "Are you sure?"

"I've always been a girl who knew what she wanted. You know this, Max. Why do you doubt me now?"

"Earl—he said terrible things to me."

"Forget them, he's an idiot. He doesn't know me and what I want."

Max laughed after he thought about it. "Look at this; the stupid wetback ended up with the beautiful girl."

She grinned. "And the truck."

Back at the ranch, Earl Wilson struggled to his feet. His head spun and he held it in both hands until the world slowed. If he could just make it to his truck, he'd show that goddamned wetback what was what. Earl burned with hatred so hot he was sweating. He crashed out of the barn to see that his truck was gone.

Terrance Judd looked up when his boss' son came dragging in. "What happened to you?"

"That wetback stole my new truck."

"Which wetback is that?"

"Max Pacheco." He spit the name as if it was something nasty in his mouth.

"Why would Max steal your truck? What have you done, Earl?"

"Why do you always blame me?"

Judd glared at the younger man.

Earl yelled, "He's left in my truck! Don't you understand English, you asshole? Call the sheriff and tell him to put out an APB!" He slammed out the door.

Terrance Judd picked up the phone, but his call was not to the sheriff.

Chapter 21

Kiko Valentino was brought into the visitor room the same way as before, chained and shackled, but he looked like a different man. It was hope, I realized. He had called me when he was allowed to, and I told him I had a piece of good news.

Hope had even changed his looks. His eyes twinkled and his black hair shone. Color had returned to his face. He had become a handsome Mexican man again instead of a washed-out version of one.

He couldn't contain his excitement. *"Digame, digame,"* he begged as soon as the guard left us alone. He wanted me to tell him what I knew.

"There was a lab report that never made it into the trial, Kiko."

He whooped before I could finish.

"I don't know if it was suppressed or ignored, but it shows that your wife was raped a short time before she was stabbed. Alone, it doesn't exonerate you, but it changes the story enough to make it hard to believe someone raped Evie and you came home afterward and stabbed her and your children. That doesn't work."

"Oh my God! Oh my God!" He bounced in the chair. I thought he would fly if his feet weren't bolted to the floor. He reached his cuffed hands towards me and I took them in mine. They were shaking.

"I'm not an attorney, but I think you have solid grounds for a mistrial. If I can locate the rapist, I believe you'll have a chance at being freed."

Huge tears stood in his eyes. "Does my mom know? My brother?"

"I haven't told anybody but you. I probably won't see them again until after I locate the missing man."

"Do you think you can?"

"Yes. It might take a while, though." *Just let me fire up my super-powers.* "You'll have to be patient."

He grinned. "You'll keep me informed, right?"

"Of course I will. Kiko, have you ever heard the name Del?"

"No. Who is that?"

"I don't know, but his name was mentioned in my investigation."

"Wait! His name was on the 911 tape."

"Right."

"I'm so sorry. I forgot about that. I think he's the same as Donny."

"Why do you think that?"

"I guess it's because I don't believe she had two lovers. I don't want to believe it anyhow."

"Del could be Donny's last name or part of his last name."

"That's what I thought. Will there be another trial?"

"I don't know. We'll need to ask an attorney, but first things first. An attorney won't be much help until Zeke and I gather all the evidence we can."

"I won't have to keep the same attorney, will I?"

"Oh, no. That guy is a jerk."

Kiko grinned. "You met him already?"

"I don't like your attorney, Kiko. He made me think that all along he believed you were guilty primarily because you're Latino."

"Que cabrón," he spit. Then he flexed his biceps. Kiko was firing up his own superpowers. *"¡Viva la Raza! ¡Soy inocente!"*

"Si, Kiko, y voy a probarlo." He proclaimed innocence and I was going to prove it.

Evelyn Valentino's brother, Jaime Mendoza, agreed to meet me during his lunch hour at a café near the office building he was remodeling. He worked for a construction company and was foreman of his crew. He was a good-looking, stocky man, dressed in typical cold weather construction gear, insulated overalls and a thick jacket. When he removed the outer layers of clothing, I saw that he was less stocky than I'd assumed, but he had a powerfully built upper body.

At first, he came at me with so much attitude I thought he was going to be worse than his sisters. "Why should I help you? And what if I do know something? What of it? Who are you to this? Why do you care?" His questions were rapid-fire and in Spanish.

He settled down when I answered. I was just as comfortable speaking Spanish as English. *Don't mess with me, hombre.* I've spent half my life in Mexico, and my bet was he'd never been there. I spoke Spanish better than he did, and it changed his attitude for some reason.

"Look, I'm doing the job I was hired to do. If you would let me speak instead of giving me grief, I'll explain what I know. Kiko claims to be innocent and I have reason to believe he is. I don't care how macho you are; surely you don't think it's fair to keep an innocent man in prison?"

A waitress came and Jaime ordered. I asked for hot tea and it stressed her out, so I changed that to hot chocolate. I didn't care, I just needed something warm.

The minute she left, he said, "It wouldn't be fair if he was innocent, but he did a fucked-up thing and we know he did it."

"Why do you think he did?"

"Did you see those pictures? The evidence proved he did. They proved it in court. The jury said he did it for Christ's sake!"

"What if I told you that not all the evidence was brought into the trial?"

"Oh yeah? What did they miss?"

I explained in detail about the semen evidence and what that meant. He listened and didn't interrupt. As understanding dawned, he calmed down.

Jaime glanced around. His nervousness caused me to check over my shoulder. Nobody was paying any attention to us.

"Can I trust you?" he whispered.

"Yes. You can trust me, but depending on what you tell me, it might have to come out in court."

"That's okay. I don't want you to run to my mother with what I'm going to tell you. She's been through enough."

"I don't have a reason to tell your mother anything."

"Women don't need a reason to talk."

"What did Evie tell you, Jaime? You were her big brother, and I know she must have confided in you."

"She did." He hesitated and looked around again. "She told me she'd gotten involved with a man from work. He came to see her after the baby was six months old. She'd gone back in to see about getting her old job back." He stared down at his hands on the table. "She wasn't a slut," he said with enough heat to singe my hair.

"Nobody is calling her a slut. These things happen."

"She was a good mother."

"You don't have to defend her. Everybody makes mistakes. Kiko says she was a great mom. He didn't want to split up with her, Jaime. He loved her. He asked her to break up with her boyfriend or move out."

"He wanted to stay with her?"

"That's what he told me. They were working things out. He believes she was going to break up with the boyfriend and when she did, he killed her in a rage."

"I told the police I had never heard of him. I lied in court to the judge and everyone."

"That can be undone. The police lied, too. A lot of things conspired to put Kiko in prison, but we can still get him out. I need your help, Jaime. Please help me."

He hesitated a long time, watching me as he made up his mind. At last he said, "His name is Donny Delmar. A lot of people call him Del or even Delmar. His brother owns the restaurant. Sonny is his name, or that's what he's called. Donny is younger than Sonny."

I nearly fell out of the chair.

He stopped talking when the waitress brought his order and resumed when she left. "Donny never had any patience for the kids, and it was like he resented them. Evie told me she made a terrible mistake getting involved with him. He thought only of himself. She said he hit Freddy once. Freddy had seen him in his underwear and was making a big deal about it, the way little kids do. It was nothing, but he hit him.

"She was terrified Freddy would say something to Kiko. I told her she should come clean to him, beg his forgiveness, and get her shit together. She loved Kiko; I know she did. He was good to her. I think he was so busy working, and maybe he wasn't treating her like a queen the way he had at first, but damn it, she knew he loved her, and she still loved him."

He paused and stared at the food as if it was something foreign. "If I'd helped her get rid of Donny, she and her babies would still be alive." His voice broke and he stopped talking.

"Don't do that, Jaime. Blaming yourself won't help. You did what you thought was best at the time. She was a big girl and had to clean up her own mess."

"That's what I thought. B-b-but she shouldn't have had to die." He put his head in his hands. "I didn't want her to die."

"You couldn't have known Donny Delmar was a rapist and a murderer."

But if you'd told what you know instead of protecting a delusional old woman from the truth about her daughter, the right man might be in prison. Why, after all the evidence to the contrary, do I persist in thinking that life should be fair?

"Oh, God. Donny is free and my brother-in-law is in prison."

"Listen, Jaime, you can help get him out."

"I have to go see him—Kiko I mean. He has to know how sorry I am that I believed what they said at the trial. He has to know I'm on his side."

"I'm sure he'd love to hear those words from you. You should visit him."

"Doesn't he have to put me on a list? He'll never do it. He thinks I hate him."

"Have you ever been in prison? To Kiko a visitor means he gets out of his cell. He won't care if you've come to smack him around."

"But we can't afford a good attorney."

"Let's worry about that when I have more evidence. Does Donny Delmar still work at Sonny's? Do you know where he lives?"

"I don't know if he ever worked at Sonny's. He was there because his brother owns it. I think he lives near the restaurant, which means he lives in Kiko and Evie's neighborhood, or not far. I wish I knew more, but I've told you all I know."

"You've helped a lot. Now I have a name."

"If he killed Evie and her kids, he probably took off, don't you think?"

"It's hard to say. Maybe he thinks he got away with it and feels safe going about his business. His name never came out in court."

"If you're going to look for him, you should be careful. He's already killed three people."

"Right, I won't forget that."

"Are you even armed?"

"Yes."

"I don't see anything."

"I'm sneaky."

He laughed and then sighed. "I wish I could help you, but I have to work. My wife and I are expecting a baby in a month."

"Congratulations. Your mom already told me. She's excited."

"Poor mom, she lost her only grandchildren. I lost my niece and nephew, and Kiko lost his whole family. When you find Donny Delmar, I hope you convince the justice system to make him pay."

I went back to the hotel and changed my clothes. I didn't want to look too professional. I wore jeans, a ribbed t-shirt, and a long-sleeved shirt over that. I had a 22-calibre palm-sized pistol in a shoulder holster hidden by my shirt in case things got dicey. I also wore brown leather boots and a girlie ball cap. I wanted to look like a woman looking for an old boyfriend, but not too slutty. There's a fine line. Maybe Sonny or Donny or anybody who knew anything might take a second to speak with me if I looked just right. Whatever that was.

Sonny's was like a Denny's with two rooms and less hype. It was busy, even though it was after the lunch rush. I took a seat like any other customer and ordered hot tea and pecan pie, neither of which I wanted. It was difficult to breathe when I thought about being in the presence of a sick wacko like Donny.

The waitress in my section was an attractive platinum blond with an old-school do. Nobody teases their hair like that anymore. Well, except her. She was about ten years older than me, so it was weird but what did I know? I wanted to tell her that back home we tease boys, not hair, but I doubted she would appreciate my little joke. This was Dallas and things were different and her nametag read "Jessie." That was the extent of my knowledge.

When she came to see if I wanted more tea, I declined.

"Honey, you haven't touched your pie. Is something wrong?"

"No. I guess I'm not as hungry as I thought." Then I smiled, thanked her, and asked, "Do you know Donny Delmar?"

She hesitated long enough to make me think she had a personal interest in him. It was a subtle thing, but there it was. Crap!

I never considered he might be working another waitress in the same restaurant.

"I'm an old friend of his," I added as if I didn't care if he was there or not.

"Really? Are you from here?" Her body language said she cared.

"No. I'm just passing through and thought I'd look him up to say hi. He works here, right?"

"Yes, but he's not here right now. I could give him a message."

"That's okay. Forget it. He probably won't remember me." I knew what I needed to know. He was still working there.

"He'll be in at seven," she volunteered. "He's been out of town a while. I'd be glad to give him a message."

"Tell him Vicky Morales stopped by to say hey. Don't be too surprised if he doesn't have a clue."

She laughed. "He often has no clue."

"How is he doing?"

"He's fine. He's been working hard since his brother got sick." She paused. "But he had almost a year off before that so he should be rested up."

"Did he move away?"

"I think it was more like a long vacation."

"Well, I'm sorry to hear Sonny is sick. Is it serious?"

"Cancer," she whispered with a knowing nod.

There I sat with pie, tea, and a vague sense of impending doom. *What now, Batgirl?* as Barney would say. I didn't have a clue. But then my phone rang with a piece of a different mystery.

"Ms. Ricos, this is Mattie Sherwood from the Waverley Home. Your information is here. It's ready for you whenever you wish to look at it."

"I could come now if that would be okay." I didn't want to sound too eager but I was and besides, I needed something to take me away from murder for a while.

152

During the taxi ride, I realized I hadn't thought about Emilio Martez for at least the last twenty-four hours. That was good. But since I was thinking about him now, I'd have to start over in my count.

It's the same way with drinking. You can't say you've been clean and sober for two years if you got drunk thirty days ago. I'd been all-the-way sober for thirty days. It might not sound like much, but it was another touchdown for Team Ricos.

Going twenty-four hours without thinking of my former lover was a big deal. Maybe I would recover.

The other thing I thought about was the fact that all this time, Zeke could have seen the same information I was about to see if only he'd asked for it.

Chapter 22

"I made you copies of everything because I can't let you take the originals," said Mattie Sherwood. "But I put the original photos in your folder and kept copies for us. I think Mr. Pacheco would want to have these photos of his mother, don't you?"

"Oh yes. Thank you." I was so excited I felt ill. I was about to see my grandmother. She handed me a file folder marked "Ezekiél Pacheco."

"You'll be comfortable over there if you'd like to sit." She must have known I was about to collapse. She indicated a sofa and chair grouping on the far side of the reception area, near large floor-to-ceiling windows.

Somehow I managed to walk that far on legs I couldn't feel. I sat down with the file on my lap and stared out the window. Now that I had the information, I was terrified to look at it.

When I opened the file, on top of everything was a photo of a striking woman holding a baby. Her hair was deep black and cascaded over one shoulder, so thick it had to be called luxurious. The baby's chubby hand clasped a curl of it. His mother's complexion was flawless and her eyes were as black as her hair. There was a heartfelt smile on her lips and laughter in her eyes. She was amazing and I had seen her before, in her son.

The young woman looked so much like my father there was no doubt about her identity. This had to be Zeke's mother. A grandma should be old, but this one was so young.

I turned the photo over. On the back was printed, *"Lucia, diez y seis años y Ezekiél Pacheco, seis meses."* She was sixteen, her baby six months. Zeke's mother. I had a name! My grandmother was named Lucia Pacheco. I had to let that sink in. She looked happy and obviously adored her child. I wondered what Zeke would think and if it would make him happy or cause him more sadness.

There was another photo of the same gorgeous woman and an older baby. He was standing beside her, his dimpled fist gripping her index finger. She grinned at the camera with the same grin I'd seen before on Zeke. On the back she had written their names and ages. They were seventeen years and thirteen months respectively.

I knew something terrible happened to separate the two. I didn't believe she'd died on the streets, but she was surely dead. Otherwise, she would never have let him go. I hoped Zeke would see that as clearly as I did.

I studied the photos a long time before I moved on in the folder. There was a form signed by Mr. and Mrs. Herman Winchester that surrendered the baby to the orphanage. There was a statement from them regarding the circumstances, in which they claimed their housekeeper had left him behind. They said she had taken off to Mexico, but to go without her baby? How did they know she'd gone to Mexico? They mentioned she was "illegal," something they didn't realize until after she was gone. Yeah, right.

There was paperwork adopting Zeke to a couple named Hamilton but, after less than a month, they brought him back saying he didn't understand English and cried a lot. What is wrong with people? They made a signed statement of their intent not to finalize the adoption.

My father spent a little over six months in the orphanage after that and was then turned over to Family Services to be placed into foster care. There was a letter to that effect from the then-director of Waverley Home. They didn't keep children older than two years. Zeke was no longer considered adoptable. He had gotten "too old" for most couples looking for a child.

My heart hurt so much. What would he think of this? Would it hurt him like it hurt me? It would be worse for him, I thought. He'd already been through the pain of it over and over. Before, it had been the pain of rejection. This would be a different pain, but still, wouldn't he want to see his mother?

I decided I'd go see the Winchesters first. I didn't believe their story of the so-called illegal housekeeper who left her baby with them. Lucia would never have willingly abandoned her child. I knew that in my heart.

I pulled out Zeke's birth certificate. It showed he was born on the Triple Bar Ranch in Dallas County. His mother was listed as Lucia Pacheco Rodriguez, as was Mexican custom. Rodriguez was her family name. She was age sixteen. His father, Maximiliano Pacheco, was age eighteen. My grandparents were only children when Zeke was born.

Zeke's tiny fingerprints were at the bottom of the form. He was declared a healthy male, born January 1, 1967 to Mexican Nationals. His father's occupation was listed as cowboy/ranch hand and his mother's as homemaker.

The birth certificate was signed by a Dallas doctor, but he did not deliver the baby. He was swearing, though, that the baby had been born in the U.S. The current place of residence for both parents was listed as the Triple Bar Ranch, Dallas.

I closed the file and sat staring out the window. I had even more questions than I had before. What had Lucia's husband done that landed him in prison? Was the prison part even true? Without a doubt, Zeke had family in México, but how would I find them? Would they want to be found? What was the truth of my grandparents' past? As was often the case in investigations, the more I knew the more questions I had.

I asked the taxi driver to take me to Fort Worth even though it would cost a small fortune. I was in deep. I owed it to Zeke, since I'd messed around where he hadn't asked me to mess. I had to figure this out and pronto. I had forgotten everything but the baby. He was adorable! I stressed on that for the ride to 35654 Royal Court in suburban Fort Worth.

We arrived in front of a mansion of intimidating size. The driver asked me if I wanted him to wait. Yes, I said, that would be great. If I was going to be a long time I'd come out and tell him. He agreed to that.

I walked up to the door, wishing I'd worn different clothing. I intended to beg and plead for the sake of the baby they turned away, and I would have liked to look older and more intimidating. Once again in my life, I had jumped out of a plane with no parachute in sight. I always jumped and then thought about the parachute. No wonder Barney called me Batgirl. I was always flying around without a clue.

The door was answered by a maid in a uniform. The place was a palace. I felt glad Zeke didn't grow up there, the spoiled son of wealthy people. But maybe they wouldn't have ruined him if being pulled out of bed and beaten before dawn didn't do it.

I ordered myself to get a grip and asked in a polite way to see either or both of the Winchesters.

"Are they expecting you?"

"No. I apologize for that, but I'm here on an urgent matter. Please ask them to see me." I handed her my card which showed I was a deputy sheriff from Brewster County. I wasn't there as a deputy, so if they agreed to see me, I'd explain that.

I waited in the foyer a long time. When the maid came back, she said, "Mrs. Winchester will see you now, ma'am. Just come with me."

I followed her down a long corridor and into a sunny, plant-filled room at the back of the house. It looked out onto a huge expanse of manicured lawn.

"This is Mrs. Winchester." With that, the maid left us. It was difficult to spot the person among all the plants.

I was standing before a regal-looking woman about seventy. I can never tell. She had silver hair piled on her head, which made her seem taller than she was. Her clothes were casual but still looked more expensive than anything I owned.

"Won't you sit down?" She indicated a chair near hers. "How can I help a deputy sheriff from Brewster County?"

I took a deep breath and prepared to tell her the truth. "I'm not here in the capacity of deputy, but that was the only card I had with me. I'm the daughter of a man who was left at the Waverley Home by you and your husband a long time ago. You stated in a letter that he'd been abandoned by a housekeeper you employed. You said you couldn't keep him and thought it best for the child to leave him there."

She was staring at me as if I'd started laying eggs on her carpet. Since she said nothing, I continued. "I'm trying to find out about my father's family, and I've come to get your help, Mrs. Winchester. Anything you can tell me would be appreciated."

"I don't know what to say." She was clearly stunned. I bet she never expected this day to come. "A young Mexican woman worked for us a short time and then she disappeared and left her baby. We waited a few days, assuming she'd return for him but when she didn't, we took him to the orphanage."

"Do you know where she was from?"

"No. We had difficulty communicating since she spoke Spanish."

"Do you know if she had a husband? Well, I know she had one, I just don't know what happened to him."

"There was no man with her while she was here."

"How did she treat the baby?"

"I seldom saw her with him. I was busy back in those days, and I left the housekeeping to the staff. I suppose she loved her son. I always thought something bad must have happened for her not to take him with her."

I opened the file and showed her the two photos. "Is this the woman?"

She looked at the photographs in surprise, as if she had never seen the woman before. This was probably because Mexican maids were invisible in her house.

"This could be her. I'm sorry. It has been a long time, and I can't say for sure. The woman who left the baby was extraordinarily beautiful, like this woman."

"Were you the one who left the photos at the orphanage?"

"Yes. I—I thought since she left them with the child, they should stay with him, you know, in case one day he might want them."

"My father never knew his mother. He hasn't seen the photos yet, but I know he'll appreciate your thoughtfulness. It will mean a lot to him to be able to see her."

"You're the daughter of the baby boy who was left behind?" She seemed amazed, as if she had just figured it out.

"Yes ma'am. This is my grandmother."

"I wish I could tell you more, but I don't know any more about it."

"I thank you for your time and help. If you think of anything else, you have my card. My personal cell phone number is written on the back."

"I'll talk to my husband when he comes home, and if we think of something, we will certainly call you. I wish you much success in finding your family. It would be terrible not to have family."

"Yes, I think that, too."

"I wish you the best." She walked me briskly to the door.

I felt certain the woman was holding back something she knew, but how would I force the truth out of her?

During the long cab ride back to the hotel, I called Barney

"I guess you want me to describe the Chisos?" He assumed I'd called for that.

"Yes, but that's not why I'm—yes, please go ahead." I closed my eyes and laid my head against the seat.

"The clouds are on the mountains today, Ricos. I was thinking about you because this is the kind of day you love. The Chisos are half in and half out. The bottom half is the same reddish rock we usually see, but the top half is, well, I guess you could say the Chisos have their heads in the clouds."

For just a second, I was looking at them.

"So what's up, my pard?"

"I might have made a big mistake."

"Oh? That would be so unlike you."

"I could use some moral support right now instead of wisecracks."

"Tell me what's up."

I told him, but only what I thought didn't infringe on Zeke's right to privacy. In other words, I didn't mention that my father had fallen apart the evening before or that he was an alcoholic.

After I told him about Zeke being parentally-challenged and raised in foster homes and thinking his parents had died as criminals, Barney took a breath and let it out slowly. "My sense is you shouldn't withhold what you know. Show him things and let him be the one to say what happens next. Please hear this, Margarita. If he asks you to give it up, you should give it up. Do you comprehend what I'm saying?"

"Yes, Barney. I hear you."

"I know how you are. If there's a mystery, you want to solve it. Realize that in trying to do something good you may hurt him worse. It could go either way."

"I don't want to make it worse, Barn."

"You should've thought of that…never mind. I know you don't want a lecture."

"I'm already beating on myself. I thought I could find his mother, but now I think she's dead. No matter what, Zeke still doesn't have a mom and there doesn't seem to be a way to find out what happened to her."

"Maybe it would be better not to know."

"Maybe, but that's never my take on things. I always think it's

Border Ghosts

better to know. That is until I know, and then sometimes I wish I didn't know."

He laughed. "I see the problem. The thing you have to remember is whatever you find out, you have to tell Zeke and then let it go. I know this goes against the Batgirl grain, but you're talking about your father. If you cause him more hurt, it might damage to your relationship. You can be his family now. Hell, Ricos, you are his family."

"Right; I know."

"That's my opinion. I'm here for you if you get in trouble."

"Thanks, Barney."

"Set your detective skills aside when it comes to your father. That's my two cents worth."

I recognized that as sound advice. Recognizing it and following it were two different things.

Chapter 23

MAX AND LUCIA, 1966

Max and Lucia took Earl's truck as far as the county line and left it sitting off the road but visible. It was too risky to take it farther. They assumed Earl had awakened or been discovered by one of the cowboys and was now missing his vehicle. He would say it had been stolen, and anyone caught with it would go to prison, and that was even more likely if they were people without papers.

Max thought he'd rather walk than give Earl the satisfaction of sending him to jail, so they got their meager belongings out of the truck and trudged to the next town. By the time they reached the edge of it, dark had come and brought the cold with it. A blustery wind was blowing from the north.

"We have to find a safe place to sleep and something to eat, Luce." Max felt vulnerable walking into a small Texas town in the dark. People might get the wrong idea and besides, he was chilled through to his bones and knew Lucia was, too. She would never complain, but he knew if he felt the cold, she would be miserable. They were wearing most of the clothes they owned and it wasn't enough.

They approached a convenience store and watched it a while, trying to judge the risk of entering. It was impossible to tell anything.

"I'm going in," Max decided. "You stay here with our stuff. I don't want the man working in there to see us with our packs and think we're wetbacks."

She laughed but agreed to wait in the shadows across the road. Within a few minutes Max ran up to her, breathless with excitement.

"Come on!" He grabbed up their packs. "The man working is Mexican. He came here when he was my age from a small town near Monterrey. He lives down the street and has invited us to stay with him and his wife for the night."

"I can't believe it!"

"He says their children are grown and gone and they get lonely. They have plenty of room. He seems to want us to stay there, Luce, and I couldn't say no. They have heat and an extra bed. You can get some good rest."

"Not if you're going to be in the same bed."

"Be serious. Is it okay that I told him yes?"

"Yes, of course; you did the right thing."

"Come with me and I'll introduce you. It's warm in the store. He has hot coffee and hot chocolate and they come out of a machine!" Max was walking backwards, talking to her and bouncing with excitement. He held his arms out. "Come on, Luce!"

"I'm coming, Max. I'm coming. I'm so tired. I've never been this tired."

He ran to her, swept her up in his arms, and ran with her towards the brightly lit store.

Lucia loved everything about the old couples' house: its spacious rooms, polished wood floors, high ceilings, the green plants everywhere, but especially the warm air that came up through metal slats in the floors. It was a wondrous thing to hear the cold wind howling and yet feel such warmth.

She marveled at the heat as she wandered from room to room with Señora Gutierrez, looking at photographs of children and grandchildren and of the couple when they were young and newly immigrated to this country. They looked poor, like Max and Lucia did now, but they also looked happy and hopeful.

The couple, Juan and Rita Gutierrez, told their young visitors about their own life together as immigrants and the trials and joys they experienced. They listened with interest as Max and Lucia spoke of their adventures, challenges, dreams, and their excitement about the arrival of their first baby.

"I hadn't realized you were expecting." Señora Gutierrez stood. "Please come with me, Lucia. I have some things for you."

She took Lucia into the room where she and Max would sleep and opened the closet doors. "These things were my daughter's when she was pregnant. She asked me to pass them to someone who needs them. She's not going to have more babies. I think she is about your size, so please take anything you like."

Lucia was speechless. She had never seen maternity clothes or even knew they existed. Where she came from, women let out the waistlines of their clothes, or they borrowed clothes from larger women or made their own. Here were clothes specially made for expanding bellies. First there was the heat coming through the floors and now this. Lucia was in awe and felt joyous, too. She hugged Rita, and then the older woman left her alone to try on the beautiful things.

As Lucia changed from one thing to the next she wondered if Max knew about these clothes or understood how the heat worked. She would have to ask him. She shrugged into a full-body stretchy-thing. It was a leotard, but she had never heard that term. It felt wonderful, warm and soft to the touch. Max would like it on her.

Over the black leotard she pulled on gray wool slacks then added a silky red blouse and a gray vest. She looked at herself in the mirror and couldn't believe her eyes. She looked like a fine lady, not a poor country girl. Maybe someday she'd wear clothes like these, but not now. It would be ridiculous to dress like that and work on a ranch. Worse, it'd make Max feel bad.

She dug around in the closet until she found jeans and simple blouses. The jeans had panels to allow a baby to grow. She sat on the edge on the bed wearing only the black leotard.

When Max came in, she jumped up, ashamed of herself for putting so much attention on clothes she couldn't take on their journey, clothes that didn't suit the life she led.

He stood frozen in the doorway. He had never seen anything like what she wore. It hugged every curve and accentuated the shapeliness of her calves and the muscles in her slender arms. He was afraid to move, afraid she would disappear.

"Max…" She was fearful he'd think the clothes were important to her.

"Lucia…" He was afraid to touch something so exquisite. He couldn't take his eyes off the tiny swell of her stomach, his child growing in her. The tight thing she wore drew attention to it, drew attention to all of her.

His eyes moved to the clothing spread out everywhere. Lucia saw the misery in them as he realized she couldn't wear them where they were going.

"Max," she began, "I'm just looking at these things, not taking them. Señora Rita said I could have them, but I can't wear them.

"I want you to have them but…"

"I don't want them, Max. I'm just playing with them."

"I want you to have beautiful things. You deserve the best clothes made, Lucia." He knelt in front of her and placed his head against the swell of their baby. She held him against her. He added, "My son agrees."

"What if it's a girl?"

He put his hands on the roundness. "A girl would make me happy, but I sense a male growing here. I can't explain it, but I feel it strongly. I would love a girl too, Luce. Surely you know that."

"Yes, I know." She placed her hands on his head and pressed him against her belly again.

"One day I will buy you anything you want."

"Yes, I know that, too, Max. I also know I'll never be happier than I am right now. It wouldn't be possible."

"You can't mean that."

"I do mean it. I have everything I need right here in this room."

"You mean the heat, don't you?" he teased, knowing how much she liked it.

"No, I mean the man kneeling in front of me, Max, the man with his head resting against our baby."

Chapter 24

I was relaxing in a warm bath when Zeke came into our room with a jangle of keys and other things he was dropping onto the dresser. The photos and file were at the bottom of my suitcase, but I still felt panicky he would see them before I had a chance to explain. A guilty conscience is a prickly thing.

The bed creaked and a boot dropped to the floor, then another.

"I hope that's you in there," he called.

"It depends on who you think I am."

"Now I know it's you."

A few minutes later, I came out of the bathroom bundled in a bathrobe.

Zeke was stretched out on the bed. "Did you have a successful day?"

"I know who the unknown sperm donor is and where he works."

"How in the heck did you do that so fast?"

"I'm nosy and don't take no for an answer."

"I've observed that about you."

"It's a good thing I don't suspect you of anything."

He laughed.

"I need his DNA, and when it matches the DNA in the evidence, it's a matter of getting somebody to pick him up. Do you think the Dallas P.D. would do that?"

"Hold on here. You're getting ahead of yourself. *When* you have DNA and it matches... If it matches, we'll decide what to do."

"Okay. Yes."

"You'll be stepping on toes at the Dallas P.D."

"They did wrong, Zeke."

166

"I think this case should be turned over to the Rangers instead of to them, and they'll have someone pick up your perp. I can assist once I'm out of class."

"You have to let me go, too. I've done all the work."

"I know you have and you're amazing. You'll get all the credit."

"I don't want credit. I want the thrill of helping you take the bastard down."

He laughed but then said, "No. I don't think so."

"In that case, I'll do it myself and tell you about it later."

"You remind me so much of a young me."

"Be fair, Zeke. I've done all the hard stuff. I should get to drag him in."

"Under what organizational authority would you arrest him?"

"Oh."

"Yeah. Oh. Rangers have authority all over Texas."

"Now you're just showing off. The point is that I'm coming with you when you go do it."

"We'll see about that."

"It's not fair to treat me like your daughter in professional matters."

"I can't help it. You're my daughter."

"Huh."

"Things are already hopping at D.P.D. Detective Morrison is hot under the collar. He didn't show up for class this afternoon, and this morning he made a snide comment about my meddling daughter."

"Well, in fairness, you do have a meddling daughter."

"If there's an innocent man incarcerated because of poor detective work by the Dallas police then by God, that lazy, opinionated detective had better look for other work."

"It's worse than just poor detective work, Zeke. He tried to make the evidence fit his own first impressions of the crime. And

I think he suppressed a crucial report. And the worthless defense attorney referred to Kiko as a 'macho Latino wife-beater.' He said it to my face."

"That was a big mistake on his part."

"Yes. He's stupid and prejudiced. He should be in prison and Kiko should be free. If I was in charge, a lot of things would be different."

"I'm sure. Say, are we going to Mexican town or not?"

"I'm for it."

"Look. First I want to say I'm sorry I had a meltdown last night."

"You don't need to apologize, Zeke."

"I know you've had enough sadness to last the rest of your life, and you're only twenty-six. My intention was never to give you more."

"Let's don't talk about me. We've both had plenty of sadness. Tonight, we should celebrate being alive, being together, and being mexicano."

Zeke lifted an imaginary glass. "Viva México!"

Zeke is a good man with a keen sense of right and wrong, and because he has a desire to please his daughter, he couldn't say no when I asked to start our evening by spying on Donny Delmar for a few minutes. I wanted to see my possible perp. What would a brutal, baby-stabbing man look like?

We were dressed for dining and dancing, Mexican style, but we were drinking coffee in a downtown café instead. Sometimes I'm not smart.

The thing was, Delmar had not come in and was not expected. His brother had taken a turn for the worse, according to the waitress who was not Jessie.

"We have something important for him." Zeke jumped in as if he'd been working the case. "Maybe we could leave it at his house."

"I'm sure that would be fine." Sheryl didn't care what we were doing or where or to whom. Her interest was in Zeke more than anything else going on in her life right then.

Waitresses and other females embarrass themselves around him; it's pitiful. I think it's that thing he does with his eyes. No. It isn't that. It's that he has eyes, and they are killer.

"I know he lives just a few blocks from here, but I've forgotten the exact address." Zeke kept on, oblivious to the fact that Sheryl was about to faint into his lap. It made me not want to go with him to the Mexican joint. Women would be all over him. "Would you refresh my memory, Sheryl?"

"Are ya'll married?"

"No." I answered because I was losing patience. "He's my *father*." I hoped she'd realize he was too old for her.

"So, you're not married?" She addressed Zeke. I was a splattered gnat on her windshield.

"No."

"In that case, are you busy? I get off at nine and there's this party—"

"I have a date tonight, but thank you. It's sweet of you to ask."

She sighed. "Maybe another time."

He smiled at her, and she fell right into those eyes. It was hard to watch.

She struggled out of the daze and remembered he'd asked her a question. "What was it you wanted to know?"

"Donny's address."

"He lives just two blocks over on Campbell, 355 Campbell."

"Right, I remember that now." He smiled at her again.

She smiled back as if they were alone in the room. Someone yelled "waitress!" and she looked towards the voice as if just realizing there were others there, and she was supposed to be serving them.

"Do ya'll need anything else?"

"No, Sheryl, you've been a big help. Thank you."

"Anytime, Sweetie. I hope to see you again. I didn't catch your name."

That's because he didn't give it.

"My name is Zeke."

"Oh, I love that name!"

"Thank you. I've grown fond of it."

She giggled and wandered off.

Zeke shrugged. "I got it."

He meant Donny's address, but I said, "No kidding. You've got it, all right. I thought she was going to fall into your arms."

"Don't be silly."

In my experience, men who've "got it" don't know they've got it, and that's what makes them irresistible.

Sheryl came back right away with an offer of more coffee, and Zeke started chatting her up again. They joked back and forth, and I was irritated until I saw where he was going. "Would you mind calling Donny for us? I want to let him know I'll be leaving the stuff at his door so he'll know to look for it."

He smiled and handed her my cell phone.

She dialed Possible Perp's number, which put it into my phone! Zeke was not looking at me, but I was watching him in awe. He looked like he was about to laugh. The waitress handed the phone to him. "It's ringing." She walked off.

"Hello; Donny? This is Ernesto." He paused while Donny spoke. "Ernesto Padilla. Rita and I are going to leave that stuff at your door, okay?" Another pause. "Very funny. I don't remember you either. Ha, ha. Right. Gotta go." He flipped the phone shut. On the other end, Donny saw "unknown name, unknown number." On my phone, I now had Donny's cell phone number.

"That was brilliant, Zeke."

"They don't let just any old dude into the Texas Rangers, you know."

"I've heard that." I grinned at him. "Here comes Sheryl again. Let's go dancing, Ranger Man."

"Didn't you want to spy on your perp?"

"Are you kidding? I don't want to think about perps. I can look for him later. I want to go dancing with my padre."

On the way to dinner and dancing, Zeke surprised me by asking, "Did you find the right orphanage?"

"Yes, I did. It's called Waverley Home."

He groaned. "It sounds like a place for old people."

"They seem nice; I think they care about the children they have there."

He didn't say anything. I had plenty to say but didn't want to tell him and take a chance of spoiling the evening.

"I'm afraid to ask what you know. Are you getting anywhere?"

"Yes. Zeke, I—I have a photograph of your mother."

"You have a photograph of my mother?" He looked incredulous. "Why didn't you say so? For God's sake, Margarita, when were you going to tell me? Wait. How do you know she's my mother?"

"You only have to see her to know, Zeke."

"Why didn't you mention it before?"

"I wanted to get more information and present it to you then."

"Do you have it with you?"

"No. It's at the hotel. I have your birth certificate, too."

"You *what?*"

"I have your birth certificate. I was—"

"So you're sitting on a photo of my mother and my birth certificate and—"

"I'm not sitting on them; they're in my suitcase."

He gave me a look. Then he made an illegal U-turn.

"What are you doing?"

"We're going back to the hotel."

"What about eating Mexican food and dancing?"

"I want to see my mother! Besides, aren't you the smart aleck who said the Mexicans will still be here tomorrow?"

Chapter 25

1966, MAX AND LUCIA AND THE
TRIPLE BAR RANCH

At first, the Triple Bar Ranch was an intimidating place to Max and Lucia because of its size and the number of people working there. Augustín, Max's cousin, had met them at the bus station in Dallas and brought them to the ranch. He explained things along the way and entertained them with stories about the happenings and the diverse mix of people on the Triple Bar.

Max and Lucia were assigned a room in the largest bunkhouse they'd ever seen. It was much like the room they'd occupied at previous ranches, except it had a double bed. When they were shown the room, Max couldn't keep the glee off his face. Before, the room they'd occupied had twin beds and no room to shove them together. They'd spent a lot of time in one bed or the other, but sleeping had been uncomfortable. That was one of the reasons they had enjoyed so much time outside under the stars.

An elderly, wrinkled *curandera* served as midwife and doctor to many of the workers. It was impossible to guess how old she was, but she had been at the Triple Bar as long as anyone remembered. When she examined Lucia, they argued about her due date. The curandera said the baby was too small and not far enough along to come in January. It would be more like March.

"No," insisted Lucia. "I know my body. I got pregnant in April. My baby will come in January, around the time of my own birthday or before."

"No dear, you're wrong," Señora Villa insisted gently. "You will have a healthy baby, but not until March."

When Lucia told Max about her visit to the old woman, he agreed with his wife. "You're right, Luce, our baby will come in January, just like you think and we need to be ready. I know exactly when you got pregnant."

She stood with her hands on her hips. "Oh? And how would you know something like that?"

"Remember the night when we made love under the full moon all night long? It was magic. That's the night. The next morning you seemed different somehow. I can't explain it, but I know it's true."

Lucia blushed. "You can't know it was that night. It could've been any night."

"That's true, my love, but I know it was that night."

She let it go. Her husband was convinced and it didn't matter. If he wanted to think it was that night it was okay with her.

"Our son might start off small," she said later, "but he will grow up to be a large, fine man, just like his father. He will grow tall and straight like a sturdy tree." She had her shapely legs wrapped around Max and he was in no mood to argue. Besides, he believed what she said was true.

Life on the Triple Bar Ranch was good. There were many Mexican workers. It resembled a small village in many ways. Working hours were long, but there was always plenty to eat. This made Max and Lucia feel prosperous even though their pay was low. They had known hunger, and at the ranch it was kept away.

Max had proven himself a cowboy and was put to work as one. One day the head cowboy watched him shoe a horse in his quiet, confident way. Max had been doing it since he was a small boy. His father had taught him well. As the older man oversaw the work, Max did the job quickly and perfectly. The horse never flinched, kicked at Max, moved, or tried to bite him. He spoke to the animal the whole time in a calm, affectionate tone. From then on, Max did the shoeing and taught others how to do it, too.

The young couple was surrounded by friends of all ages. Many older couples were more than happy to take the place of their parents. The advice was never-ending, sometimes confusing, and often ignored.

When it came to matters concerning her baby, Lucia believed she knew what she was doing. She didn't know where the knowledge came from, but it was there. She wasn't afraid of the birth; she looked forward to it and to holding her child.

She hadn't gained much weight and this was a point of concern to all the older women. She had gained enough, she knew instinctively. Her pregnancy was hers and unlike any other. She didn't look as far along as she knew she was, and everyone still argued with her about her due date.

Before Christmas, the old midwife examined her and declared that her body was preparing to deliver the baby.

Lucia knew that. "It'll be the first week of January," she said.

For Christmas the couple received gifts for the baby including clothes, hand-knitted items, blankets, and diapers. Max presented Lucia with a cradle he'd made from the hard wood of a mesquite tree. It was the most exquisite piece of furniture she had ever seen. It was adorned with intricate carvings and was a piece of art that would also hold their baby. She had no idea her husband knew how to work with wood. When had he had time to learn?

Lucia had knitted a soft wool sweater for Max with the help and instruction of some of the other women. It was a vibrant blue, the color of the winter sky at home when the air was cold and clear.

"When you wear it," she told him, "know that my arms are around you. Feel the love I have for you. Always know, Max, that you are loved."

His eyes filled with tears and he had been unable to speak. He had worn the sweater every day since Christmas and was wearing it the night his son was born.

On New Year's Eve, there was a big party at the ranch hosted by the owners, although they did not attend. There was more food and drink than Lucia had ever seen. There was roasted and barbequed meat of every variety, along with huge hams, tamales, picadillo, every style of potato from salad to mashed, all kinds of breads, vegetable dishes, rice, tortillas, and enough desserts to fill two long tables. There was champagne, many brands of beer, hard liquor, punch, coffee, and tea to drink.

There were two live bands, one playing Mexican music and the other country-western. The ranch owners had told their employees to invite anyone they wished, so it was the biggest celebration Max and Lucia had ever seen. People brought family from all over, and the cowboys invited friends and girlfriends as well.

Spirits were high and there was much toasting for health and happiness in the New Year. Lucia wasn't interested in food. After she danced a few slow dances with Max, she told him she was tired. He took her to bed and snuggled with her.

"I don't want you to miss the party," she said when they were awakened by the loud festivities. "You should go for a while and at least drink a beer."

"I want to stay here with you, Mi Amor. There is nowhere I'd rather be." He drew her close and nuzzled her neck.

Lucia grew restless; she was unable to sleep or get comfortable in bed. "Let's take a walk, Max. There's a full moon and we should admire it."

He agreed because as long as Lucia wasn't sleeping, he wasn't sleeping either.

Moonlight streamed in the window, and Max wanted to tell her he had been admiring the way it shone in her hair and added to the glow that came from within her. Instead, he gathered two blankets. It wasn't a cold night, but if they decided to lie down, it might feel colder.

They slipped out a back way so they wouldn't disturb the partiers or be disturbed by them. Max had the blankets slung over one shoulder and his other arm around his wife.

"Don't panic, Max, but I'm having a few pains," Lucia admitted after they'd walked about half a mile.

"Shouldn't we head back?"

"Not yet. It will take a long time for the baby to come, and walking is good for the delivery. It makes it easier."

"But Luce, you've never had a baby before, and you don't know for sure how long it will take."

"Please let me rest and then we'll head back. I just want to sit for a while in the moonlight."

He knew she would not be deterred. They made their way to the top of a small rise where they could see the party lights and hear the music. Max spread out the blankets and helped his wife sit on the makeshift bed.

When the New Year came, they knew it because of the loud sounds of the well-wishers, the noisemakers, and the music the bands were making to welcome it. The two hugged each other without saying anything for a long time.

"I'm glad our baby is small," Lucia said. "He has to come out a very small place."

Max laughed and agreed with her.

"I have a lot of pain now, Max. The baby is coming. I feel like I'm being ripped apart."

"We have to go back." He felt panicked. "I can carry you."

"There's no way you could carry me so far. Let's stay here."

That horrified him further. "No, Lucia. I don't know anything about having babies. Who will help you? We need the old woman."

"It will be okay."

"But—"

"I'm having the baby, Max. All you have to do is stay with me and hold my hand. Everything will be fine. I promise you I can do this."

He wanted to believe it but felt it was irresponsible not to go for help. The old midwife and the other women would know what to do, how to comfort her, how to help the baby come. He realized, as the thoughts passed through his head, that it wasn't going to be that way.

By two that morning, Max was wild with panic, convinced he should run for help. Lucia was in great pain although she wasn't complaining. She held his hand so tightly he was sure she would crush the bones in spite of the difference in the size of their hands.

By two-thirty she was sweating and panting.

"Lucia, listen to me. I'm going for help."

"Don't you dare leave me," she gasped and gripped his hand even tighter.

"But I don't know what to do."

"There is nothing for you to do. The work is all mine. Just stay with me; that's all I'm asking you to do."

A little later, he was frantically pacing and she said, "I feel something, something different. I have to push." She was trying to stand.

He couldn't believe his eyes. "What are you doing? Lie down! Our son is going to fall on his head!"

She laughed in spite of everything. "Don't be an idiot. I'm going to squat. It will make pushing easier."

When he looked incredulous, she added, "Women have given birth like this for centuries, Max. Trust me, please."

How did she know that, he wondered. How would she know any of the things she knew? He did trust her. He had always trusted her. He felt so useless he wanted to cry from the shame of it.

"Will you steady me, Max?"

He put his hands on her shoulders and pressed his legs against her gently from behind. Then he watched in awe as his tiny wife pushed and pushed, holding onto his legs for support. In spite of the cool night air beads of sweat stood on her forehead. Her face was wet. Max wiped her with his bandana, using only one hand. The other still held her shoulder.

"He's coming." It was three o'clock. "Please hold me up. I don't want to fall over on him."

Max watched in silent wonder as she pushed some more and then held a tiny boy out in front of her. He seemed to glow in the light from the moon. His wet hair glinted as if drenched in silver.

"Sit down and take him," Lucia said.

Max stood staring like a statue.

"Did you hear me, Max? He's still attached to me by a cord. You can't take him far."

She fell to her knees and then lay down on the blankets, exhausted. Max knelt beside her and covered their tiny son with a blanket. Then he pressed him against his jacket, close to his heart.

"Are you all right, Luce?"

With her usual good humor, she answered, "I feel okay, considering a dump truck passed through my vagina."

He laughed and looked down at his son. "Don't we have to cut his cord?"

"Now is the time to go for help, Max. Hand him to me and run. Please bring a truck so you can take us home. I don't want to walk."

"I won't be gone long." He knelt and kissed her. Then he stood and ran, yelling the whole way, "I have a son! I have a son!"

When they were alone in the big bed with their son between them, they looked him over and declared him perfect in every way. The old midwife had said it too, as if amazed that such a tiny boy could be so healthy and well-formed.

"He looks like you," she said to Max.

"I was thinking he looks like you."

"I guess he looks like both of us."

That was the wonder of it for the new parents. He did look like a combination of the two of them. And he seemed content to have arrived in the world. He hadn't yet cried but looked towards the sound of Lucia's voice when she spoke to him. When Max put his face close to the baby's and welcomed him, he seemed to listen as if he understood everything his father was saying.

They decided to name him Ezekiél Antonio, after both of their fathers. Ezekiél was Max's father, Antonio was Lucia's. Wouldn't their parents be delighted to know they now had a healthy grandson? They couldn't wait to send them word.

"We'll call him Zeke," said Max, "if that's okay with you."

"I like it. He'll be big and strong and handsome, too, like his father."

"When will he eat?" Max was curious about how that worked.

"He'll eat when he's ready, I guess."

"How will you know when he's ready?" He put his face against the baby's to breathe in the sweet scent of him.

"I haven't done this before either, but I think he'll cry. That's how I'll know he needs something."

"It seems like he'd be hungry by now. Come on, Zeke, you can't grow if you don't eat."

"Let him sleep, Max. Being born was hard work. I don't think he enjoyed that any more than I did."

"Sleep then, Son." Max kissed his forehead. "Sleep now, my precious little dump truck."

Max put his arm around his wife and Zeke, thinking that in all his life, nothing would ever be better than that moment.

Chapter 26

Zeke stared at his mother's photograph so long I didn't know what to think. He took a deep breath, and I realized he was trying not to cry. "Do you think this woman is my mother?" The words were tightly controlled.

"Yes. I think so. Look at the back. She wrote her name and yours on both. How likely is it that a beautiful woman who happens to look like you would also have a baby boy named Zeke? And it says right there the last name is Pacheco."

"Lucia. Her name was Lucia. Lucia Pacheco." It was like he was testing the feel of it on his tongue. "My mother. Tell me the story again."

"These photos were left at the orphanage when they left you there. I think it proves that—"

"I don't need you to tell me what it proves," he snapped without taking his eyes off the photograph.

Fine. I sat on the bed and looked at my phone to be sure Donny's number was still there. Yup.

After a few minutes, Zeke sat down next to me and put his arms around me. "I'm sorry. This is hard to get my head around."

He let me go and went back to studying the birth certificate, but with one hand he held his mother's photos against his heart. I wondered if it was conscious. "Do you think this birth certificate is real?"

"Yes, I think it is. It looks like the real thing, but if you doubt it, you could have the prints compared."

"I was thinking that." A few seconds passed. "According to this certificate, my father was Maximiliano Pacheco. Lucia and Maximiliano Pacheco. I never knew their names." His voice caught and there was another long pause. "It's true that I was born on January

181

first. I didn't know if that was correct or a date that was picked for me at random. It's nice to know."

"There's a little more to the story of my visit to the orphanage, Zeke."

He turned to me. "What is it?"

"Mr. and Mrs. Herman Winchester left you there."

"How did they get me?"

"They made a statement that your mother had been working for them as a maid. They claimed she abandoned you, so I went to see them."

"You went to see the Winchesters?"

"Yes. I didn't learn much, but she did say your mother would never have left you behind, so something must have happened to her. I'm trying to find out what, but I'm not there yet."

Zeke tried to speak and failed. I thought I'd overwhelmed him and he needed time alone, so I kissed him on the cheek and bowed out to take a walk. When I returned to the room, Zeke was asleep on the bed, still holding his mother's photos against his chest.

The next morning, I headed off to work on both of the mysteries I had going. Zeke let me take his truck and reminded me not to drive a Texas Ranger vehicle like a bat out of hell. I thought it was the perfect opportunity. Who would stop me?

I went first to 355 Campbell Street, parked two blocks away, and walked over to the house. There was no car in the driveway and, after observing the place a while, I saw nothing going on. It appeared nobody was at home. I thought for a while about breaking in and taking something with DNA on it so I could confirm my suspicions. Reason took over and I decided against it. DNA gotten illegally is not usable in court and might come back to bite me hard, and worse, hurt Zeke.

I went to the door and knocked a while, but there was no answer. Someone passed on the sidewalk and waved and yelled, "He's not there. I don't think he lives there anymore."

"Thanks." I waited for the man to get on down the street. Then I went to the trashcans at the side of the house. Something discarded is legal to take.

I took an evidence bag from my pocket and put a couple of plain plastic cups and a paper cup from Starbucks into it. In a separate bag, I placed cigarette butts. I ran back to the truck, checked the time, and called Zeke.

"Are you still in the room?" I could hear the television.

"I've been watching T.V. I never get to watch it. What are you doing?"

"Would you call the crime lab and ask them to take a look at some things for me?"

"You went to Campbell Street?"

"Yes; I lifted some items from the trash. With any luck, we've got him."

"I could call, but you already have a buddy in the crime lab."

"Oh?"

"Sure. Michael Wingman is a big fan of yours."

"Maybe so, but I don't think I can just start taking him things without some kind of authority."

"Use my name if you need to. He knows me and after yesterday, I think he'd do anything you asked. He's quite taken with you."

"I doubt that."

"I've been watching *Walker, Texas Ranger,*" Zeke said. "What the hell is that show based on? Who writes that crap?"

"It's a show for entertainment and it's from long ago. Walker gets to kick ass in every single episode, and thanks to him, there is no crime in Texas anymore."

Zeke laughed. "I'd like to be like him," was the last thing he said.

I went to the crime lab with the trash and put the items directly into the hands of Michael Wingman.

"I'll do this for you, but I want to take you to dinner tonight."

"But you're doing me a favor. I should take you to dinner."

"I don't care who takes who as long as you'll go with me."

"Thank you, but I can't. I'm here with my father and I shouldn't abandon him."

"Do you want me to clear it with Zeke?"

"No. He'll say it's okay to give up the plans we already made, and I don't think that's fair. I hardly ever get to see him."

Michael held up his hands. "Okay, maybe some other time."

"Thank you for understanding."

"If you'll give me your cell phone number, I'll call you when I know something. I'll give your evidence priority after I finish what I'm doing."

"Oh, thank you so much, Michael."

He held up my card. "I'm not saying I'll never call you for personal reasons."

I grinned and got out of there. The last thing I needed was a Dallas boyfriend, and especially not one who'd be up to his wrists in bodily fluids every day.

Because I was so close, I went back to the hotel and up to our room. Zeke had left for his class. I turned on my laptop and Googled the Triple Bar Ranch where my father was born. It was still going strong and had an engaging website advertising purebred Angus cattle as well as quarter horses. It was one of the largest ranches in Texas and was less than an hour's drive from Dallas if you could believe their ads.

I decided to go. Just to take a quick look.

As I was heading in that direction, my cell phone rang. I expected it to be Zeke but was surprised when a woman's voice said, "This is Greta Winchester."

"Hello, Mrs. Winchester." I pulled off the road.

"Ms. Ricos, when my husband came home last night, we talked a long time about your visit. We decided that you should know the truth."

My heart did a flip-flop.

"I told you a lie about the circumstances surrounding Baby Pacheco. You took me by surprise, and I wasn't sure what to tell you. He wasn't left with us by a Mexican housekeeper."

"What happened?"

"This is going to sound awful to you, but we bought him."

"You bought him?"

"Yes, you see my husband and I had been trying to have a baby, and when that didn't happen, we decided to adopt, but that takes forever. A man who worked with my husband understood our desire for a child, and he knew a man with a baby to sell. So they agreed to meet." She paused, and when I didn't speak, she continued, "He only wanted twenty thousand dollars for a perfect baby. He said the parents had abandoned him in the street. The father had been killed in prison, and the mother had taken off to Mexico."

I couldn't have spoken if my life depended on it.

"I never believed that, Ms. Ricos, to be honest. We did a terrible thing buying him, but I've told myself that perhaps we saved him from a worse fate. I hold to that thought to keep the guilt at bay. I know we should have called the police, but we wanted that baby when we saw him. He was an adorable little boy."

"He was fourteen months old?"

"Yes. We met with the man and his wife and gave them the money in cash."

"It wasn't the parents who sold him?"

"Definitely not, but the young woman who had him seemed to care about him. She didn't speak English, but she tried to tell me about him, or that's what I thought she was attempting to do. She gave me the birth certificate and the two photos I left at the orphanage. She also gave me a letter which I couldn't read but had translated."

It was difficult to make myself speak. "What did it say?"

"I don't know why I kept it, but I found it last night and would like for you to have it if you want it. Your father will want it, I'm sure. It reads: 'Beloved parents, I'm sending my son Zeke to you with Claudia because I know you will love him and care for him until I can return. My precious Max was killed in a Border Patrol prison. I don't know any of the details, but my heart is broken. I will come as soon as I can. I'm having trouble getting away, but I should be there within the month. Your loving daughter, Lucia.'"

"I want the letter, Mrs. Winchester. It explains a mystery that haunts my dad. He needs to hear that his mother loved him and didn't abandon him."

"I felt awful when I understood the letter. The child we paid for was stolen from someone who loved him."

"Yes."

"Will you come for the letter?"

"Yes, later today if that's all right. May I ask you something?"

"Certainly."

"If you paid for him, why did you leave him at the orphanage?"

"I wasn't prepared for a toddler. He cried for his mother, and his baby talk was Spanish. Much of it was about 'mama.' We just didn't bond like I thought we would. I know I should've given it a little more time and he would have adjusted, but I was a spoiled, head-strong young woman who wanted an image of motherhood, not the real thing. God was wise not to give us children."

I was crying and made no comment, although a few choice things came to mind. I had no desire to hurt her. She couldn't have known Zeke's fate.

For a while, I sat at the side of the road above the Triple Bar Ranch to observe. I wondered what it would've been like there in the sixties and if the Mexican workers were treated well. They were probably undocumented for the most part and not treated all that well. Things would be different now, I hoped.

After I quit crying, I called Barney and asked him to look at prison records in all of 1967 and through 1969. He had access to them via the Sheriff's Office, and I didn't unless I was on my work computer.

"Who am I looking for, Ricos?"

"Maximiliano Pacheco. I don't think he had a middle name."

"Would this be your father's father?"

"Yes."

"Are you sure he was in prison?"

"Yes, but I'm not sure if it was Texas. I suspect it, though."

"I'm on it, Pard."

I thanked him and decided to go see if the ranch had records. I seemed to be getting somewhere in the Pacheco mystery, but it wasn't turning out the way I had envisioned. Like eight-year-old-Zeke, I thought I would find his parents alive and well and—surprise! They'd been looking for him, too.

I checked my face for evidence of tears, adjusted my clothing, took a deep breath, and went to see what I could find. I introduced myself to the secretary and asked if they had employee records from the sixties. She went to get the ranch manager because she didn't know.

"Ms. Ricos, I'm Edward Matthews." He was a tall, sun-baked man in his thirties wearing jeans, a fancy western shirt, and enviable cowboy boots.

I took the hand he offered, introduced myself, and asked if I could speak with him about people who worked at the Triple Bar during the sixties.

"Of course I wasn't here in the sixties, but come on in." He took me to his office and indicated a chair. The walls were cluttered with photos of ranching scenes.

"This couldn't be about payroll records after all this time?"

"No sir, it's nothing like that. I'm trying to find information about a couple from Mexico who worked here. They were Maximiliano and Lucia Pacheco."

"Were they undocumented?"

"I think so. I assume they were."

"What is your interest in them?"

"They're my grandparents. My father was born on this ranch. I'm trying to help him find his parents."

"Oh, I see. We had undocumented workers here up until the late eighties. I'm sorry to say there are no records of them. They were kept under the radar, of course. To have records would be admitting that we had illegal workers, if you know what I mean."

"Yes; I understand."

"I wish I could help you. Wait, I do have an idea. There are a few people here from those days. Old Joaquin Flores might remember them, or Chico Gutierrez. He was here then, too. Chico was born here and both men had children born here. Maybe they'll remember something."

"I would love to talk to them."

"They're working cattle up by Salty Springs. If you'll wait a few minutes, I'll take you up there."

"That would be great. I'm going to get some old photographs out of my truck that might help them remember."

"Meet me back here in twenty minutes."

Edward Matthews left me alone in his office. I looked at the photos of cowboys branding, roping, riding broncs, working with cow dogs, doing cowboy things in other words. My eyes came to rest on one old picture. A group of Mexican men stood around a campfire. One had a guitar and they all appeared to be singing except one. He was laughing and looking right at the camera. It wasn't so much that he looked like Zeke. It was the expression more than anything, and he held himself the same straight, proud way. It would've been difficult to explain why, but I was sure that happy cowboy was my grandfather.

I glanced around and since I saw no one, I slipped the framed photo under my jacket. They wouldn't miss it, and I would return it after I had it copied.

I went out to my truck and put the photo upside down on the seat and placed my file over it. The photos of Zeke's mother went into my pocket.

Because I'm compulsive and had time to kill, I called Barney to see if he knew anything yet.

"For cryin' out loud, Ricos, you just gave me this job twenty minutes ago. I'm good, but if you want instant results, you need a magician."

"Sorry, I'm a little keyed up."

"Ya think? I told you I'd phone and I will. This might take a long time because it was in the sixties."

"I know. Thank you for doing it."

"Wasn't everybody smokin' dope and dancin' to funky music back then?"

I laughed. "There must've been somebody paying attention. I'll let you go, Barney. Thanks for everything."

"Peace, man."

I missed him more than I would've thought and a lot more than I wanted to admit, especially to him.

Edward Matthews and I bounced along in a big Dodge pickup, heading towards a part of the ranch he called Salty Springs. He told me about the registered cattle and claimed they had bulls worth thirty-five thousand dollars and up.

No bull for me, thanks.

We arrived at some large pens where cowboys were working extra hard when the boss drove up.

"They'll be here," Matthews said as we waited for the dust to settle.

He greeted everyone by name, all of whom stared at me, probably hoping I was not the latest addition to their outfit.

No worries there, guys.

"Hey, I need Chico and Joaquin. Send them over here, please."

We waited by the fence while he smoked and my heart felt like it wanted out of my chest and would crawl out through my throat. A couple of cowboys rode up and dismounted. They had pleasant faces, wrinkled by age and years of work under the broiling Texas sun.

"Hey Boss," they greeted him and tipped their hats to me.

"This young lady is looking for relatives who lived here in the sixties."

"Who is that?" Chico asked. "Who are you looking for?"

"I'm trying to find out what happened to Maximiliano and Lucia Pacheco." I pulled out the photo of Lucia and handed it to Chico. He glanced at it and passed it to Joaquin. They exchanged knowing looks and had a back-and-forth in Spanish that I didn't quite catch over the racket the cowboys were making.

"You know them?" I asked in Spanish.

"Yes, we do. Were they your relatives?"

"Yes. They're my grandparents."

"I see." Joaquin looked sad.

"Boss," the one called Chico said, "this could take a while, and we don't want to be rude, but we have to speak Spanish. There are some things that can't be said in English, not by us anyway. You understand?"

"Sure, I'll go check on a few things with Rudy and Tommy. Just yell for me when you're through here."

They indicated we should go to a couple of picnic tables a few hundred yards from the pens.

"I wish we had good news," began Chico. "They were great people, those two. They were young and so in love, and they were both hard workers."

"Go ahead and tell her," interrupted Joaquin, the older of the two.

"Max was picked up by Border Patrol and taken away. He was working out in the Cottonwood Grove section of the ranch, and Lucia was at the bunkhouse in the kitchen. The baby was with a sitter."

Chico wasn't telling the story fast enough for Joaquin, so he finished it. "Max was killed in prison while he was waiting on a hearing. Some Argentinean gangsters stabbed him to death."

"They thought he was someone else," added Chico. "We wish we had happier news for you."

I couldn't get my breath. This was so not how I wanted this story to go. "And what about Lucia?"

"There was this big cowboy who bothered her," said Chico. "She was beautiful, as you can see by her photograph. Without her husband to protect her, it got worse with him. He went to her room one night and got into bed with her. She stabbed him and didn't intend to kill him but she did. It was self-defense, but it was hard for Mexicans back in those days. The cowboy was a white man so, no matter what, Lucia would've been executed or sent to prison. Mexicans were less valuable than farm animals and were more easily replaced."

"A bunch of us helped her get away," Joaquin explained. "We hid her that night and smuggled her out the next day."

"Where did you take her?"

Chico removed his hat, ran a dusty hand through his hair, and replaced the hat. "We carried her into Dallas. We figured it would be best. They would never find her in the city. We took her to a mission, a shelter for the homeless. It's long gone now. We never heard from her again."

"But we did get word of her," added Joaquin. "Someone passing through said Lucia and the baby had been taken in by a man who owned the factory where she went to work. He didn't want the baby, so she sent him back to México to her parents and planned to join him as soon as she could get away."

"That's all we know." Chico's eyes were sad, and I thought he had cared about my grandparents.

I let out a long breath, tried to speak, and couldn't.

"We're so sorry. I wish we could tell you something better."

"Do you know the name of the factory where Lucia worked or the name of the man who took her in?"

They looked at each other and shook their heads. "No."

It seemed like I had come to a dead end.

"Your father's parents were good people," Joaquin said, "and they were crazy about him. All of us were. We always argued about who was going to hold him. He was happy and loved people. He used to have the sweetest laugh. The cowboys would take him riding and he would laugh and laugh."

"When you talk to your dad," said Chico, "tell him his parents were innocent of any wrongdoing. They suffered the fate of many immigrants. Life is hard when you're different and poor and not educated in the cruel ways of the world."

Joaquin put his hand on his heart and glanced over at Chico. "We were two of the lucky ones."

For a while, we talked about the positive changes that had happened on the ranch over the last thirty years.

Then Chico brought the conversation back to my father. "What is little Zeke doing now?"

"Little Zeke is forty-seven years old and works as a Texas Ranger."

"That fits." Chico grinned. "We thought he would grow up and do great things. Of course, nobody thought that more than Max and Lucia."

"He's a good man," I said. "His parents would be proud."

"I know they would," agreed Joaquin. "You should also tell him his mother was happy—always. She would kid around and make jokes. Her joy at being alive made life easier on all of us."

Chico smiled at me. "You resemble her, you know."

"Thank you. And thank you for sharing your memories with me." I was too choked up to continue.

When I left, they hugged me as if I were family. In a way, I was.

Chapter 27

LA FAMILIA PACHECO AT
THE TRIPLE BAR RANCH

A month before the birth of his son, Max and four other cow-boys were working with horses in a corral. One of the men, Bart Jenkins, liked to hassle Max. He was a large, rough, Anglo man, and he looked down his nose at Max for being mexicano. He referred to Max as The Wetback, a term he never used for anyone else. The real problem was not Max but Lucia. Bart wanted her and it wasn't a secret.

Bart wondered loudly if Max was really married to Lucia or if other men "still had a chance." The cowboys laughed. Max didn't like hearing Lucia's name come out of that man's filthy mouth. He assumed he was being disrespectful but didn't understand what was said until one of the English-speaking Mexican men translated for him.

"Of course I'm married to Lucia. We were married in a church in México last February. Why do you ask?" *Why are you thinking about my wife?*

"She doesn't wear a ring. If she's married, why isn't she wearing a ring?"

"A ring isn't important. I love Lucia and she loves me. That's all we need."

"In this country, *boy,* women wear rings."

"Marriage is only about love, *muchacho."*

The subject was dropped, but it bothered Max. None of the people he knew had wedding rings, but they were poor. Many were married by an old Mexican custom. If you fell in love with a woman, you made love to her and brought her home. Bringing her home meant you intended to love and support her. That arrangement seemed to work fine. His parents had never married in the church

194

and yet they were happy, faithful to each other, and had provided a loving home life. Everyone respected this form of marriage as well as one made in a church. Marriage is about love and making a commitment.

Lucia would have her sixteenth birthday in January, the same month their child would be born. Max wanted to give her something besides his body and soul and words to show her how much he loved her. She never asked for anything, and he knew she understood how he felt about her, but the thought of a gift persisted. He wanted to buy her a ring.

When a friend headed back to México for Christmas, he gave him money and asked him to buy a simple gold band and have it engraved. His friend returned on the night the baby was born and gave Max the ring the following day. It was smooth and shiny, especially in the sunlight. It was beautiful and had been engraved word for word as Max had specified.

On the morning of her birthday, Max awakened to see Lucia and their son asleep in a rocking chair. She had been nursing him, and one of her breasts was still exposed. Zeke's sleeping face was mashed up against it in contentment.

Yes, Son, he thought, *you definitely have it made. Surely there is no better way to sleep.*

Taking care, Max moved the baby to his cradle. He made a little snuffling noise but didn't waken. Max stood a moment to admire the tiny perfection of him.

When he looked back at Lucia, she was awake and smiling. "He's beautiful, isn't he?"

"Oh yes. The only person as beautiful as my son is his mother."

"Oh, Max."

He went back to his wife and knelt at her feet. "Do you know it's your birthday, Luce?" He wondered if she ever regretted growing up so young.

"It is?"

"Yes, it's today. Happy birthday, Mi Amor." He kissed her and then rested his head on her lap.

She stroked his hair lovingly. "Thank you, Max."

He straightened up and faced her. "Are you happy?"

"Of course, I couldn't be any happier. Why do you ask? Aren't you happy?"

"Yes, I'm about to explode I'm so happy. But it's different for a woman. You are so beautiful, Luce. I think you could've done anything you wanted."

"I did exactly what I wanted, Max. How many times do I have to tell you? The only thing that would make me happier is for you to lie down with me a few minutes before you go to work and tell me all those romantic things you tell me."

He lay next to her and whispered sweet words to her and later, pulled the ring from his pocket. "I want you to wear this, Lucia, as a symbol of my never-ending love for you." He read the inscription to her, "Lucia, I will always love you, Max."

She was tearful and speechless, but he could tell she was pleased with his gift. The gold ring was beautiful against her dark skin and she held it up to study it in a ray of sunlight streaming through the window. She sighed contentedly, lowered her hand, and then raised it again.

The ring's message of love and commitment was clearly under-stood by its recipient as well as its giver, but in the end, didn't make a difference to anyone else.

Zeke Pacheco was a little over a year old when his father was picked up in a Border Patrol raid. Max and seven other men were working in a section of the ranch known as Cottonwood Grove. Four were American citizens. Two of the Mexican cowboys had work permits and two did not. The two who didn't were Max Pacheco and Jorge Ramos.

The big green and white vehicle seemed to come out of nowhere and screeched to a halt by the corral in a cloud of dust.

"Max! Jorge! Run!"

They took off. Running away was a matter of economics more than fear. Getting picked up and taken back to the border would mean at least ten days without working and often more. Neither man could afford time off.

Max and Jorge jumped the corral fence and ran hard for a small woodland area about a quarter of a mile away. Two of the Border Patrol officers took off after them, yelling in Spanish for them to stop. Both officers had guns drawn but would maybe not have used them if Jorge hadn't been fumbling in his jacket for his inhaler.

"Drop to the ground right now," ordered one of the officers in Spanish. "United States Border Patrol." He identified himself to make his demand official.

Max was ahead and had no way to know the officers thought Jorge was reaching for a gun until a blast shattered the quiet. Max stopped in his tracks, thinking they were shooting at him. Jorge lay sprawled in the dirt behind him, his inhaler clutched in his hand.

"Do not move," growled the younger, more eager of the two officers. "Put your hands above your head and stay right where you are."

Max did as he was told. He was terrified and stood still, afraid to breathe. He watched his friend Jorge for some sign of life. There was none.

"Why did you run?" the young patrolman asked Max. "I should shoot you, too."

"You killed Jorge." Max was stunned.

"I asked why you ran."

In English, the older officer admonished the younger. "That's enough, Jerry. Just take him back and put him in the vehicle."

Max didn't understand what was said and for a hellish few moments, thought they meant to shoot him, too. "Please don't kill me," he begged. "I have a family."

"Yeah, sure. Don't we all?" Again, Jerry spoke in English although it was evident Max did not understand.

Max continued to plead for his life. By the time they neared the Border Patrol vehicle, Max had a plan of escape in mind. When his captor relaxed and let go of his arm, he ran as hard as he could.

"Stop! You son-of-a-bitch, I *will* shoot you!"

Max understood even though it was yelled in English. He ran as hard as he could in a zigzag pattern. When he came close to the fence line, another Border Patrol vehicle was waiting. The officer commanded him to stop and he did.

Max was charged with resisting arrest and endangering a federal officer, even though he had never been a danger to anyone. He had seen his friend shot to death, and he ran in fear for his life.

Max was handcuffed and shoved roughly into the back of the vehicle. He was told nothing. The men took him to the Dallas County jail where he spent two nights as a prisoner of the county. He was not mistreated or threatened, but he was still terrified. He had always promised Lucia he would be fine if caught. Now he wasn't so sure.

On the third day, Max was transferred by Border Patrol to a large Immigration & Naturalization holding facility where he would await a hearing. He had no way to get word to Lucia, which caused him stress and sadness. He knew she would be as lonely and worried as he was.

Lucia was making tortillas in the ranch kitchen when one of the cowboys burst in. "Lucia! Lucia! They got Max!" She didn't have to ask who had him.

She tried to stay calm. "Do you know where they took him?"

The cowboy took a few seconds to get his breath. "They'll hold him at the county jail overnight and take him back to the border tomorrow."

The women gathered around, expressing concern and trying to be of comfort.

"Everything will be all right," Lucia insisted. "Max and I talked about this, and he'll come back. If he can't return, he'll send for me."

"Oh, he'll be back before you know it," one of the older women consoled her.

Lucia left the kitchen to go to her son. An older woman cared for him while she worked. As she held him, she tried to keep her mind on the plans she and Max had made and the happy, successful life she envisioned for her child. It was a comfort to know Max had been wearing the sweater she knitted for him.

There was nothing she could do but wait.

The day after Max's arrest, Lucia began having trouble. Chico Gutierrez had made advances before and pledged his undying love. He begged her to leave Max. She had been kind but didn't take him seriously. He was her age, old enough to have better manners. Had he never had a mother?

Lucia picked up Zeke from the babysitter and headed home, but Chico blocked the doorway to her room. He was not a large man, but he was large enough.

"Please let me help you, Lucia. You shouldn't be alone. Anything could happen to you or Zeke."

"I'm perfectly capable of taking care of myself and my son. Max will be back soon. Please move so I can get in my room."

"But I love you, Lucia."

"Chico, I told you before, I love Max and I'm married to him. We have a son."

"I'll stay with you until Max returns. I could comfort you, Lucia."

She wanted the protection, and even the company, but she knew it would come with a price she was unwilling to pay. "Move, Chico."

He did, but he followed her into the room. "Lucia, you don't know what it's like. I burn for you. I feel like I'll die if I can't have you."

She set her son down on a blanket with a few handmade toys. He began to babble and examine the playthings.

"Please sit down, Chico."

He sat.

She took a deep breath. "You're making a fool of yourself. And what if Max found out how you pursue me? Wouldn't you be ashamed? You work with him and he likes and trusts you. Your attention flatters me, but shouldn't you have it on a single woman? Max and I can't continue to be your friends if you act this way."

Chico thought about it. After a while he stood. "I'm sorry, Lucia. My feelings haven't changed, but if you love Max, I guess that's that. No hard feelings?"

"No, Chico, no hard feelings. Buenas tardes."

"Buenas tardes, Señora." He bowed and left.

Lucia let out a long sigh of relief. "Momma doesn't understand men, Zeke."

He looked up at her and laughed.

An Anglo cowboy called Little Mike worked on the ranch, too. His name was a joke; the man was huge. Lucia had never seen such a big man and was afraid of him and his hungry, wandering eyes. Several times he had come up behind her and put his arms around her. He whispered words in English she didn't understand, but she got the message. She knew she should tell Max but didn't dare. Little Mike would kill him if confronted. Max was not small, and he was strong and muscular, but he was no match for a man the size of Little Mike.

News of Max's capture spread around the ranch and within a couple of hours everyone knew Lucia was now alone with her son. Little Mike heard the news, too.

When the cowboys came for dinner, his eyes followed Lucia everywhere. As she served their table, he made comments to the others. While she didn't understand the words, she understood he was saying nasty things and speaking disrespectfully. She tried to ignore him and kept her eyes on the platters she was placing on the table.

Towards the end of the meal, Lucia was bringing dessert, and Little Mike tried to touch her breasts. She snapped at him in Spanish and backed away from the table. The head cowboy, who spoke Spanish, heard her outraged comments and demanded to know what was going on.

"He touched me. Even if I was not a married woman, it's rude and demeaning to be groped. I don't deserve this treatment. Nobody can touch me like that. He'd better not do it again."

The head cowboy spun around to Little Mike. "You're out of line, partner. Apologize to Lucia, and in the future, keep your goddamn hands to yourself. You know better. For Christ sakes man, she's married."

"I'm sorry, Lucia." Mike spoke the words, but not with any sincerity.

Lucia understood the words and that he hadn't meant them, but she let it go.

When she left the dining room, one of the cowboys whispered to Little Mike, "She says you're not man enough to satisfy her."

Mike's eyes flashed with anger. He would show her.

Chapter 28

I went from the Triple Bar to Fort Worth to pick up Lucia's letter from Greta Winchester. That went well, considering traffic was obscene and there was almost no opportunity to go the speed limit, let alone speed, and there were still no mountains anywhere. They have tall buildings though.

Mrs. Winchester had left the letter and its translation in an envelope for me. The maid handed it to me when she answered the door. That made the visit easy and painless. All I wanted was the letter anyway.

I drove back to the hotel and shoved the envelope in my suitcase. How was I going to tell Zeke what I knew? It made me feel sick in my stomach and heart, so I did what I do when the world goes upside-down. I ran.

The afternoon was brisk and it felt good to be wearing sweats. It also felt good to run. Dallas Police Headquarters appeared too quickly, so I kept going, dodging people and traffic and imagining my mountains.

The sun dazzled tall buildings, pavement, and small patches of grass when it should have been shining on the craggy mountains of Big Bend and bouncing off the waters of the Rio Grande and warming the desert soil. You're wasting yourself, I thought towards it. The sun kept right on; it was obviously less judgmental and more generous than I was.

When I ran back, I sat on a bench to watch the goings-on and noticed a man who seemed to be watching me. He was aiming a camera in my direction, but when I caught sight of him, he lowered it and tried to act casual. It was comical and also creepy, but I wrote it off to the weirdness of the city. If a random dude wanted a picture of me so what? My body was covered, I was sitting alone, and I'm not a famous person, so I figured it wasn't about blackmail or selling my photo to the tabloids. Then I started making up possible headlines: Single Female Seeking Solitude or Desert Deputy Destroys Dallas. How about Lonely, Needs Mountains? Zeke came out the door and saved me from myself.

I looked around, but my photographer friend had moved on.

My father sat next to me on the bench. "Just seeing you sitting here lifted my spirits when I came through the door." He flashed one of those bright Zeke smiles that would melt a glacier on an icy day.

"Thank you, Zeke. You make me happy, too."

"How is that?"

"I don't know. I guess I'm starting to fall for you."

He laughed. Then I noticed that man again, peering at us from the sidewalk less than a block away.

"Zeke, don't look yet, but there's a man to the right with a camera. He's on the sidewalk wearing dark clothes and sunglasses. Will you glance over there and tell me if you've ever seen him before?"

He waited a few seconds and then took a casual look around. "I've never seen him. Is he bothering you?"

"No, but I think he's taking photos of me. Isn't that weird?"

"Maybe he collects pics of beautiful women. Do you want me to go over there and ask him why he's photographing my daughter?"

"That won't be necessary."

We watched him a while and decided he seemed harmless. Maybe he was just strange or thought I was someone else.

"Did you run here?"

"Yes. I hope you don't mind walking back to the hotel."

"That's perfect. I need to walk."

I tucked my arm in his and we strolled more than walked, looking in shop windows and taking our time. At the hotel, a doorman, but not the jazz musician, opened the door for us and Zeke stood aside to let me go in first. I glanced back and thought I saw that odd man again. I was about to say something to Zeke, but when I looked again, the guy was gone.

While Zeke took a shower, I tried to mentally prepare myself to tell him what I knew. He already knew his father died in prison, he just didn't know how.

Barney called me before I got too worked up.

"I've looked for Maximiliano Pacheco in the Texas State Prison records and don't find him. He may have been listed under another name. It wasn't uncommon for undocumented immigrants to use aliases."

"That's true, but there's another explanation. I'm sorry I didn't call you."

I filled him in.

"Well that sucks. Did you tell Zeke?"

"No, but I'm about to."

"Good luck, Ricos." He paused two seconds. "You haven't asked me how the new deputy is working out."

"How is that going?"

"You don't really care, do you?"

"Of course I care, but I haven't had time to think about him. I have my hands full here, and I know that you have everything under control there."

"You take a lot for granted."

"That's because I know you."

"Good luck with your dad and whatever else you're doing up there."

"Thanks, Barney. Hey, has anything changed on my hill?"

"No. Everything seems to be holding together nicely without your supervision."

"I guess that's good, but it makes me feel kind of sad."

He laughed. "You'll be home soon, right?"

"Right, it won't be long."

We signed off.

Zeke came out of the bathroom toweling his hair. "It's your turn."

"I have something important to tell you." I sat on the bed.

"Is it bad?"

"Yes, but it explains something that bothers you, so it's not all bad."

"You found out something about my father?"

"Yes. Zeke, your father did die in prison, but his only crime was being in this country without proper documentation. He was picked up by the Border Patrol and was there pending a hearing. Some South American gang members mistook him for someone else and stabbed him."

He came and sat next to me. "How do you know?"

"I visited the Triple Bar Ranch and met some guys who knew your parents."

I told him about Joaquin and Chico and what they said. Zeke was quiet, taking it in. It was hard to tell how it hit him, but I thought he was sad. And naturally it was frustrating that the story of his mother was still a mystery.

My cell phone rang. When I answered, Chico Gutierrez said, "Margarita, we thought of something else you should know."

"Please hold on." I motioned to Zeke that I was going to step into the hall.

"Okay, Chico."

"When we left Lucia at the mission she was using another name. She went by Soledad Rodriguez, her mother's name."

"Thank you so much for calling me, Chico."

"We thought it would help in your search. We sure would like to know if you find out what happened to her."

"I'll be in touch," I promised.

Zeke looked up questioningly when I came back in the room. He had been crying, I thought.

"That was Chico calling to tell me your mom was using a different name when they left her at the mission."

"So she killed some guy in self-defense and went to Dallas to hide with a baby in tow? Can you imagine how hard that would be?"

"I know. It makes me so sad for her."

"She would've been lost in Dallas. You've met men who knew my parents?"

"Yes. I could take you to meet them if you want."

"I'll have to think about that. You know what? I feel like such a traitor for saying what I did about my parents."

"Ease up on yourself. You were a child. You can't blame yourself for believing the lies those people told you. The reality of it is that they did leave you, but not willingly. How does that feel?"

Zeke flopped back onto the bed. "It feels wonderful. It feels right."

He turned to face me. "I think my heart is going to burst if you want the truth. How can I ever thank you for what you've done?"

"It was easy. You could've done it if you hadn't been so busy making something of yourself."

He had gotten his parents' photos out. He held up the one of him on his mother's lap. "I was worth a lot more than twenty thousand dollars, don't you think? Look how cute I was."

I laughed. "Yes; I agree."

"And look at my mother. Was she beautiful or what?"

"She was amazing."

"She looks so happy, and she clearly adored me."

"Yes, it's obvious. So Zeke, did I do the right thing?"

"Oh yes. It's weird that it took my daughter to bring my parents to me." He hugged me and then set the photos on the dresser. "Now, if she would get ready, I'm going to take my kid dancing. That's providing the Mexicans are still here."

We ate tacos and enchiladas and talked about various things not related to our lost family members.

Zeke said, "I want you to just keep talking to me and don't look or be alarmed. That strange man is here, on the street. He must be following us."

"But why would he? It doesn't make sense."

"I'm going to confront him. Are you sure you don't know him? Could he be a man you dated once or someone you had dealings with as a deputy?"

"I never dated him. I don't think I've ever seen him before."

"That doesn't mean he doesn't know you. He could be some guy you arrested who had to do time and—"

"I haven't made many arrests that resulted in prison time, Zeke."

"Yes, but you've made some."

I was going over them in my head and feeling more nervous by the minute. "Nobody would be out yet, and a couple of them aren't getting out."

"People plan and schedule hits from prison all the time."

"Zeke, get a grip. I haven't sent any mafia goons to prison."

"In general, criminals are bitter and blame everyone but themselves. You'd be shocked to know the things they can pull off from inside." He glanced around again. "There's something about this guy that says he's not a hit man. Maybe he's a stalker. Whatever he's doing, I don't like it." He wiped his mouth and set the napkin next to his plate. "You sit tight."

"I'm coming with you."

"Do *not* argue with me. Stay right there."

Zeke was so forceful I did what he asked. He left the restaurant moving at a normal pace and for a few seconds I couldn't see him anymore. Then the photographer took off at a dead run. Next, Zeke flew by the window giving chase.

Chapter 29

MAX AND LUCIA

Max paced the cell he shared with two other mexicanos and a man from El Salvador who was seeking political asylum.

"It's so boring and we're never told anything," Max complained. The tedium of life in the holding facility pressed down on all of them.

"Some guys have been here seven months," one of his cellmates responded. "I been here four. They got no reason to hurry."

"You need an attorney if you want out sooner," a different man said. "Even then, it won't be as fast as you want."

Max spun around. "I have less than ten dollars in my pocket, hombre. How will I get an attorney with that?" He had around two hundred and fifty back at the ranch, still not nearly enough. He and Lucia had been sending most of their earnings back to their families in México.

When he went for meals, Max read the notices tacked on bulletin boards by various immigration lawyers. He called a few when he was allowed to use the phone. All of them wanted a retainer of two thousand dollars, an amount far out of Max's reach.

There was a bright spot in the day when he was allowed to call Lucia. The ranch manager accepted his collect call and sent someone to bring her. It took so long Max had little of his fifteen minutes left by the time she came to the phone.

"Oh, Max." She was breathless from running. "How are you?"

Max leaned against the wall and shut his eyes and tried to absorb her through the telephone. "How I miss you, Luce."

"I miss you too, Max."

"How's Zeke?"

"He's fine. Please don't worry about us. All is well. We're here waiting for you."

"I can hardly breathe without you by my side."

"I feel the same way."

A guard stepped forward and told Max to get off the phone.

"I have to go, Mi Amor. Kiss our son for me. Oh Luce..." He broke down.

"Max, I love you so much. My heart is there with you. Please don't be sad."

"I'm okay." His last words, "Never forget, Lucia."

"I won't, Max. Of course I won't."

Their call was disconnected.

After a week of waiting, Max was appointed an advocate. He felt hopeful, but the man seemed overworked and under-concerned. He half-listened when Max explained what happened on the day he was taken into custody. It was his word against theirs, and they were federal officers. He was an illegal alien with no rights. That was clear.

Max asked the advocate if he would get word to his wife at the Triple Bar Ranch. She needed to know he was being charged with not just evading the Border Patrol, but with endangering them, something he hadn't done.

"Those charges will be dropped," the advocate assured him.

That would turn out to be true, but by then it didn't matter.

When Max had been gone two weeks, Lucia was called to the ranch headquarters by the manager. She assumed he had news of Max, but she had no idea it would be so devastating.

With Chico Gutierrez standing by to translate, the manager said, "Lucia, I'm so sorry to have to tell you this, but Max was stabbed to death by gang members who mistook him for a member of a rival Mexican gang. It happened fast, before anyone could respond."

Lucia heard the foreign words and watched the man's mouth as he spoke to her. Then Chico translated in a somber voice.

"No. That's wrong. It wasn't Max. It can't be Max." Her knees buckled but the two men grabbed her and led her to a chair. She buried her face in her hands and sobbed. It couldn't be true. Max promised to come back to her; they were going to be together forever. He couldn't be dead. He was young and so alive. How would she live without his love?

"You're lying," she snapped at Chico. "You want Max out of the way so you're making this up."

"I told you what he said word for word. I'm sorry, Lucia, but Max has been murdered. It's the truth."

"You're a liar. I hate you for this, Chico."

After she calmed down, Chico took Lucia back to the workers' compound. She picked up her son from the babysitter and took him to their room. She held him close and cried for his father.

It can't be; it can't be, she thought over and over. Yet she knew it was. Max wasn't coming back. She was on her own.

She repeated, "It can't be" to all the friends who came to see her. If she said it enough maybe Max would come back. Various people tried to take Zeke so she could have time to herself to think about what to do. She refused to be separated from her son. He was all she had left of Max, and his happy babbling kept her alive.

Chico knelt in front of Lucia. "I've loved you since the first time I saw you."

She was rocking her child to sleep and said nothing.

"I would be a good husband to you and a good father to Zeke. I will always treat you right. I'm a good man, Lucia, and a hard worker, like Max."

"Please, Chico. The love of my life has just died. I can't make any decisions right now. I can't even think about another husband. Please have respect for how I feel." She didn't explain that she would never accept a man who had pursued a married woman in such a relentless way.

Lucia felt that Chico was a good man, but he had a lot to learn. He didn't have the respect most of the Mexican men showed to her and other women. He was young and thought of his own needs before anyone else's. She didn't hold it against him or dislike him for it, but she would never take any proposal from him seriously.

She had decided to return to her home in México. Her son was an American citizen, and her dream had been to raise a family here, but she didn't see a way without a husband. A woman without proper documentation would never make it alone. Without Max, she didn't see how she would make it anywhere.

Her friends encouraged her not to be so hasty and reminded her that there were many eligible men on the ranch. Good men, hardworking men, even attractive men. She knew it, but she was not moved by any of them. For Lucia, marriage was about love, not convenience.

The next morning the ranch manager came to the kitchen to tell Lucia that Max's father had claimed his son's body and Max was being returned to México to be buried on his father's ranch.

Zeke, Max's father, had called with a message for Lucia to come home as soon as she could get away. She decided then to take their savings and go back to her family until she could decide what to do. She needed to be with her parents and other people who loved her and understood what a terrible loss she had suffered.

That night, Lucia slept for the first time since she'd heard the news of Max's death. She and Zeke were curled together in the center of her bed. His warmth and innocence and the clean baby smell of him gave her comfort.

Exhaustion caused Lucia to sleep through the stealthy opening of the door to her room. When a man crawled into bed beside her, she at first thought it was Max. She woke in stages, groggy from deep sleep and couldn't immediately understand what was happening.

"Max?" she murmured.

"Hello, Baby." The voice was deep and spoke English. Unfamiliar arms reached for her and she smelled liquor. It was not Max. Panic rose, and she screamed and tried to get out of bed but he pulled her back down.

"No," was the only word he said that she understood. His big hand was rough and was placed across her mouth. "Shut up." She understood that, too.

She struggled against him but it was useless. "Por favor," she begged when he removed his hand. "Please," she added in English, "Please no. This no good."

He laughed. "This muy bueno. Understand?"

"Please, my son." She tried to tell him that her son was in the bed. "My son, my son," she repeated as Little Mike began to kiss and stroke her. She was terrified the huge man would crush Zeke and maybe crush both of them.

Since he'd been gone, Lucia slept with Max's knife under her pillow, her sole protection in a world that no longer felt safe. Her instincts had been right. Here was proof in her bed, moving his big hands along her body.

"No, no," she continued to beg.

She tried to reach the knife but couldn't get her hands on it from where she was. Her head was no longer on her pillow. Zeke's small body had rolled against her when Mike pulled her next to him. Her baby was behind her, flat up against her back, blocking her only path of escape. She would risk injuring him if she tried to move in that direction and she couldn't crawl over Mike.

Meanwhile, Mike had moved closer. He was breathing heavily and getting more and more out of control. He whispered but not sweet, seductive words like Max would say. They sounded filthy and one of them was a word she knew, "fuck." She'd heard it used as a curse. Like the Spanish equivalent, she knew it could be used in a variety of ways, including its literal meaning.

With her right hand, she continued to feel around for the knife and at the same time begged him to understand that the baby was in bed with them. Mike's roaming hands discovered Zeke at her back. He lifted himself on one elbow, angry. "What the hell?" he growled.

Lucia didn't want him to hurt Zeke.

As he made a move to push her son away, her hand closed over the knife. She let it rest under the pillow, her arm above her head. When he rose over her to push at the baby, she stabbed him in the side. She couldn't see well in the dim light and wasn't sure if she had hurt him enough to stop him.

Mike was suspended above her for a moment, surprised and furious. He began trying to strangle her, cursing and spitting words, but soon lost strength. Then he collapsed with his leg on top of her. She could smell and feel the blood. It was all over her and Zeke, too.

"Bitch," Mike groaned.

Gathering Zeke into her arms, she scrambled out of bed, wrapped a blanket around herself, and flew out of the room. Two doors down from her lived her friend Claudia Ortiz with her husband Beto. She banged on their door until Claudia answered.

Her eyes widened in horror when she saw her friend standing there with her baby boy, both bloody.

Claudia reached out a hand and pulled Lucia into her room. "What happened to you? Are you bleeding or is it someone else?"

Lucia tried to calm herself enough to speak. In fits and starts she told her friend what had happened.

"I think I killed him," she sobbed.

"Get up, Beto," Claudia addressed her husband. "This is an emergency and we need your help."

"What's going on?" Beto was still half asleep. He sat up quickly when he saw Lucia at the door covered in blood and holding her son.

Beto went to get Chico who lived down the hall in a room he shared with another single worker. Chico and Beto went to Lucia's room and came back a few minutes later with the news. "He's dead."

Chico took Lucia gently by the shoulders to steady her. "Mike was in your bed?"

Lucia began to sob. "He tried to rape me." She started shaking and Claudia helped her to a chair. She took Zeke and placed him in the center of her bed. He continued to sleep peacefully.

"We have to get you out of here." Claudia turned to the men and they agreed.

"But he was trying to rape me, and he was going to hurt Zeke. I had to stop him."

"Yes, we know." Chico came forward. "But when the police come, you'll go to jail. You killed a white man."

"He was raping me!"

"Yes, Lucia, but they won't care. Please try to understand what I'm saying."

Claudia shrugged. "Who knows what they'll do?"

"You're Mexican and you killed a gringo," said Beto. "That's all they're going to know or need to know."

Everyone knew that was true. Even with an attorney, it could go either way for Lucia. The courts never protected illegal aliens.

A decision was made to hide Lucia and Zeke for the rest of the night and then to sneak them away from the ranch at first light.

Lucia thought the answer was to return home right away. "Will you take us to the bus station?"

"That's the first place they'll look," said Chico. "A beautiful Mexican woman with a baby will be memorable to everyone they ask. I doubt if you would make it to the steps of the bus."

Lucia heard the truth of that, and her heart sank to a new level of despair. She returned to her room long enough to pack their few belongings. She had to leave Max's things behind, along with the beautiful cradle he had made. It hurt her heart, but it didn't make sense to lug them in addition to her clothes and a baby and all his things. She asked Chico to give them away to people who needed them. She took along only one of Max's old t-shirts because she thought it still smelled like him.

Chapter 30

When Zeke didn't return after twenty minutes, I thought that was odd. I called his cell phone and got a voice message, so I paid the bill and went to look for him. I was wearing a dress but it had a skirt made for dancing, so it didn't hamper my movement. The shoes were a drawback though. They were espadrilles, better than the spiky pumps I favor, but still not great for running.

After a few blocks of no Zeke and no weird photographer guy, I realized my dad could be lying injured in an alley, and it became stop and look and start again more than anything like running. I saw no sign of him and it was worrisome. On one hand, he's a lawman with many years of experience, but on the other, where in the hell was he? Had he been lured into a trap? But who would lure him and for what?

I called Zeke again and left a message. Then I waited three seconds and called the police for a frustrating runaround. Nobody can be a missing person until twenty-four hours have passed. The officer wanted me to come in and fill out paperwork. I thought not, hung up, and called the Dallas office of the Texas Rangers. If those guys wouldn't come for one of their own then there was no hope for the brotherhood of law enforcement.

My call was answered by a recorded message that advised to call 9-1-1 after hours. I should have known that. Those were not the guys to call for an emergency. Crap! The only people I knew in Dallas were a couple of old Mexican cowboys, a ranch manager, a prisoner and his family, and a waitress named Sheryl. She would want to help Zeke, but would she be any use? It was frustrating, but since I didn't know what else to do, I kept searching. Do you know how big just the "Little Mexico" section of Dallas is? It was daunting.

I made myself stop and sit on a bench to focus. *Think!* When Sheryl came to mind, so did Sonny's Restaurant. That brought me to Donny, my likely perp. Why would Donny have my father? I was the one running around asking nosy questions, so how would he even know about Zeke? Could Donny know we were on his trail? Of course he could know; criminals find out things they have no business knowing, and it was useless to sit there trying to figure out how. Somebody had my father!

I took a taxi back to the hotel, made a mad dash for the room, changed into my running shoes no matter how stupid they looked with a dress, yanked the keys to the truck off the dresser, and checked my phone. Still nada.

Before long, I was stewing in the white Rangers' truck in the shadows of trees across the street from 355 Campbell. There was no vehicle in the driveway and the scene radiated loneliness. The house was dark and appeared as deserted as before.

Since it was late there was nobody on the street. I jumped down from the truck and went to look in the trash. That would tell me if anybody had been there since my last raid of the bins. They were empty, as I suspected. It made me think the perp had taken off, but why would he? None of it made sense. He was never even questioned about the murders. Since Kiko went to prison, he'd have no reason to think he would ever be a suspect. What did any of this have to do with Zeke? Something stank and it wasn't the trash.

I didn't know what else to do, so I tried the doors on Donny's house. They were still locked. I listened at the windows to see if I could detect any sound. Not even a mouse. Then I went back to the rear door and glared at it. I wanted to kick it in so badly that for a second I thought I had.

I went back to the truck before somebody called the cops. Then I called them myself and asked the officer on duty to give me a list of phone numbers for every hospital in Dallas, Ft. Worth, and the surrounding areas, including private treatment facilities for cancer patients. I spent an hour calling those places and found one that had a record of Sonny Delmar. They had treated him, but couldn't give me details due to confidentiality. The interesting thing was that

Donny had checked his brother out of there three months back, and they hadn't heard from Sonny since.

It seemed like nobody had seen Sonny in a while. Maybe Donny had moved him to a better treatment facility or was taking care of him at a residence somewhere. Did Sonny matter to my case? If it was a lie that Donny was caring for him, then where was he? Was Sonny involved in this case somehow? Why would he be? Did he see the murder? Had he been enjoying Kiko's wife, too? At the same time, maybe? Oh, gross. My mind was more tired than my body, and I didn't feel sharp enough to start the truck, let alone figure out what was going on with the elusive Delmar brothers.

Within a few minutes, my cell chimed to let me know I had received a text. It showed Zeke as the sender. Relief washed over me until I saw the message: *We have your father. Hold for proof.* A photo loaded and it was Zeke tied to a bed wearing his underwear and nothing else. It was the most chilling thing I'd ever seen. It was hard to tell, but he appeared to be unconscious. *Please don't let him be dead.*

What do you want? I texted with trembling fingers.

The reply was: *Leave the Valentino case alone. Valentino is where he needs to be.* I thought Kiko would take issue with that.

Who is this? Yeah, that would cause them to spill it.

I want what's best for everyone, the unknown evil answered.

Punishing an innocent man is not best for everyone.

He's not innocent.

If you have proof, please come forward.

Already proved, replied the kidnapper.

How do I get my father back?

Do you love him?

Yes, of course. It felt weird to admit to an evil stranger something I hadn't yet admitted to myself.

You have one chance. Are you ready?

217

Yes.

If you continue to investigate, I will kill your father.

Okay. You've made your point.

Western Sky Inn rm 12, downtown but not nice part like where you're staying. Don't make me kill him. Adios, amigo.

Two things: He knew where we were staying, which was creepy. Also, he didn't know much Spanish or he wouldn't have called me an "amigo." A female is "amiga." Nit-picky distinction? True. Important? Maybe.

As I drove, I called 911 from the no-hands phone system in the truck and asked the dispatcher to send an ambulance and the police to the Western Sky Inn, room 12.

"Ma'am, what is the nature of the problem?"

"My father was kidnapped. Did you hear me? He needs an ambulance!"

"A crew has been dispatched," he replied in that cool, impersonal way they have. Somebody has to stay calm in a crisis.

I got the address of the inn from dispatch and put it into the truck's GPS. It wasn't far from where I was, which cemented Donny Delmar as Suspect Numero Uno in kidnapping as well as rape and murder. He was racking up felonies. But at this point, what did he have to lose?

The Western Sky Inn was on the seedy side, a rent-by-the-hour sort of place. I was just in time to see police officers bust down the door of room 12. They rushed in, followed by two medics with a stretcher. I wasn't far behind but as I entered, I was grabbed by one of the policemen. "You can't be in here."

"He's my father!"

"Stay back."

Officer Grabby was hurting my arm. He was more attractive than is decent for a policeman. The other officer offset him though. With his scowling face and southern drawl, he might as well have worn a sign with "humorless redneck" in block letters. He didn't even need a sign.

I broke away from Grabby yelling, "Zeke!" and ran to the bed.

"He's coming around," said one medic to the other. My legs nearly caved with the relief of it.

I continued talking to Zeke until Officer Grabby put his powerful arms around my waist and lifted me out of there. It was tempting to use a self-defense move on him, but he was an officer of the law and I didn't need jail time in Dallas. I needed to see if Zeke was going to be okay, and I tried to explain that to Grabby.

"Are you going to behave, or do I need to cuff you to the railing?" The officer was young—who else would be on duty at four in the morning? His blue eyes sparkled with suppressed laughter.

"That's my father in there."

"I understand, but unless you're a doctor you don't trump a medic."

"A daughter trumps everybody." I slid into a sitting position against the railing of the second story walkway. "I've been looking for him all evening, and it's not fair to keep me from him."

"Why didn't you call the police?"

"Are you kidding?"

"They told you to wait twenty-four hours, right?"

"Right. The police were useless. I had to search for him myself."

"That's not fair. We're here now, aren't we?"

"Well yeah, but where were you guys when I needed you? Never mind. Will you let me speak to my father? He's surrounded by strangers and he needs to see my face. And I still don't know how badly he's hurt. Please, Officer Grabby."

He smiled down at me. "Man, you're annoying."

"Thank you. I do my best."

He laughed and gave me a hand up. "Let's see what's going on in there."

"Listen, the perp was texting me using my dad's cell phone. There's a good chance it's still in the room, so you shouldn't let anyone touch it until the crime scene techs get here and handle it properly."

"Really? We would never have thought of that."

"Sorry."

"That's protocol at any crime scene, Ms…?"

"Ricos."

"Ms. Ricos. May I see your phone?"

"Sure, if you'll let me see my father, Officer Wardley." According to his nametag he was Jeff Wardley.

"You drive a hard bargain, Ms. Ricos."

"I'm tougher than I look," I said because he was looking.

There was a short conference between police and medics and I was allowed to see Zeke. He was covered by a blanket and a medic was taking his pulse. I knelt by the bed. "Are you all right?"

"Groggy."

I was overcome with emotion that was more relief than anything I could have articulated. I took his free hand in both of mine. It was icy.

"Your. Hands. Warm," he whispered hoarsely and tried to smile at me.

"Was he drugged?" I asked the closest medic.

"It appears so. He's stable now, but we'll take him to the hospital for evaluation and observation. You can ride along if it's okay with the patient."

"Yes," Zeke said before anyone asked him.

"Has he been injured?"

"We don't think so," one of the medics said, "but he'll be checked over more thoroughly once we get him to the emergency room."

I had to get out of the way so they could load Zeke onto a stretcher. Then I walked along beside them as they carried him out.

"Hey—" Jeff Wardley grabbed my arm again as we passed near him.

"Yes, Officer Grabby?"

He laughed, turned beet red, and released me as if my skin had burned him. "I'm sorry. I'm used to grabbing the guys." He went a shade darker. "Oh boy, that came out wrong."

I couldn't help but laugh. "What did you want to say?"

"How can I see you again?"

"Well, I'm going to the hospital right now, so I don't know."

He followed me out of the room. "I have your phone."

"Isn't that what you wanted?"

"No—I—just—yes. I just remembered I have it."

"Do you have to keep it?"

"Not long, maybe, but yes I do need it for now. How can I get it back to you?"

"Do you have a card? I'll call you."

He dug around in his shirt pocket and handed one to me. "How will you call if I have your phone?"

"Um. There's an old-timey desk phone in our hotel. I think those still work."

"Very funny, Ms. Ricos. I was thinking—never mind. You're staying in a hotel?"

"Yes. Is there a problem?"

"You're not from here then?"

"No. I have to go; the ambulance is going to leave."

"I'll call you," he called after me.

I started to remind him that he had my phone, but he'd figure it out.

Zeke was taken into the emergency room but it wasn't long before they settled him into a regular room with two beds. Once he was sleeping soundly, I collapsed on the extra bed. A dim light glowed in the eastern sky but that didn't keep me awake.

I don't know if it was the banging and clattering of breakfast being served or the blue-eyed man calling my name three inches from my face, but something woke me with a start.

"Ms. Ricos?"

It took me a minute to recognize him. "Hey, it's Officer Grabby."

"Man, you're so annoying." He laughed. "Good morning." He had changed from the D.P.D. uniform to jeans and a blue pullover and the improvement was one hundred percent.

"How can it be morning? I just went to sleep." I looked over at Zeke. He was watching us with so much amusement I knew he was better without having to ask.

I got up, gave Zeke a hug, and went in the bathroom to clean up. I needed a toothbrush and other things, but soap and water were better than nothing.

Zeke was scheduled for various tests and would most likely be released later in the day. He seemed like his old self, so when Officer Grabby invited me to breakfast, I accepted the offer.

While waiting for the elevator, we invited each other to use our first names. He didn't care for "Officer Grabby" for obvious reasons, and "Ms. Ricos" sounded like someone I didn't know.

Once we exchanged names, I asked if we could go to Sonny's Restaurant.

"I'd like to take you somewhere nicer than Sonny's," he said.

I liked that a lot, but I said, "I have some unfinished business there."

He gave me a questioning look but agreed. He had no idea how single-minded and stubborn I was. That Delmar pervert had kidnapped my father. He was going down if it was the last thing I ever did.

Chapter 31

PRESENT DAY, DALLAS

"Hey! You're back." I was amazed Sheryl recognized me since she had taken so little notice of my presence before.

We greeted her and she said, "Have a seat wherever you like and I'll be right there with coffee."

I asked for grapefruit juice instead of coffee, and we slipped into a booth and perused the menu.

Sheryl set down a juice for me and poured coffee for Jeff. "Where is Zeke?" she asked, getting right to the point.

"He couldn't come today. He said to tell you hey."

"No he didn't, but it's sweet of you to say that."

She took in Jeff and her eyes lit up as she realized he was no slouch in the looks department. That blue pullover made his eyes look like the Big Bend winter sky. He was at the light end of the tall, dark, and handsome scale. Tall, light, and handsome works, too. Except for the eyes, he reminded me of Kevin, my former husband, which was a fond thought I noticed didn't hurt as much as it used to.

"Do you know every good-looking man in Dallas?" Sheryl spoke to me but winked at Jeff.

"Not yet, but I'm working on it."

"I want to start hanging out with you."

That got a laugh from us.

I killed the fun by asking, "What have you heard from the Delmar brothers? Zeke and I left that stuff at Donny's house, but we haven't heard if he got it. How is his brother anyway?"

"I don't know. Donny hasn't been here in quite a while. I guess Sonny isn't doing so well."

"How long have you worked here, Sheryl?"

"About a month," she said absently. She was still admiring Jeff.

"Have you ever met Sonny?"

"No; he was sick when I got here. I've only met Donny and haven't seen much of him, either."

"Who's in charge when the brothers aren't here?"

"Eddie Newsome. He's the general manager."

"Is he here now?"

"No. Is there some problem?"

"No. We left some samples for Donny, and I'm thinking we should've left them for Eddie if he's the manager. When does Eddie work?"

"Mostly in the day, unless someone gets sick."

"Was he here this morning?"

"I think so, but he was in the back. Then he left. Do you sell supplies or what? If that's what you're doing, then Eddie is the one you should see. Donny doesn't have anything to do with buying things for the restaurant."

Another employee called to her and she walked off with a, "Be right back."

As she left, I had the clear thought that Sonny and Donny were the same man. Maybe there were no brothers. Maybe I just needed to sleep.

"Do you and Zeke sell restaurant supplies?" Jeff asked.

"No, but we're trying to find the Delmar Brothers."

"For?"

"They're old friends of Zeke's."

"Please don't lie to me. I'm not an idiot. It sounds like you're trying to get to them secretly. If you don't want to tell me, then just say so."

"I'm sorry, Jeff. I can't talk about it."

"I found out last night that Zeke is a Texas Ranger. Is that what you do?"

"No. I'm a sheriff's deputy. I'm helping Zeke with an investigation."

Sheryl came to take our order. I asked for the special pancake breakfast, but I wanted to substitute potatoes for meat. "I'm a vegetarian," I said. Wow, that rolled off my tongue as if I'd been saying it for years. It might have been a lie, but I was determined to give it a fair try.

"Aren't you afraid of getting fat?"

"Saturated fat is one reason to avoid meat."

"I meant aren't you afraid of *being* fat?"

"No. I'm a runner."

Jeff asked for the same thing and added, "I'm a runner, too."

After Sheryl left I asked if that was true.

"Nah, I was just trying to show solidarity. If you don't want to eat meat, that's your business and not hers."

I was starting to like the guy.

"I'm interested in your investigation," Jeff said. "Maybe I could help you."

"You wouldn't be able to talk about it."

"Of course not. I understand the concept of detective work; I just don't get to do it. I want to, though. I'm working up to that in my department."

"Don't you need to sleep?"

"Probably, but I'd rather do something exciting."

He was a man after my own heart. How could I say no to him? "If you'll lend me your cell phone, I'll call Zeke and run an idea past him."

I stepped outside and talked to my father. He said if I trusted Jeff, I could talk to him about getting me into the house. He asked me not to give away the details of the investigation since it was not yet an official Texas Rangers' case or official in any capacity or anybody's business.

I went back to the booth. "I need to search a house."

"Does it belong to the brothers?"

"It belongs to at least one of them."

"Did you try to get a warrant?"

"No. I don't think I have a sound basis for a warrant. I only have strong suspicions and a gut feeling. I think he's the one who took Zeke."

"Have you thought of searching without a warrant?"

"Well of course, and I almost kicked the door in last night. I don't want to go to jail in Dallas—or anywhere."

"If we find something useful we could get a warrant tomorrow."

"But how?"

"We'll make up a reason for going in. For instance, if there's a corpse, we can say we smelled it."

"Have you done this before?"

"No, but I've stood outside while detectives did it. Please don't tell anyone that."

"I won't."

"Sometimes the detectives just need to look around and it's the only way."

"Would you want someone to invade your privacy without a legit reason?"

"No. I guess I wouldn't."

"If I don't like something done to me, I try not to do it to someone else."

"The Golden Rule."

"Yes. It works."

He studied my face a while before saying, "There's one more way."

"What is that?"

"We could talk to my dad."

"How would that help?"

"He's a judge."

I explained who I was and showed the judge my deputy identification even though it had nothing to do with the subject at hand. At least I could prove I had law enforcement training. Then I laid out my case for a warrant. I did it with so much passion he paid close attention. It helped that he'd heard of the Valentino case. He said he knew there was a question of a second semen deposit and thought that should have been explored more thoroughly. He didn't say the defense and the judge had screwed up, but I thought he was thinking it.

At last he said, "I'll issue a warrant for today only, based on the testimony of members of the victim's family, since they now admit there was a lover and gave you a name. This warrant is for evidence pertaining to that in a direct way. You need to be able to locate Donny Delmar, and I'm signing this hoping you can get an idea of his whereabouts from his home. If you find something not related to that, ignore it. Understand? This warrant is limited."

"Yes sir; I understand. Thank you."

He turned a stern look on his son.

"Yes. I understand, Dad."

I picked the lock on the back door at 355 Campbell and we entered the dark, musty house. It appeared nobody had lived in it for a while. I supposed the perp stopped by on occasion to check on things because it was clean. That led to the question of where he lived now and why he came to the Campbell Street house at all. The electricity had not been cut off but all the appliances were disconnected with the exception of the central heat. That was set on fifty-five degrees to keep the pipes from freezing, we supposed. It got cold in Dallas in the winter. The fact that he had left the heat on indicated he might not be living nearby.

"If he lived in the area," Jeff said, "he could come to the house and turn on the heat whenever cold weather is predicted. But maybe he's lazy or busy."

"He's not receiving mail or newspapers."

"Did you check with the post office?"

"Yes, and they have no forwarding address. That would've led me right to him."

"Maybe."

We snooped all through the house but didn't find anything. It had been stripped of the things that make a house personal: books, curios, movies, magazines, clothes, and nearly everything else but the furniture.

"Let's look in the basement," I said, even though I didn't want to.

"It's probably freezing down there," was Jeff's comment.

I flipped on the light at the head of the stairs. "Anything could be living down here, or dead down here. Do you smell that?"

Jeff's eyes were wide. "Putrefaction, there's no mistaking it."

I hadn't smelled much of it in my career, but I had no doubt. "Maybe it's a dead cat or rats or…"

"Victims," Jeff said, taking the words right out of my head. "God knows what he might have hidden down here."

That was the truth. We found human remains in a barrel near the farthest wall from the stairs. It wasn't even surprising considering this perp, but it was horrifying. When we took the lid off a barrel that had once contained chemicals, we were almost knocked out by the smell. We held the necks of our clothes over our mouths and noses but it didn't help. The odor and sight of human soup with bones will stop the blood in your veins.

"Now what? This is unrelated to the warrant, I think. I don't know."

"We need crime scene investigators. I guess we should call it in."

"Wait," I said. "Let's think this through. If we call the police, it will be all over the news in a few hours. Donny will just go deeper into hiding. We need to find him and the sooner the better."

"I see your point, but what about this body, or what's left of it?"

"I'm thinking."

"Even if it was just an arm we would still have to report it."

"Yes, I know. Before we do anything I'm going to call Delmar."

"The perp?"

"Yes, I have an idea."

When we were back in the living room I said, "I suspect the soup in the basement is what's left of Sonny Delmar, Donny's brother."

"It doesn't matter who it is. The fact that he has a dead body in his basement tells us what we need to know about him, don't you think?"

"Definitely. I'm going to call him and try to lure him into meeting me or to at least tell me where he is."

"Good plan. Ask him about Sonny and see what he has to say."

"Officer Grabby took my phone. That's where I have Donny's number."

"I wonder if you could be any more aggravating," he mock-grumbled.

"You haven't seen anything yet."

"I was afraid of that."

He took out his cell and called the crime lab. It took about fifteen minutes, but he got the number. He also said, "Michael Wingman wants you to call him. Also, your mom called."

"Thanks. Officer Grabby made things difficult for me; it's very inconvenient."

He reddened. "God, you are more and more annoying. Stop whining. You'll get it back soon." He handed me his.

"Will he be able to see your number?"

"No. That's my work phone. It'll display the info as unavailable."

A man answered on the third ring.

"Hello, I'm calling for Sonny Delmar," I said in my sweetest, most wide-eyed-innocent voice.

"Who is this?"

"I'm Victoria Morales." I pulled the name of my best high school pal out of the air. Using a name I know keeps me from forgetting what name I'm using. "I'm a friend of his," I added.

"What kind of friend?"

"I'm a personal friend."

"If you were close you'd know that Sonny died of cancer a few months ago."

"Oh. I'm so sorry. I didn't know he was ill."

"Yeah, it was sudden."

"Who are you?"

"I'm his brother Donny. This is my number."

"This is the one they gave me at the restaurant. They said it was Sonny's."

"They shouldn't give it to people. This was never his number. It's always been mine."

"I see; well, I was sure hoping to see Sonny again. He um… loaned me some money, and I wanted to repay him. Does he have children or a charity he'd like to receive the money? I feel I have to repay him. He helped me start a business that is now successful. I owe it to him."

"How much money did he lend you?"

"It was twenty thousand dollars." I winked at Jeff.

I heard a sharp intake of breath on the other end.

"I could get it to his wife for you," Donny volunteered. "His children are too young to handle money, but I can give it to her. I see his family often, of course. I've been trying to help out as much as I can."

"That would be great. It would make me feel better. I promised to pay him back, and he knew I would. It just took longer than I'd hoped."

"His wife would appreciate having some extra cash."

"Should I bring it to you now?"

"I—uh—I'm not in Dallas right now."

"I guess I could mail you a check," I offered, hoping for an address.

"I think it would be better if we met in person," he said. "I can be there late tomorrow. I'm traveling right now, and I don't know where I'll be. Would tomorrow work for you?"

"Sure. That would be fine. Where should we meet?"

"I have a house in Dallas. It's at 355 Campbell Street, near downtown. We could meet there and then go somewhere else. I think the house will be too cold."

"That works for me."

"Could I have your number so I can call you if I run into any problems getting there on time?"

"I share this phone with my husband, and I'd rather he not know anything about it. Why don't I call you tomorrow mid-morning and we can check in with each other? I could call you again in the evening if you like. I hope you understand about my husband. He's jealous and doesn't know about the loan."

"So this was just between you and Sonny?"

"Yes, and I'd like to keep it that way."

"I can understand that." He chuckled. "I don't want you to have trouble with your husband."

"Well, it's nice talking to you, Donny. I'll be in touch tomorrow."

"Yeah, thank you Victoria." He sounded like a happy camper.

When I clicked the phone shut, Jeff grabbed me, scaring me half to death. "You're brilliant! You've got him coming to you instead of having to chase him down."

"I'm good." I strutted around. "He's meeting me here tomorrow evening."

"You are good. It's scary the way you lie without taking a breath. It makes me wonder…"

"What do you wonder?"

"I wonder if that isn't a bad trait in a woman I want to date. You might use that talent against me."

"First of all, lying to a heartless killer is not the same as lying to a real person. Secondly, we won't be dating, Jeff. I live in Terlingua."

"I don't care where you live."

"Terlingua is nine hours from here, and if that isn't discouraging enough, I'm not ready to date anyone."

"Did someone hurt you?"

"Yes. He died."

"I'm so sorry." He seemed sincere, and I liked Jeff Wardley even more for that. "Would you at least go to dinner with me, with no strings attached?"

"Yes. I think that would be fun."

"Good. I can guarantee I won't grab you if you won't be annoying."

"That's a deal."

"I'm a good liar myself," he admitted a few minutes later. "What's your plan now? There's still the problem of dead guy soup in the basement."

"We should go talk to your dad. I think we overstepped the warrant by looking in that barrel, don't you?"

"Hell no. For all we knew, that could've been Donny in there. Dad issued the warrant so we could look for him, right? But we can talk with my father if you want. You don't want Delmar to get off on some obscure technicality."

"You've got that right."

"I think we should take one of those bones in the barrel to the crime lab and see if the DNA matches someone in the system," he said. "But we won't tell them where we got it."

"Sonny's DNA should be on file since there's a restaurant permit in his name. He had to have a blood test for the health department."

"That's true," he agreed. "I'll take the bone to the lab if you'll fish it out. If I have to go down there again, I know I'll throw up."

"Just thinking of going down there makes me want to throw up," I said.

I did it anyway, using a will of steel, kitchen tongs, and a doubled-up zippered plastic bag. When I came back up the basement stairs, I handed the bag to Jeff. He grimaced and set it down.

I sat down on the edge of the sofa.

"Get up!" he screeched, alarming me.

I jumped up as if I'd been bitten. "What? What is it?"

"There could be anything on that sofa. Think spilled food, think semen, think spit, think vomit. Never, ever sit down on anything in a perp's house. Never."

"Yuck. I hope I didn't get something nasty on my dress. That reminds me. I need to change my clothes. I forgot I was wearing running shoes with my Mexican dancing dress."

"You totally rock that look," he said with a straight face.

Chapter 32

PRESENT DAY, DALLAS

After I showered and changed clothes, I went back to the hospital. It had been determined by various docs that Zeke's health was excellent, he had not been raped or physically abused in some other way, and he would have no lasting ill effects from the ordeal. They suspected he had been drugged with Rohypnol, but by the time they tested him, there was no detectable amount in his system. A red needle prick mark on his neck told a story he couldn't remember. For Zeke, everything about the incident was fuzzy or forgotten, a side effect of the drug. The doctors said his memory of the attack might come back or it might not.

Zeke was anxious to get out of bed. The hospital cooperated by releasing him, and I took him back to our room.

It upset him that he couldn't recall the incident. He had an investigator's eye and was used to being able to describe things in minute detail. I tried to take his mind off that by telling him how Jeff and I had set up Donny Delmar. He thought that was great but continued to fret about his lack of memory and the fact that he'd missed the last day of class. It didn't do any good to point out that it wasn't his fault.

We had just returned to the room when I received a call from the front desk that I had a visitor, Chico Gutierrez. He was waiting in the lobby.

Chico was cleaned up and wearing western-style dress-up clothes, going-to-a-dance clothes. He looked different without the dust and dirt of his job and was not as old as I had thought.

He lifted his hat and greeted me warmly but seemed ill at ease. "This is one fancy place." He gaped at the opulent lobby. It was a little much for me, too.

"Would you like to get coffee? There's a small café around the corner that serves great coffee day and night, or so I'm told."

He was quiet on the short walk. Once we were seated and had ordered, he set his cowboy hat on the seat next to him. "I guess you wonder why I'm here. I've come to tell you a few things I didn't want anyone else to hear. And I would appreciate it if you'd keep this to yourself as much as possible."

"Okay, Chico. What do you want to tell me?"

"I started thinking about Lucia and Max, and I was worried that in your research you might find out I was one of the men who tried hard to get Lucia to cheat on her husband."

I didn't say anything so he continued. "I was the age of Lucia but not as mature as she was. I wasn't married then. From the moment I saw her smile she was all I could think about. She was the most beautiful woman I've ever seen. It wasn't just about her looks, either. She had personality and there was a kindness about her that seemed to radiate from her pores. All the cowboys were filled with lust for Lucia, but she only had eyes for Max. I'm ashamed to admit it, but I made her life miserable." Chico swallowed hard.

I had faith he was going somewhere so I let him roll.

"I wanted her to be my wife," he continued, "and I was stupid enough to think that if Max was out of the picture she might be mine. Even when they had a baby, I was still telling myself I could win her over."

He paused to drink coffee. "I'm married now and happily so. That's why I don't want this story known around the ranch. I've been married forty-four years and they've been good years. My wife and I have three children, all born on the ranch. They're grown now and all of them have done well. We are very proud of them."

"Why are you telling me this, Chico?"

He fidgeted and didn't seem able to answer.

I said, "It doesn't matter what you thought or did so long ago. Everybody does stupid things when they're young."

"I don't want you to think Lucia was a slut."

"Of course I won't think that."

Chico drank more coffee. Then his eyes caught mine. "I haven't told you everything."

For a few seconds, the whole world hung suspended by a fragile thread of conversation. Blood rushed in my ears. Dust motes rode golden rays of sun that warmed the window next to us. In the quiet of the deserted café, it seemed like I could hear every beat of my heart.

"She was 'kept' by that man."

"What man, Chico? I think you should start at the beginning."

"She didn't have a choice."

I tried to be patient. My papi spoke in the same roundabout way.

"John Teshman was his name."

I watched him, expecting more.

"She did what she had to do, and I know she did it for her son." Chico looked at me and his face was full of pain. "Once Max died, she had a hard time. If I'd had any sense, I would've helped her get back to México." He sighed and slumped in the chair.

"You're talking about when you and the others took Lucia to Dallas?"

"Yes. It was done out of panic. We were terrified she'd go to prison and didn't have time to think it through. I thought of it later and tried to go back for her and Zeke, but I had already lost them by then."

"I assume you checked at the mission?"

"Yes. I went there first. The woman told me Lucia had trouble with some men and was forced to leave to protect herself. She said she didn't have any idea where she'd gone. I asked around and ran into a man who thought she was living in a rooming house with other women and working at one of the factories, but he couldn't say where. I searched and searched but got nowhere."

Chico stared into his coffee. When he looked at me there were tears in his eyes. "What I'm trying to tell you is this. John Teshman killed your grandmother. He claimed it was an accident, but only he and Lucia know what happened."

"How do you know he killed her?" The news hurt my heart; I didn't want her to be dead. She was as alive to me as my mother was.

"It was in the papers, and the ranch buzzed with the horror of it. He did time, but it wasn't much."

"The news was in the Dallas papers?"

"Yes. There was a big scandal in Dallas high society."

"How did Lucia know John Teshman?"

"I'm sorry. I haven't done a very good job of telling this story." He took a long breath and let it out slowly. "Teshman owned a factory where Lucia went to work. He saw her and you can guess the rest. He was a rich man and could get whatever he wanted. He took in Lucia and Zeke, or that's what I heard."

"Lucia and Zeke lived with him?"

"Teshman was a married man, so it was more like he gave her a place to live in exchange for—for—sex. Lucia was his mistress." The words pained Chico Gutierrez, even all these years later.

"When we heard that Soledad Rodriguez had been killed, we knew it was Lucia and got word to her family. It must have been terrible for them."

"Yes. I'm sure it was."

"Sometimes beauty is a curse," he said. "It's a gift and a curse at the same time. If she wouldn't have been so beautiful, things might have been different."

"But then she wouldn't have been Lucia."

"That's true." He appeared to ponder it. "No man could ever have taken Lucia from Max if he had lived. She loved him and he loved her, too. I'm so sad their son never knew either of them."

***

When I entered the room, Zeke held out the phone. "It's Michael Wingman for you." He winked.

I took the phone from him. "I'm sorry I haven't called you, Michael. It's been one thing after another."

"Zeke was filling me in."

"Did Jeff bring you the toothbrush and the bone?"

Zeke's head practically spun around. I hadn't had a chance to tell him about the remains in Donny's basement.

"Yes, but first let's talk about the evidence you brought me from the trashcan. I did a preliminary on it, and it doesn't match the semen. The full report will give more detail, but I'm sure it won't be a match."

I collapsed into a chair.

"It's possible it wasn't his trash," Michael said.

"True. I don't think he lives there anymore. But wait. What about the partial print?"

"Not his."

"The toothbrush?"

"Again, a preliminary shows a no-match to the semen."

I was so stunned I couldn't move. Was it possible Donny wasn't the perp?

"I'm sorry," Michael said. "I think you have your sights on the wrong man."

I had to run or my head was going to explode. As I put on my shoes, I told Zeke about the barrel in Donny Delmar's basement and explained what Michael Wingman had said about my evidence-turned-back-to-trash.

"Let me think on this a while," he said, but he was back to watching *Walker, Texas Ranger.* I thought Chuck Norris would be just as clueless at solving the Valentino murders as I was. But the man had moves.

When he saw me running towards him, the doorman held the door as wide as he could open it. It had become a standard joke between us.

"Stop calling me fat."

He looked as guiltless as a newborn kitten. "Where's the fire, Running Gal?"

I wordlessly indicated my hair.

Damn it. My feet beat out the curse in a steady one-two rhythm. Damn it. Damn it. Damn it. Maybe Kiko was guilty after all. No. There was someone else. I could almost smell him just out of reach, gloating in the shadows. I let my mind run over it a while, came up with zilch, obsessed a little more, and then went back to damn it, damn it, damn it. I needed to not think. I needed to drink. I needed to let myself grieve over the death of Emilio Martez and let him go. I needed my mountains. Damn it. Damn it. Damn it.

A public library stopped me in my tracks. If Zeke was fourteen months old when his mother was killed, that would've been 1968. I went to the desk and spoke with a helpful woman about researching old newspaper articles. She set me up at a computer, and then I sat in front of the screen staring. Was this something I wanted to know? Would Zeke want to know? I couldn't seem to answer for either of us, so I jumped in.

The Dallas Morning News has archives as far back as 1885, not that I had to go that far. I put in the year of death for Soledad Rodriguez and then her name. Nothing came up. For the sake of obstinacy, I used the name Lucia Pacheco. Still nothing. So, using the search engine, I looked for murders during 1968. A lot of articles came up. One caught my eye: *Local Man Jailed in Death of Woman.* That wasn't it.

Teshman Pleads Guilty to Manslaughter popped up. Unless he'd killed others, that had to be it. The article didn't give the woman's name but called her an "illegal immigrant and Teshman's sometimes girlfriend." Steam nearly shot out my ears.

I kept looking until I found an earlier article: *Teshman Industries Scandal/John Teshman Arraigned.* The article stated that Teshman, the 33-year-old son of Arnold and Katherine Teshman of Dallas, had admitted to accidentally killing a woman whom he described as his mistress. Towards the end of the article, the woman's name was given as Soledad Rodriguez, age seventeen, illegal Mexican immigrant.

She was my grandmother, you bigoted assholes.

The size and scope of the scandal was enormous because it involved a wealthy, well-connected, and white, man of means. I read the article with care, feeling worse all the while. There were scores of juicy articles. Well, not juicy, but they alluded to plenty of juiciness.

John Teshman was sentenced to three years in prison. I tried to be removed from it, but they were talking about Zeke's mother, my grandmother. Three years. He was wealthy and important, a well-known member of Dallas high society. She was an "illegal immigrant." Do the math.

Teshman claimed he didn't intend to kill her; he had pushed her during an argument. She fell back against a stone fireplace, hit her head hard, and had bled to death before paramedics arrived on the scene.

It was speculated that he would've served no time if he hadn't been so slow to call the ambulance.

Holy crap on a stick.

Chapter 33

I ran back towards the hotel, but I was slowed down by my heart; it weighed at least a ton. *Better take that door all the way off its hinges, Mr. Doorman.*

I plopped onto a bench to contemplate the one hundred percent fucked-up nature of things. Soon I was crying and couldn't even blame Dallas. Mountains or buildings, trees or desert, I had been heading for a meltdown and putting it off by sheer force of will.

The tragic fates of Lucia and Max, the wickedness of a system that begs our starving neighbors to come here and then treats them like dirt, my two lost loves, a society that values money and status over goodness, the way the wrong man had been convicted for the murder of Kiko's family, the bloody, broken bodies of a Terlingua family of four, the damned general unfairness of life, the thought of my sweet father being dragged out of bed and beaten and sexually abused—it was too much. I was melting all over a Dallas street.

I sobbed as people passed with a nervous glance in my direction. A kind soul stepped out of the crowd of faceless persons and slid in next to me on the bench. He put his strong arms around me and cradled me against his chest. He whispered into my hair that everything was all right.

"Everything will be all right."

"Officer Grabby," I sobbed.

He laughed softly. "Man, you're so annoying."

"Stop sweet-talking me."

"I knew that wouldn't fly with you."

"How did you know I was here?"

"I went to your hotel and Zeke said you were out running this route, so I came to look for you."

A few seconds passed, and he lifted my tear-streaked face to his and planted little kisses all over it. Then his lips landed on mine. It was a soft and sweet kiss at first, but it became burning and demanding and left no doubt about where this was going if I didn't stop it. Since I was in flames, I didn't feel like stopping it.

Maybe this encounter was more about seducing me than kindness, but I still thought he was kind or I wouldn't have kissed him back.

"Would you like to forget about rape and murder and human soup and other atrocities for a while?" he murmured against my ear.

I nodded and he kissed me some more.

"Get a room!" somebody yelled.

"For god's sake," a passing person sneered.

We kept on kissing.

When Jeff said, "Come with me," I put my hand in his.

Making love with Jeff was one of the kindest things I'd done for myself in recent history. I didn't beat myself up or try to second-guess things or call myself names or think about the future or have regrets about the past. It never occurred to me to wish that Jeff was somebody else, nor did I think even once about Somebody Else. It was Jeff and me and the warm, golden rays of a dying sun spilling over naked bodies in a wide bed in a nineteenth-story apartment somewhere high above the city of Dallas. Time stopped and it was a long time before it started again.

It was late when I let myself back into the hotel room I shared with Zeke. Since I preferred not to have to face him, he was sitting up reading.

He looked up from the book. "Well, did you have fun?"

"Yes." I turned beet red. That was embarrassing, so I went a shade redder.

242

"Jeff came by looking for you, and I told him you'd gone for a run. He said he would try to find you to take you to dinner."

Did he not know? Parents are sneaky.

"He found me." I tried to sound casual, but I doubt it came off that way.

Zeke smiled and went back to his book.

I went to shower and try to get my face under control, but I felt like singing at the top of my lungs.

Chapter 34

The next morning Zeke was drinking coffee and I was sipping hot chocolate. It was delicious, but I didn't really want it. It was a cold, clear, sunny morning. I was in such a good mood even the city looked gorgeous. Jeez.

Zeke said, "When Jeff came by, he brought us new phones. He said it would be a while before we can get our old phones back. They're evidence."

I tried not to allow it, but my face flamed again. I couldn't stop thinking of Jeff's hands and that sort of thinking leads to…

"Did you hear what I said?"

"Uh-huh." I sounded mentally challenged.

"He downloaded our info from the old phones into the new ones. Wasn't that thoughtful?"

"Yes. He's like that."

"Of course, I think this might've been more about his concern that you have a phone than anything, but I came out a winner, too."

I wasn't listening. What I heard was: concern, phone, winner. Yes, ladies and gentlemen, we have a winner.

Zeke kept on and then he just stopped talking.

"I'm sorry, Zeke. I have a lot of things going on."

"I was saying that I need to stay at least until Tuesday. I'm scheduled to do a make-up class on Monday. That isn't going to be a problem for you, is it?"

"No. I—I'm working on some things, and I still don't have a clue who murdered Kiko's family."

"It hurts to be wrong when you're sure about a suspect, doesn't it?"

"Yes, and it puts me back to square one. I don't know where to go from here."

"You left this with me when you went out to run, and I've been thinking about it. Go back over every interview, every single word spoken to you about the case, and every shred of evidence. Also, you need more info about Kiko's wife. It could have been someone jealous of her and it has nothing to do with Kiko. Maybe she had a stalker or another boyfriend who got sick of her shit. Basically, what you need is a list of all the people the couple knew."

"Oh, is that all?"

"If this job was easy, everybody would be an investigator."

Yada, yada, yada. My head had already gone back to Jeff and the way the gold hairs on his chest had looked in the waning light. Crap. I had to get over this dreamy teenage stuff and get to work.

You want to call him whispered that annoying inner bitch I mentioned before.

So you liked him, too? I shot back at her. Jeez, I was hearing voices and responding to them. I think people are institutionalized for less.

Zeke was busy doing whatever he was doing, so I searched John Teshman online and got hundreds of references to him in newspapers, magazines, and online society crap. I even found photos of him. He was old, but still a wealthy bastard who got away with murder. He owned manufacturing plants in and around Dallas as well as a book publishing company. He was known for his philanthropy. Right. What a guy.

I needed to see him.

"I have to go out a while, Zeke." He was watching Walker single-handedly fight a gang of five big, mean, ugly dudes.

"This is ridiculous," he said without looking away.

"I know, yet you're watching it."

"It's great to see a lawman kick ass and always win. He never fails to get the bad guys. That fascinates me."

"It's not real, Zeke. Never mind. I have to go. I'll call you later." I kissed him on the cheek.

"I wish I could take on five guys at once."

"Yeah, me too."

The fact that he didn't respond to that told how badly those *Walker, Texas Ranger* reruns had gotten to him. I ducked out before he asked where I was going.

I sat in the lobby and called Donny Delmar. He said we were still on target for meeting Saturday night. Even if he wasn't the Valentino perp, he had somebody's decomposing body in his basement.

I was about to call John Teshman next, but the phone rang before I could.

"Are you busy?" Jeff asked.

"No." *Yes you are, you hopeless little slut.*

"Do you feel like coming back over here?"

"Don't you ever sleep?"

"I slept last night."

"Did you lose your job?"

He laughed. "Not yet. I have two nights off, which means I have the day, too. If you'll come over, I'll make you a vegetarian breakfast."

"Okay. It's nice that you remember that."

"Oh, I remember every single detail about you. Your details—well—do you remember how to get here?"

"No. After a while all tall buildings start to look alike."

"Take a taxi." He gave me the address to give the driver. "When you get here, hit the buzzer of 1904 and I'll let you in. The elevator stops in front of my apartment."

When Jeff opened the door, he pulled me to him and we began to kiss. The sweet aroma of pancakes filled the air, but we never got around to eating them.

I called John Teshman at his home after I left Jeff's. I figured the guy was more or less seventy-nine now. Did I really want to confront an old man? Yes. I did.

Whoever answered his phone was so hard to get past that I pulled out my powerful secret weapon. "I'm with the Texas Rangers, and it would be in his best interests to speak with me."

Oh, brilliant.

After I waited a long time, he came to the phone. "This is John Teshman. How can I help you, Ms. Ricos?"

"I'd like to speak with you about the death of Soledad Rodriguez."

"Who?" I didn't think he'd forgotten; I had stunned him.

"Soledad Rodriguez, your former mistress."

Silence reigned while I waited. A busy, powerful man could refuse to see me. There was no law saying he had to, although I was trying to think of one.

He said, "Soledad Rodriguez died a very long time ago." He sounded so sad I couldn't be mean to him.

"Yes sir."

"My first inclination is to tell you to go to hell. I'll give you one minute to tell me why I should speak to you about Soledad."

"I'm the daughter of her son, Zeke Pacheco."

There was a long, long silence.

"You're not calling me representing the Texas Rangers?"

"No sir, but I had to get past whoever answered your phone."

"That was my housekeeper. She screens my calls."

"I need to know anything you're willing to tell me about my grandmother. That's all I want from you."

It always amazes me when honesty works. "When do you want to come?"

"I would love to come now."

"Come on then." He made sure I had the address.

The Teshman residence was grand but understated in an old money way. There was nothing gaudy or flamboyant on the outside anyway.

A uniformed maid answered the door and led me to a paneled study that was old-fashioned and beautiful. John Teshman sat near a roaring fireplace in a leather chair. He glanced up when I entered.

"I paid my debt, and I mean with far more than prison," he said.

"I would like to hear your story, Mr. Teshman."

He waved his hand at a nearby chair and I sat in it. "Want a nip of bourbon?"

Oh God, yes. "No sir, thank you."

"I knew this day would come sooner or later. I was beginning to think I had escaped the wrath of that little boy."

"My father has no wrath for you, Mr. Teshman. At this point, he doesn't even know you exist."

"Are you going to tell him?"

"I don't know. I guess it depends on what you say."

"I have some things he might want. I always thought he would show up one day."

The old man rose in the slow, determined way of the elderly, but he was not feeble. He was tall and walked with a straight spine. He offered me his hand. "I apologize for not saying hello before."

"That's all right. I know I've caught you off guard."

He chuckled. "Yes, you have."

He poured himself another nip and sat down again. "What is your father's name, young lady?"

"It's Zeke Pacheco."

"Zeke. Yes. Zeke. I remember that now."

"My grandmother's name was Lucia Pacheco, not Soledad Rodriguez." I wanted him to at least know her name.

He sighed. "I loved her, Ms. Ricos."

That he had loved her never occurred to me.

"Her death was an accident. I shouldn't have pushed her. I know that, but I never intended to harm her."

"It must have pained you to kill her, then."

"You can't imagine how much it hurt me." He looked at me with sharp, clear eyes. "I should never have gotten involved with Soledad, but I was a spoiled, privileged man who hadn't grown up. I saw something I wanted and by God, I was going to get it." He drank a sip. "You look like her, you know."

"I'm proud of that, but you should see my father. The resemblance is so strong there's no doubt she's his mother."

"Does your father know where you are?"

"No sir. He's been hurt a lot and I don't want to hurt him anymore. What you say might stay forever between you and me."

"I'm the reason he was sent away."

"Would you please start at the beginning and tell me everything you're willing to share?"

He gave me a piercing look. "I don't have to tell you anything."

"I know that, sir. But maybe it would help you to talk about it. It would help me to hear it. If you don't explain things, then I will always think of you as a wealthy bastard who got away with the murder of my grandmother." I didn't mean to use that word, but I had, and it hung there between us.

"Wealthy, murdering bastard," he muttered. "Yes, I can see how you would think that." He turned those sharp eyes on me again. "It's even true, but you don't know the whole of it."

"Please tell me. There doesn't seem to be another way to find out."

"I'll tell you, if you'll reserve your judgment 'til the end."

"I apologize for judging you at all. I shouldn't but—"

"Hush now, young one, or you'll miss my story."

I hushed.

"The first time I saw her," he began, "I knew I was in trouble.

More to the point, she was in trouble, but I never thought like that then." He stared at the burning logs as if there were answers in the flames. "Fire consumes, Ms. Ricos, and I was on fire."

I reminded myself to breathe.

"She was so young and beautiful. Her beauty was natural and shone from her eyes and in her smile. Her hair was pulled back into a ponytail that day, but I could see the sheen and thickness and length of it. I wanted to take her hair down and put my face in it. Everything about her was mesmerizing."

He stopped, sipped, and continued. "My family owned several factories and I was in charge of most of them. We hired a lot of illegals but we treated them well. We didn't pay much, but our working conditions were better than many." Then his eyes caught mine. "Oh hell," he sighed. "They were sweatshops, I suppose."

I kept my judgmental mouth tightly closed.

He shifted around in the chair. "I'm an old man, and old men should speak the truth. Don't you agree?"

"Yes sir. Everyone should speak the truth."

"But people don't."

"That's true."

"Do you ever lie to yourself, Ms. Ricos?"

"Yes, more than I want to admit."

"Those are the worst lies of all. We commit unimaginable cruelty and stupidity by lying to ourselves."

I nodded in agreement.

"Moving past the sweatshop nature of my factories, which I lied to myself about daily, I also told myself that I had improved Soledad's life. On the surface that even seemed true, but I caused her more pain by seducing her into a contract for her pride and sense of worth."

"How so, sir?"

"She was working at a friend's factory. He was showing me through it because he'd purchased some new equipment. I was horrified to see his people were locked in. What if there was a fire or some other disaster? I confronted him and then I spotted this woman who took my breath away. I couldn't quit looking at her.

"We walked up and down the aisles and eventually I was within a few feet of her. My friend saw me looking and as we walked away he said, 'She's a real beauty,' or something like that, and I asked about her. He was speechless that I would ask about an illegal worker in his factory, but I couldn't help myself."

John Teshman leaned his head against the back of the chair. "God help me, I told him I had a place for her in my organization. He knew exactly where I wanted her. He told me she owed him three thousand dollars and was working it off. My ass! The lyin' son-of-a-bitch had an eye on her too, you see. I wrote him a check for the full amount even though I knew she owed him nothing.

"He said, 'Well, Johnny, you've bought yourself a woman. I hope you know what to do with her.' With that, she was mine. Except she wasn't—nowhere near."

A tear rolled down Teshman's cheek. He wiped it away and continued. "My mother was born in Mexico, so I grew up speaking Spanish. I went to Soledad and asked her to come with me. I told her I had a job for her at my company. She looked terrified. She knew what was coming even before she heard my offer.

"I took her into the hall and told her I'd paid her debt with Freeman Industries. Man, her blood boiled. 'I have no debt!' she said with real heat. My desire for her went from sexual longing to an all-consuming fire. I hope I'm not speaking too frankly for you, Ms. Ricos."

"No. Please don't edit yourself. You're doing fine."

"I asked her where she lived and she told me. I knew from the address that it was a terrible place. It was a falling-down tenement with little heat and no air-conditioning. It was a fire trap at best.

"I must have looked horrified because she added that she lived there with a friend who worked nights and took care of her baby during the day. Christ, the woman had a child. I hadn't thought about that possibility. I had stepped off the deep end. I didn't know one thing about her except that she was an exquisite woman and I wanted her. I would've sold my soul to see her smile, and I suppose I did." He crossed his legs. "Are you sure you don't want something to drink?"

"I'm sure. Thank you."

"I was married. I never thought for a second of my wife. I've spent all the rest of my life trying to get my soul back from the devil." He affixed me with those piercing eyes again. "Are you sure you want to hear all of it?"

"Yes sir. I'm sure."

"I had mistresses before. I was the product of wealth and was spoiled and egotistical. I kept an apartment in downtown Dallas where I sometimes took women and that is where I wanted to take Soledad. I asked her to have a look at it, as if she had a choice. I pointed out that where she was living was not safe for her child. I used her son against her and more than once."

He released a long, shuddering breath. "It gets worse."

"It's all right; go ahead."

"I took Soledad to the apartment and showed her around. It had two bedrooms, so I pointed out that her son could have his own room. I watched as she tried to take it in. After she had seen all of it, she said, 'I can't live here, señor.' I asked her why not and she said she couldn't afford it. I understood clearly that she meant I should keep my dick in my own pants.

"So I told her it would be part of her pay. She looked skeptical but asked what she'd be doing. I told her she would be my escort to company functions and things like that. She saw right through me. 'But I don't speak any English,' she said.

"I told her it didn't matter, that she could learn and I wanted to be seen with a beautiful Mexican woman. I had my reasons. She raised an eyebrow. 'And what about my son?' she asked.

"I told her I would get a babysitter when I needed her. Then I asked her to show me where she was living. She was reluctant to take me there, but again, I used her son. Lying asshole that I was, I said I wanted to meet him. He was dressed in every piece of clothing she could find for him, I guess. It was early April, but we'd just had snow and a cold front. There was no heat to speak of, and the boy's little hands were like ice. The babysitter had the oven turned on with the door open for heat.

"I was horrified and yet the place was spotlessly clean. I begged her to bring him and come live in an apartment with heat. I promised her that her son would never want for anything. What a fucking liar I was."

He sat up straighter and cleared his throat. "Forgive me. I forgot you were here for a moment."

"That's all right, Mr. Teshman. I know the word."

"Well I hope you're not in the habit of using it."

"No sir."

"Soledad struggled with my offer. God, I hate myself when I think of it. She agreed for the sake of her son. She had no illusions about the deal she'd made. Soledad was as smart as she was beautiful.

"I took her and her small boy to the apartment and got them settled. I missed three meetings that afternoon and my secretary was hysterical looking for me. This was before there were cell phones, back when a man could disappear for the day and nobody could interrupt him."

He shifted in the chair, drank a bit of bourbon, and continued. "In the interest of time, let me just say that I bought her everything. She was a queen in rags, and being dressed up made her even more regal. In truth, we seldom went out because she claimed she liked to cook. It wasn't that as much as shame that kept her home.

"And all the while, I did things for her I would never do for anyone, such as shop. Wealthy people don't shop. We spend money but we have people to shop. We have people to do everything. Being in love with Soledad prompted me to do things for her. She made me into a man, but she never loved me."

He paused and took out a handkerchief and blew his nose. "What I came to want as much as the sex was for her to smile at me the way she smiled at her little son. But at first it was more about sex, and I took the life right out of her, Ms. Ricos. When she fell against the fireplace and died that was only her body. I had already taken everything else, even her son."

"How did you take him?"

"He was in my way, and I convinced her to send him to her parents for a while. From that moment, I believe she planned her escape. How stupid can a man be to ask a woman to give up her son? Damned stupid, it seems."

I knew for a fact that my grandmother had planned a getaway, but I didn't comment. What would have been the point?

"I was thirty-three years old and not unattractive, but to expect Soledad to fall in love with me was ridiculous. A wild bird would never love the hand that crushes it. She knew what her work was and all she asked was that her baby be asleep and that I not hurt her. I wouldn't have hurt her for anything.

"One night when I was lying beside Soledad, I thought I would give up my fortune for her. If I'd had the guts to do that things might've been different. I wasn't enough of a man for Soledad, but she did bring out the best in me. I tried to be the man she deserved."

Mr. Teshman wiped his teary eyes. "Do you want me to go on?"

"Yes sir."

"Along the way, I found out about her husband, who she still loved with all her heart. I knew she was just having sex with me. On her part, there was no love. She went somewhere else in her mind when I was making love to her. It hurt me but what could I do? I kept on loving her. I never loved anyone like I loved her."

I was convinced by then that he had not meant to kill her, but I wanted to know the whole story.

"I told Soledad that we'd send for her son once I bought a house so we'd have more room. I nagged her. One day a friend came and took him. She was distraught when I came to her that evening. She was crying and said she missed him so much she didn't think she could bear it. 'Please let me bring him back,' she sobbed. As mean and selfish as I was, I couldn't deny her. I couldn't bear to see her cry, so I promised her I would take her to get him as soon as he arrived in Mexico. That was going to be in about a week. The people she sent him with weren't sure how long it would take them to get there. My promise made her feel better and she was counting the days until her son's arrival at her parents' home.

"About that time I began to realize she was not spending the money I gave her for food and other things. She was saving it. I became obsessed with the idea that she was planning to leave me and go back to Mexico to live in peace with her son.

"I yelled at her and threatened to turn her in to Immigration. I threatened to put her onto the street. I'm so ashamed, Ms. Ricos. She was never anything but good to me and I lorded over her like a typical privileged asshole.

"We argued and I pushed her away in anger. She stumbled backward and fell against the stones of the fireplace and hit her head hard. She slumped to the floor and bled to death right in front of me. I've done bad things in my life but watching that surely was a punishment even a man like me didn't deserve. She didn't deserve it either." His voice broke.

After he composed himself, he continued. "The reason—the reason I didn't call the ambulance right away was that I held her."

He swirled the bourbon around and I wondered if he saw her in it. "I guess I don't need to tell you what a scandal ensued."

"I can imagine it."

"They made it worse than it was. My wife left me, of course. On top of everything else I had to do prison time. That will change a man, no matter what."

There was a long pause during which I thought he was trying to keep it together. I sure was.

"If you don't take away anything else from this meeting, I want you know that I loved your grandmother. I deeply regret sending her son away. I regret so many things, but I will never regret knowing Soledad Rodriguez. If you decide to tell Zeke about this conversation, I want you to tell him that. He had one hell of a mother."

I nodded, unable to speak.

"I also want to tell you that she's buried in Greenlawn Cemetery here in Dallas. You might want to move her to wherever her beloved Max is buried."

We contemplated the fire which had died down to glowing embers.

Teshman rose and set his drink down. "I have some things for Zeke, and I send them to him with my blessing and my apologies for not doing better by him."

He went to a wall safe, put in the combination, and opened it. He removed a small box and shut the safe again.

"I took this ring from her finger the night she died." He held it up. "It doesn't have much value, except to you and Zeke. Maybe it was wrong not to bury her with it, but my intention was to send it to her son if I ever found out where her people were or if he came looking for me.

"Thank you, Mr. Teshman. My father will treasure it."

"Take a look at these pictures." He handed me a stack of them.

They were of the most beautiful, elegant woman I'd ever seen. There were four photos of her dressed in various evening wear. She looked as if she belonged on the society page. In one, Lucia was bending down to her son who was speaking to her. One hand held back the long dress, the other reached out to him. Her smile was bright and love shone from her face.

"Zeke will treasure these," I said past a lump in my throat. "I will treasure them."

"You know, the name is wrong on her headstone," Teshman

said. "And there's no date of birth, only a date of death. Will you take care of that?"

"Yes; I promise I will."

He laid a hand against his chest. "That makes me feel better. I'm so glad you came here today, young lady."

"I'm glad I came, too. Thank you."

"Does Zeke need my help financially?"

"No; I don't think so. He makes a good living as a Texas Ranger."

"Oh, so he's the Ranger, not you."

"Right."

"Is there anything I could do for him?"

"I don't know. He would have to answer that."

"If you decide to tell him about me, will you ask him?"

"Yes. I will."

"If you think of something, will you call me?"

"Yes. I sure will."

"I have money, and there is no joy in money unless you can use it for good. It took most of my life to figure that out. It would make me happy to do something for Zeke. I want you to write down his full legal name and his address because I'm going to name him in my will."

I hugged John Teshman when I left him. He seemed to badly need it.

Chapter 35

I sat on the curb outside Teshman's house. My plan was to call a taxi, but for a while I just sat. The fat as well as the slender branches of the leafless oaks conspired with the sunlight to dapple the street in intricate lined patterns. I watched for a while and then brought my knees to my chest and rested my head on them. It seemed like I wasn't the only human who messed up their life with un-thought-through decisions and wrong moves. Good grief; we start out knowing nothing and by the time we start to get it, we're gone. That was reason enough to drink.

My phone rang and I saw that the caller was Jeff.

"What are you doing?" he asked when I answered.

"I'm just sitting here on the curb thinking."

"About?"

"How messed up people are."

"I hope you don't mean me specifically."

"No; everybody is a mess in one way or another."

"That's why we need each other."

I didn't comment, although I agreed.

"Are you all right?" Jeff asked.

"Do you ever feel so sad you can't even cry?"

"If you feel that sad, I should come there."

"Thank you, but I need to be alone a while to think."

"Do you want to get something to eat?" he asked after a word-less pause.

"You can't keep luring me with promises of food."

He laughed. "I swear I'll be more restrained this time. Besides, we'll be in a restaurant."

258

We worked out where to meet, and that's where I asked the taxi driver to take me. During our meal, I told Jeff about the whole of the Valentino case because he knew almost none of it, including my frustration with solving it and my fear for Zeke. My father had blown off the threat to his life with, "It's nothing. Criminals try to intimidate me all the time," but I wasn't reassured.

"You've obviously stepped on somebody's toes," Jeff said. "You must be close without realizing how close you are." In the next breath he said, "I could help you if you want. I have until Sunday night at eleven. Zeke is feeling okay now, right?"

"Right."

"When we finish here, let's go talk to him. If the three of us work on this, we ought to be able to figure it out by Sunday night."

I was skeptical but he only grinned. His enthusiasm reignited my interest in Kiko's plight. Besides, there was a raping murderer on the loose.

I dragged myself out of a past I could never change, no matter how badly I wanted to. Maybe I could help to change what would be Kiko's past someday—and my own.

Jeff and I left the restaurant with the conviction of soldiers heading off to do battle with all things wicked, except we were unarmed and not planning to kill anyone.

Zeke jumped on Jeff's plan with both boots. He admitted he didn't want to face Kiko or his family if he didn't have some answers for them. Besides, now that he'd been threatened, he was angry and humiliated.

"Nobody intimidates me off an investigation and then gets away with raping and murdering," he said with a dark look.

Even though it was Saturday afternoon near dark-thirty, Zeke announced his intention of going to the prison. He needed to see Kiko anyway, and maybe he could jog his memory about something he'd failed to tell me. I reminded him that we had a scumbag to pick up at nine.

"I hope you didn't think I would forget that," he said.

Jeff and I started making a list of the interviews I'd made and what I'd learned, the places I'd been, and places we needed to revisit.

When I mentioned looking at the evidence again, Jeff said, "I shouldn't go with you when go there. They won't like it that I'm working to discredit a DPD detective."

"That's not at all what we're doing. We're trying to find a murderer."

"Well, they see it differently. Nobody over there likes it that you and Zeke are sniffing around, even though it's unofficial."

"When Zeke was abducted it became a Texas Rangers' case, but I'm sorry if they feel like that. Detective work should be about getting to the truth, finding justice for the victim, and getting criminals off the street. The men who worked the Valentino case went the easiest route to a conviction. They were wrong, Jeff. An innocent man is in prison for life, and a murderer who is also a rapist is still out there."

"Hey, I'm on your side. I'm just telling you what's happening at headquarters."

Zeke came back from the prison with a list. It was all the men Kiko had interacted with during the month prior to the murders and every person he could name who had anything to do with the investigation, trial, or post-trial follow-up. It was a daunting list.

Jeff and I had put together a copious amount of information as well, but everything was set aside as Zeke and I prepared for our nine o'clock date with a murderer.

Once again I sat in front of 355 Campbell, but this time I wasn't hiding in the shadows. I was in a bright blue unmarked car that belonged to the Texas Rangers. Zeke and a Dallas-based Ranger were somewhere nearby.

Zeke didn't want me there at all but I had set up the meeting, and they needed me to keep Donny occupied long enough for them to grab him. It was too much like a movie extra role for my tastes, but there I was.

Jeff couldn't have a role because of his position with the Dallas P.D. In addition to being an off-duty rookie, the D.P.D. was not involved yet. He didn't like it, but Jeff stayed at the hotel going over the notes from my interviews.

We were a few minutes early, but I kept checking my phone for the time. I was tempted to look around for Zeke, but I figured I would never spot him. Besides, I was supposed to act like a person alone in case Delmar was watching. For a while I sat on the hood of the car but got back inside. Either place felt wrong. Everything began to feel wrong. Coming to Dallas was wrong. Getting involved with Jeff was wrong. Digging up Zeke's past was wrong. Waiting is hard. Delmar was late.

At 9:25 a small car pulled up behind me. The lights went out but the door didn't open. I was nervous as hell. *He knows!*

A man got out and strode up to my window. "Ms. Morales?"

I recognized my fake name just in time to avert disaster. It was hard to see clearly, but Donny looked about my age and was dressed up. He had an air of self-confidence and a nice smile. It's always hard to come to grips with the fact that perps look so normal.

I smiled at him. "Are you Donny Delmar?"

"That's me." He grinned. "So you were a personal friend of Sonny's?" He went from happy grinning to lecherous grinning.

I tried to ignore the heavy intimation that I had been his brother's lover. "Yes. I was so sorry to hear of his illness." I needed to move the talk away from Sonny, a man I had never even seen.

What if Donny asked what I thought of his brother's tattoos or his missing leg? I didn't even know what color hair the man had.

I took a deep breath. "Would you like to sit in here while I write the check? Should I make it to you or in the names of the children?"

"It'll be easiest if you make it to me." He came around the front of the car.

My heart was doing the thump-bang.

Donny got in and watched me expectantly. My checks read *Margarita Ricos*, so I didn't want him to see one. I smiled because it calms me, it's a good stalling tactic, and people like smiles.

Nice and easy. This isn't hard.

As I smiled at Donny, I saw Zeke creeping down the driveway from the direction of the house, his pistol drawn.

"Do you go by Donny Delmar?" I asked. "Is that how you want me to make the check?"

"Yes. Donny or Donald, either way is fine."

I pretended to look for my checkbook.

"Did you have any trouble getting away from your husband?" It wasn't so much the question as the way he asked it. This dude thought he was getting the money and the girl, but in fact he was only getting a surprise. And it was nearly on him.

"No, my husband is busy with his own business." I flashed another smile because it never hurts.

Then, so fast it even startled me, Zeke yanked open the door with one hand, his weapon trained on Donny with the other. "Donny Delmar, I'm Sergeant Pacheco of the Texas Rangers. My partner and I are taking you in for questioning." The other guy popped up seemingly out of nowhere. "Partner" must have been his cue.

Zeke's tone scared the crap out of me, but I had to hand it to Donny. He was unperturbed and asked insolently, "For?"

"We have questions about the human remains in your basement." Zeke dragged him from the car and his partner helped get him cuffed. Donny was so surprised he didn't even fight them.

"What the fuck? What the hell's going on? What about the money?" He was ranting and looking at me for answers.

I shrugged innocently. It was tempting to laugh. Donny didn't get it that he was screwed, only not in the way he hoped.

"What money?" Zeke winked at me.

The other Ranger, Bob Angell, recited Donny's rights even though he was not technically under arrest.

Then Donny started to get it. "You lied to me, you bitch."

"Watch your mouth," growled Zeke.

Delmar continued to give me brooding looks. The gravity of his predicament hadn't fully hit him.

Zeke negotiated Donny into the back seat and sat next to him. Bob drove, and I rode shotgun without a shotgun or any other type of weapon.

"Where are we going?" the detainee wanted to know.

When nobody answered, Donny called me a cock-sucking Communist cunt. *Nice alliteration,* I thought, but Communist?

Zeke took Donny's attack in a more personal way than I did. "One more word and I will stuff something in your filthy mouth."

Donny ignored him, called me a few more choice combinations, and then started on my mother.

Zeke ordered, "Stop the car." He got out and looked around for something to use as a gag. Then he took off a boot and removed one of his socks.

The perp's eyes were wide. "You aren't going to put that in my mouth?"

"My sock is cleaner than your mouth."

"That's police brutality."

"I'm not the police."

"Who are you?"

"Say one more word, Delmar; this is your final warning."

Not another word was said.

The guys left me at the hotel. I wanted to be in on the questioning and, at the same time, I didn't. Regardless, I couldn't be. Donny had more than likely killed his brother out of greed or jealousy. It was depressing that he wasn't the culprit in the Valentino crimes. That would've been a nice, neat package to tie up with a bow so I could work on my other Dallas interests. Jeff Wardley, for example.

Now that I had met Donny Delmar, I wondered why Evelyn Valentino had gotten involved with him. More importantly, if he had murdered her and her children, I now knew that he would've left behind clues—something—because he was not the brightest color in the parade. A faulty condom could happen to anyone, but it took someone intelligent and focused to leave no clue at a chaotic scene like that. All we had was one partial print that possibly had nothing to do with the crimes. Past that, there was only the semen and no match to it.

Jeff lifted his head from the table when I walked in. He was disoriented and had obviously been asleep. He yawned and stretched and then held out his arms. I went to give him a hug but he pulled me onto his lap. "How did it go?"

"It was dull; you didn't miss anything."

"That's easy for you to say since you were allowed to be there."

"It's bad for your macho police officer image to whine."

He began nibbling my neck and everything else faded to gone.

"You know," I said in a show of incredible will, "Zeke is coming back here."

"What time is it?"

"It's only ten-fifteen. Do you feel like working a little longer?"

"I feel like taking a shower with you in that great big bathroom."

"I love that idea, but my father will be back soon."

"We could lock the door."

I smacked my forehead. "Ah man, I never thought of that."

"How did you get to be such a smart-ass?"

"I don't know. It's one of many wondrous things about me."

"Lord."

"Sometimes I can't stop myself. Kissing me works."

That did it all right.

When we heard Zeke at the door, we began pouring over stacks of notes. Sure, that would fool him.

"What happened?" I asked when he came in.

Zeke shed his jacket, kicked off his boots, and undid his belt. I smiled because the first thing I do when I come home is strip out of my work clothes.

"He admits that it's Sonny in the barrel," Zeke said. "At first he tried to tell us his brother died of cancer, and he didn't have the money to bury him." He took the badge off and loosened the top buttons of his shirt. "He got his various lies so messed up it became easier to tell the truth. Long story minus a bunch of horseshit, he poisoned Sonny because he needed money."

"I assume you spoke with him about the Valentino murders."

He gave me an exasperated look. "We never once thought to ask about that."

"Now I see where you get it," Jeff said to me.

Zeke looked back and forth between us but we said nothing, so he continued. "He admitted to having an affair with Evelyn Valentino, but he 'cut that bitch out for lack of respect,' which translated to 'she dumped me, man.' He has an airtight alibi."

When Zeke sat at the table with us, Jeff moved his shoeless foot and caressed my ankle. Then he inched it under the cuff of my jeans and as far up my leg as he could get it. That wasn't far, but he kept stroking me until I almost cried out.

Zeke was looking over our lists and notes, but I don't think he was reading anything. "Have you two come up with anything here?"

My eyes cut to Jeff but he wouldn't look at me. Nor did he speak. I wanted to kick him and, at the same time, I wanted to take off my clothes.

"We've just started," I managed to say.

"We'll get this more organized tomorrow," Jeff said in a raspy voice. He cleared his throat. "Zeke, will it upset you if your daughter spends the night with me at my place?"

I could not believe it.

"Of course not, young man, but you'll have to ask her. Margarita is a grown woman, and she speaks for herself."

I spent the night at Jeff's.

Chapter 36

It was a bright, crisp Sunday morning. I lay in Jeff's bed in a tangle of sheets, feeling sweaty and contented and with pleasure still burning. He was singing in the shower. He wasn't a great singer but he was loud and heartfelt. He had made me forget, for a while, the difficult news I still had to tell Zeke about his mother's demise.

In general, Jeff had stopped sadness from chewing at my heart and had lifted my spirits and made me feel alive again. Maybe it was only a reprieve, but if so, that was okay. I had needed it.

The phone rang and I almost jumped up for it. Then I realized I didn't have to answer; this wasn't my house. If it was a dispatcher, he wouldn't be calling for me. I lay back down with a grin on my face.

After four rings, a machine answered and Jeff's recorded voice asked the caller to leave a message. There was a beep, and a woman said, "Hi Baby. I tried your cell but if I know you, it's still in your pants. I'm sure you have to work tonight, but could you call me sometime today? It's about the guest list your mom sent. There's no problem, just a question. I don't think the chapel will hold that many people." She laughed and sounded so happy it felt like a cold hand was squeezing my heart. "My mom is just as bad as yours. Whose wedding is it, anyway? I'll be home Wednesday night. You can't imagine how much I've missed you. I love you, Sweetheart."

I looked around for my clothes and realized I had left them in the bathroom, along with my hair clip. I would wear something of Jeff's if I had to, but I was getting out of there before he came out of the shower.

I looked in the closet and found a few feminine stay-over clothes way in the back of it shoved out of sight. Those were hers and anyway, they were not appropriate for running through the Dallas streets. Next I opened a drawer of t-shirts and hidden there were five photos of Officer Grabby with his fiancée or somebody he seemed to adore. Whoever she was, he was the wrong man for her.

I found sleep pants that I tied below my breasts with a piece of cord to keep them up. His t-shirt fit me like a short dress, but so what? I was making an escape, not a fashion statement.

I had kicked off my boots in the hallway not the bathroom, so I put them on and tucked the pants in so I wouldn't trip and fall any harder than I already had.

Then I looked around to be sure I had what I could take. The jerk could have my clothes. I opened the door of the steamy bathroom and tried to keep my voice even. "You have a message on the machine, Jeff."

"Okay. I'll get it in a minute. This feels great. Want to get in here with me?"

I shut the bathroom door gently.

"I think not," I said as I let myself out of his apartment.

Zeke looked up in surprise when I came in with wild hair wearing too-big clothes and a scowl. "This does not bode well," he commented dryly.

I threw myself onto the bed. "He has a fiancée, and she called and left a message while he was in the shower."

"I'm sorry, Honey."

"I guess I should've asked if he was attached. Silly me, I assumed he was free because he acted that way."

"You shouldn't have to ask a man if he's single."

"I wanted to yank up that phone and tell her the truth. Save her the heartache. But then I thought I should stay out of it. With any luck, he'll accidentally kick my bra behind the toilet and it can do the talking."

Zeke laughed. "I'm glad to see you haven't lost your sense of humor."

"I'm okay. My pride has taken a hit, but it'll mend."

"Maybe this will be a wake-up call to him. He has a lot to learn. But then he's only twenty."

"How do you know that?"

"I asked about him at Headquarters. Did he tell you something different?"

"He told me he was twenty-five."

"He's a liar on several fronts, then."

"Zeke, I want to say that I didn't mean for this to happen. I was shocked when Jeff told you we were going to spend the night together."

"I'm not scandalized, if that's what's worrying you. I'm well aware that you're a grown woman."

"It's not like me, though."

"It's all right to take comfort when you have the chance. Sometimes it's nice just to be held by another human being."

"That's true. I don't usually like short-term relationships, but I enjoyed that one."

"Well then? No harm done. You shouldn't be so hard on yourself." After a few moments he asked, "Why did you leave your clothes?"

"They were in the bathroom and so was he. I didn't want to go in to get them. He can have them."

My cell phone rang. I picked it up, looked at it, and then dropped it.

"Was that Jeff?"

"Yup."

Then Zeke's phone rang. I only heard his half of the conversation, but it wasn't hard to imagine the other half.

"No, Jeff, I don't believe she wants to speak with you." Pause. "Well she would have answered her phone if she wanted that." Pause.

"How would she have misunderstood?" Longer pause. "I don't think she's angry; it's more like disgusted."

I gave Zeke the thumbs-up.

"No. No, I don't believe you did anything as dramatic as break her heart." Zeke winked at me. There was another pause. "Stop talking, young man. Yes, I know, but apologizing to me is futile, and I don't believe Margarita wants to hear it either. You acted in bad faith, and to try to justify it is folly."

There was another pause and then Zeke said, "I'm her father for God's sake, not a priest! I don't have to absolve you of your sins, nor do I want to know them."

I couldn't stifle a laugh.

Zeke paused again while Jeff whined or whatever.

Then Zeke cut him off. "It would be wise if you brought my daughter's clothes and anything else she left at your place. Leave them at the front desk. I'll take your pants and shirt to headquarters when I go tomorrow morning. If you return her things today, I won't feel the need to mention your behavior in class as an example of conduct unbecoming an officer of the law."

Zeke had this. I went to shower.

After we ate, my father and I knuckled down on the Valentino mystery even though the sun was bright and warm and there were more enjoyable things to do on a Sunday. I wanted to find a park with grass and trees and run until Officer Grabby was a comically sad bump on a wrong turn. Zeke still wanted to go dancing. I was all for that and anything else except rapin', murderin', cheatin', lyin' sons-a-bitches.

Valentino was now an official Texas Rangers case, but there was no rule to say I couldn't help my father with footwork and thinking. For a while we discussed the interviews I'd done, but whatever information I had gleaned seemed solid and no probable culprits popped up.

"I have an idea," I said after a long time of blank brain. "Maybe we should go see Donny Delmar."

"What are you thinking?"

"He's had some time in jail, right? That means time to settle down and think. He was intimate with Evelyn Valentino, so there's a possibility he knew if someone bothered her or caused her problems. Maybe she was afraid of someone. And it's not out of the realm of possibilities that she was having an affair with someone else."

"You have a good point. I think you should go alone, though."

"But I'm not even officially a part of this case."

"I'll go with you; I just won't go in to see Donny because I think he's the type of man who'll respond more openly to a woman, don't you?"

I stared at him. "Oh. So you want me to slut it up and go in there and work him like a pro."

"Aye Dios mío." Zeke rubbed his forehead with the fingers of his right hand. "I don't want to think about what 'slut it up' would look like on my daughter."

"I guess you're about to find out."

"No; I will not."

"Isn't that what lawmen expect from lawwomen in the way of help?"

"Hold on here. What are you trying to say to me?"

"There are only two women in the Texas Rangers. Why do you think that is?"

"You know what? I'm *one* Texas Ranger. I'm not the Texas Rangers any more than you're the Brewster County Sheriff's Office." He took out his phone. "Let's call the director and ask him why more of us aren't women."

"Okay, forget I said anything."

"I think you're angry with one lawman and now you want to take it out on me because I'm a lawman. I have some anger issues with women. Would you like it if I jumped on you about them? I mean, one woman is the same as another, right?"

"Okay. You've made your point. I get it."

"Why are we fighting? All I'm thinking is that Delmar sees me as the lawman who brought him in and therefore the enemy. He's unsure who you are. He may still think you'll give him twenty thousand dollars for all we know. He's not the brightest crayon, as you noticed."

"I see what you mean."

"If you'd rather not do this, then just say so."

"I want to do it."

"Don't pick fights with me, Margarita. You're young and inexperienced. I've got heartaches older than you."

Donny Delmar was in the county jail waiting to be charged by the D.A. on Monday, or whatever was the next step in the process. Toto and I were not in Brewster County anymore.

As Zeke and I walked towards the place, he spoke animatedly and put his hand at the base of my neck in an affectionate gesture.

I put my arm around his waist and hugged myself against his side. "I'm sorry I mouthed off to you, Zeke. You're right that I'm aggravated with one lawman and was taking it out on another. I don't even know why. Jeff was only a comfort stop and I knew that going in."

"What he did was wrong. That was a rude and cruel good-bye." He squeezed my neck gently. "I'm glad he was a comfort to you, however briefly."

Zeke had arranged the jail visit with practically a snap of his fingers. There was something to this Texas Ranger thing, and I intended to find out why there were so few women. But I would do it when I was in a better mood.

Donny Delmar was happy to have a visitor, but he was surprised to see it was me. He was cuffed to the front, not chained and shackled like Kiko, and he was never bolted to the floor. It was ironic because Donny was the more dangerous one.

After we got past the macho posturing, rough language, and other bullshit, I brought up the subject of the Valentino rape and murders.

"What are you in this deal?" he wondered. "Those guys never said if you were in on my arrest or not."

"I got into some trouble, and I had to help them or go to prison."

His eyes grew wide. "You did?"

"Yes."

"So you're a bad girl?"

You better know it, buster. "Now the Rangers are trying to figure out who raped and killed Evelyn Valentino, and I have to help them."

"Who cares who offed her?"

"The law cares. And her husband does. Her family does."

"I thought her old man did it."

"They say he didn't."

"Well, why do they think I know something?"

"You were having sex with her. They think she may have mentioned that she was afraid of somebody or that someone was giving her a hard time."

"That bitch wasn't afraid of nobody."

"Were you aware of anyone giving her a hard time?"

"Nah, just me." He laughed.

"Do you think she could've been having an affair with somebody besides you?"

He frowned. "Maybe; but how would I know that?"

"She could have mentioned a name, or you accidentally overheard something you weren't supposed to hear."

He shook his head. "No, nothin' like that. I fucked her; I didn't live her life."

"If you think of something will you call Zeke Pacheco?" I handed him his card.

"He's the guy who makes you help him?"

"He's in charge of the investigation."

He leered at me. "Do you have to do sex with him, too?"

"He's a Texas Ranger."

"So they don't like sex with women or what?"

"We never discuss sex."

Donny was incredulous.

It was over. I stood. Once the prisoner got on the subject of sex, I felt I had lost control of the interview. It was either leave or smack the crap out of a cuffed man, so I got ready to make my exit.

Donny said, "I just thought of something. I don't know if it will help you, but there was a man who messed with her at work."

I sat back down. "Did she give you his name?"

"I don't know if she knew his name."

"In what way did he bother her?"

"He always made sure he got seated in her section, and he asked her out all the time, even though she explained that she was married. He patted her ass and tried to brush against her boobs. She didn't like him. She said he told her one time that he'd followed her home from work. He liked her house and especially liked it that she had children. It was afternoon, and he saw a swing set in the yard. He went on about how he wants a family and asked for personal details about the kids. She thought he was creepy."

"Did you ever see the guy?"

"Sure. I seen him."

"What did he look like?"

"He looks like an overgrown kid. He has red hair and freckles. He's kind of chubby, but not real fat. He has a babyish face. I don't think he would've killed her."

I thought differently.

Zeke had been watching the interview, but he didn't know Donny had described Aaron Franklin, Kiko's attorney, until I told him.

"This is the biggest break we've had," he said excitedly. "If it was him, no wonder he didn't represent Kiko adequately."

"He wanted Kiko to go down for it."

"Do you think Aaron Franklin is a sick freak?"

I didn't have to think about it. "I think it's possible. He spoke of Kiko with such derision. It would explain why if he was jealous of him and wanted what Kiko had."

"But wait; we don't know for sure if it was him."

"Wouldn't it be a huge coincidence if it wasn't? Aaron Franklin is pudgy and kid-faced. He has red hair and freckles. How likely is it for two men who meet that description to be involved in this case?"

"On the night of the murders, Franklin may have seen Kiko come home and make love to her. That could've put a stalker over the edge. We need his DNA."

"When you say 'we,' are you referring to you and the mouse in your pocket, or are you asking me to get it for you?"

"Yes. I'm asking my smart-aleck child to help me get it."

"I have an idea."

Zeke kept it together as I told him the tragic story of his mother. He chewed his lip, gnawed on his thumbnail, and occasionally sighed. At times his eyes filled with tears. It was an extreme relief that he accepted the message I wanted him to have: his parents had loved him until the end of their lives.

It was when I brought out the photos of Lucia dressed in finery that Zeke broke down. What did it was the one of her reaching to him as he babbled to her. Her look of adoration brought a clear message forty-six years after the fact and he got it.

We cried a while and held each other.

Zeke wiped his eyes on the hem of his shirt. "My parents didn't even live long enough to become adults by today's standards, but they lived honorably. It means everything to me to know that and to know I was loved. How can I ever thank you for bringing them to me?"

"You don't need to thank me. I found them for myself as much as for you. I'm just glad you're happy."

We expressed our wonder and gratitude that Lucia and Max's blood was in him and therefore also in me. Zeke pointed out that someday I would pass that legacy on to my children.

Chapter 37

The next morning, I called Franklin's office under the pretext of making a delivery that only he could sign for. They were expecting him in at ten. We had a delivery all right, but he wasn't going to want it.

Aaron Franklin serving as Kiko's attorney was no coincidence in my opinion and Zeke agreed. I asked if he'd call the clerk of the circuit court for me to save time. It would take me all day and "all you have to do is snap your fingers."

He gave me a look.

"Well? When you say, 'I'm Sergeant Zeke Pacheco of the Texas Rangers,' people listen up and hop to it. When I say I'm Deputy Ricos of the Brewster County Sheriff's Office, they yawn or act stupid."

Zeke laughed but he made the call. He told them he needed to know how the lawyer had been assigned in the case of Francisco Valentino. He gave the date of arrest and the date of the trial and answered a few questions. They would be glad to get that information for him, of course, and someone would call him right back.

When Zeke told me what they said my response was, "See? I rest my case."

Next, Zeke called his Austin office and told them he needed the home address of a lawyer named Aaron Franklin. I had been unable to locate that in the phone book or by cajoling his secretary.

After twenty minutes, someone from the clerk's office returned Zeke's call. I waited impatiently to know for a fact what I already suspected.

"An attorney was assigned to the case," Zeke explained when he got off the phone, "but Aaron Franklin came in and said he knew the family and would take the case pro bono."

"Yet he told Kiko the case had been assigned to him by the court."

"Yep; your theory is correct, Margarita. He wanted the case."

"Kiko had everything Franklin wanted so he took it all away from him. Yet he destroyed it, so he can't have it either."

"That's classic stalker behavior. They often destroy what they love or think they love. Stalkers are dangerous. If some man ever acts this way with you—"

"I'll call you."

"You'd better."

Zeke's phone rang again and he answered, "Pacheco." There was a pause while someone else spoke. Then Zeke began writing down an address. "Thanks Mike. Yep. You know it. Adiós." He handed it to me. "Here you go." He glanced at his watch. "It's eight-forty already. You better get going if you plan to follow him."

"I'm going. Zeke, do you realize you almost certainly have family in Mexico? You'd have uncles and aunts and cousins at least."

"Yes. I realize that."

"Don't you want to meet them?"

"Please don't start pushing. I'm trying to get used to the idea that my parents weren't what I thought. I have you, and I think that's family enough for me for now. I find the thought of a bunch of relatives overwhelming."

"But they could fill in even more information about your parents."

"You're pushing."

"Sorry." I zipped it and left to tail a sicko.

My hair was loose instead of in a French braid, and I wore sunglasses and dressed in a casual, nondescript way, with running shoes. A person who knew me wouldn't be fooled, but someone who had only seen me once would be; I hoped.

It was Monday, so my favorite doorman was back on duty. He held the door as wide as he could get it as I sprinted towards him. His mischievous grin could make a person's day. I stopped because he held up his hand.

"Running Gal, a man left something for you at the desk yesterday afternoon. They were supposed to call you."

"They did; thanks. I'll get it when I come back."

Then he flashed that grin again. "Who is it that chases you every day?"

I returned the grin. "I'm chasing somebody."

"Ah."

I put the sunglasses on and began to jog.

Franklin lived in an apartment building four blocks from his office, according to a map of Dallas I consulted before leaving. It was a three-mile run from our hotel. What I hoped is that he would walk to work and, on the way, discard a cigarette, coffee cup, water bottle, or anything.

I made it only two blocks before I had to stop for a traffic light. I didn't look around, so I didn't notice the somewhat overweight, out-of-breath man who ran up behind me. I did notice the needle prick of pain in my back and before I could cry out, the world went fuzzy and my knees buckled.

Arms caught and steadied me. As the drug took effect, he spoke into my ear, as if he were a lover who had just encountered me on the street. People passed, but no one asked if I needed help.

"Just walk with me," he whispered and an arm went around my shoulders. "If you make a sound I'll kill you."

I couldn't focus well enough to see his face, but I knew the so-called man was Aaron Franklin. "Wha…want…" Talking was useless, but I was conscious enough to know without doubt that he would kill me.

"You just couldn't leave well enough alone." He continued talking because I couldn't stop him.

There was a cell phone in my pocket, but how would I use it? I thought of Zeke only a few blocks away. Before I blacked out, I thought of Max and Lucia and how nothing about life is fair.

When I came to, my head hurt so much I didn't want to open my eyes. It sounded like I was in a hospital. How had I gotten to a hospital? I tried to think back, but it was useless. Someone was holding my hand and I thought it was Zeke. It was comforting, but I had so many questions.

"Margarita?" He squeezed my hand. "You're safe now. Can you open your eyes?" Since he was speaking Spanish, I thought it was Papi.

I opened one eye to find out and gradually Zeke came into focus. He smiled. "Everything is all right."

The last thing I knew, I was standing on a street corner and—what? Pain. Had I been hit by a bus? That's how I felt.

Zeke pulled up a chair and sat next to the bed. He took my hand again. "Do you remember what happened?"

I shook my head.

"Aaron Franklin tried to abduct you about two blocks from the hotel. Thanks to Tommy Landon, we were able to intercept him."

"Who is Tommy whoever-you-said?"

"He's the doorman at the hotel, the one who teases you all the time."

"You're saying Tommy saved me?"

"Yes. Before you went down to the lobby, he had noticed a man on the sidewalk acting suspiciously. When you ran out, that guy took off after you. Tommy yelled to one of their security team that he was in pursuit. I walked out of the elevator right after that, and the guy saw my badge and weapon. He asked me to help and we ran. When he said someone had taken off after a running woman, I nearly had a heart attack. Tommy was already sitting on Franklin when we got to the scene."

"So Tommy is a hero."

"Most definitely."

"I knew I liked that man."

"Aaron Franklin is in the county jail and a swab of his DNA is in the lab."

"So I did get his DNA."

Zeke laughed. "You sure did, but you got it the hard way."

"Anything to bag a perp for my father."

"He's refusing to cooperate, but that won't matter. Some of Evelyn Valentino's things were found in his apartment, along with surreptitious photos he took of her and her family."

"That's great."

"And those two missing knives?"

"He kept them?"

"Yes, and you'll love this. He was offered counsel but he refused. He plans to represent himself."

"In that case, he's sure to lose."

Sometimes life is fair after all.

Chapter 38

The next day I was released from the hospital, and Zeke took me back to the hotel. Tommy saluted and opened the door as wide as it would go when he saw us coming. He had a big ol' grin on his face and his dark eyes were luminous.

I hugged him and burst into tears.

"Don't cry, Running Gal." He held me tightly.

"How can I ever thank you?" I sobbed.

"There, there," he patted my back. "I didn't do a thing some other man standing here wouldn't have done. Nobody takes off after a guest like that and gets away with it." He hugged me tightly. "That goes double for you, Running Gal."

"You're a hero," I said against his chest.

"I'm just a man who does what he can."

That's exactly what a hero is.

Later, Zeke said Tommy would be given a commendation by the Texas Rangers.

I continued to express my wonder at the fact that he had saved me.

Zeke put his arm around me. "Do you remember when you commented, and somewhat testily, that you weren't being paid for your work on this case?"

"I remember."

"I reminded you that you were paying it forward. This is the kind of thing that happens when you pay it forward."

Zeke and I went to tell Kiko the great news about his case. He listened with tears running down his face, but he was also smiling.

His first question was, "When do I get out?"

"I can't tell you that for certain," Zeke said.

I thought it was wrong that an innocent man had to spend even one more hour in that horrible place, but I don't make the rules or always agree with them.

Zeke went on to explain that he needed the report from the crime lab before he could proceed with the necessary paperwork. "I have reports to make and then we'll make formal notification to the court. Margarita has taken the liberty of hiring an attorney for you, a good one. It's James Fowler. He'll stay on top of it."

"James Fowler! He's the best lawyer in Dallas people say. How much did it cost, Margarita? I'll pay you back once I start working again."

It was fifteen thousand dollars for the retainer, but Kiko didn't need to know that. "Don't worry about repaying me. I have money that was left to me by a man who died recently. He didn't always do the right thing in his life, but I'm using the money he left to right some of those wrongs by helping people in his memory."

"What was his name?"

"Emilio Martez."

Kiko looked up at the ceiling. "Well, thank you, Emilio Martez. I don't know what else to say. Isn't there something I can do for you, Margarita?"

"Instead of doing something for me, do something kind for someone else."

"That's a promise." Kiko started to stand and was reminded by his restraints that he was still bolted to the floor. "I want to hug you, but I can't even stand up."

I went to him and gave him a big hug. "If you need anything else, you'll call one of us, right?"

He nodded tearfully.

Zeke hugged Kiko and said, "I'll be in touch soon. Your attorney will be by this week to meet you and explain what to expect. If you feel he's not working out, please call Margarita or me."

"Yes. I will."

My last glimpse of Kiko was this: A guard disconnected him from the floor while another one watched. Then the prisoner was helped up by the guards, and he stood still while the chains were reconnected to the cuffs. Kiko was looking at the drab prison ceiling, but I thought he was seeing the sky.

Zeke and I went by the crime lab to say good-bye to Michael Wingman and thank him for his help.

He shrugged off our praise. "Oh, you did all the hard work. I just mix a little of this with a bit of that and—"

"And save the whole world." I finished the sentence for him.

He turned every shade of red. He started to speak but instead, hugged me. "We never had that dinner you owe me."

"The next time I'm in Dallas, we'll go."

"I won't forget. I have a scientist's mind for details."

I laughed.

"If you come back, I'll know it," he warned. "I have spies everywhere."

I promised I would call him.

We went from the lab to see the Dallas P.D. man in charge of setting up the class Zeke had taught. As we walked down the hall, a strong hand took me by the elbow and pulled me away from my father's side.

"I know you don't want to speak to me, but I need to speak to you," said Officer Grabby.

Zeke stepped towards him.

"It's okay," I said to my father. "I want to hear what he has to say."

"I'll be right over here." A threatening-faced Zeke took up a watchful post near a counter to be sure Grabby wasn't up to something sinister.

I gave the officer an expectant look, but I didn't say anything because I didn't know what there was to say.

"I'm sorry," he said. "I want to give you a bunch of excuses and reasons but it'll make you think I'm lamer than what you already think. I screwed up. That's all I can say in the way of explaining, so I hope that's clear enough for you."

"It is."

"I really, truly like you. I'm sorry I messed it up so badly."

"I liked you, but…"

"Could we just leave it at that?"

"Okay. Adiós, Officer Grabby."

"Adiós, Margarita."

That was the last time I ever saw him.

"I need to do one more thing," Zeke said. We were standing on the sidewalk outside police headquarters. He glanced at his watch and then at me. "Do you trust me?"

"Yes; of course I do."

I followed where Zeke led, which was to a building on the same block and then into a large room with about thirty chairs and twenty-odd people.

There was no sign, not one indication of what this was about, but I knew.

"Please sit," Zeke said. "If you don't like it for any reason, you're free to go after five minutes. Please give it five minutes."

I'm free to go right now, I thought in my obstinate way, but out of respect for my father I stayed. That was what I told myself.

A man went to the podium. "Hi. My name is Rick. I'm an alcoholic."

"Hi, Rick," responded the group.

Groan.

So it went around the room. It was so lame.

Zeke took my hand when it was almost his turn. His hand was trembling. I looked over at him out of concern and realized my hand was shaking, too. In a moment of sobering clarity, I knew I belonged there. Yes, it was lame all right, but how lame is it to let drinking, even thoughts of drinking, control your life?

So when it was my turn I jumped in. "My name is Margarita. I'm an alcoholic."

Chapter 39

A few weeks after we returned from Dallas, Zeke and I made another trip together. We were going to look for whatever remnants of family we might have in a pueblito that sits in the foothills of the Sierra Madre on the Cuidad Chihuahua side.

It was Zeke's idea, and I hadn't pushed him or even mentioned it again. I was excited to go, but he was much more reserved.

"I'm afraid of the whole family thing," he said more than once. "I've never had one and I can't even imagine it."

"It will be okay, Zeke. They'll love you and you will probably love them, too."

"I guess that's what's scaring me. I've never had more than one or two people loving me at one time. Will it be weird?"

I laughed. "I think you'll like it. If you don't, they're in Mexico and you won't have to see them often. I hope you keep an open mind because family is wonderful. I can't explain it; you'll have to see for yourself."

"What if we find out that my parents weren't as great as we think?"

"Stop it. Now you're just looking for problems. The chance of that is nil. Everyone they met loved them. Don't you think their own family loved them too?"

"You seem so sure of everything."

"I'm not sure of anything, but why not hope for the best? Besides, I know Mexican families. In general, they are great big loving organisms. Also, generally speaking again, they are large enough that *somebody* will love us."

Zeke laughed and appeared to calm down.

A few days before, I had called the office of the mayor in the little town that Max and Lucia had called home. I was told the

Rodriguez family still lived on a ranch near there, and the same was true of the Pacheco family. I asked about telephones, but she refused to give me that information. She said some people have cell phones but the service is terrible, and besides, she still didn't have the numbers.

She offered to take them a message but I declined. I didn't think I should leave a message about something as important as a nephew/grandson/cousin they had never seen and probably thought was dead.

When I asked if the ranches were hard to find, she said, "You can ask anybody in town and they'll tell you how to get to them. The families are well-known here and the ranches are side-by-side. When you find one, you've found them both."

So Zeke and I had family. I was excited and a little nervous. Zeke was freaking.

Before we went to meet our family, I went alone to the grave of Emilio Martez. It was something I wanted to do and, at the same time, didn't. I was near Chihuahua, though, and I felt I'd always regret it if I didn't go. I didn't need any more regrets.

The only thing I know for sure about death is that the person you love doesn't come back. You have to figure out how to go on. There is something comforting—not comforting, but final—about saying good-bye out loud even when you know the person isn't there. I guess it's symbolic.

The site was marked by a flat piece of marble into which was carved, "Rest in peace, my son. You will always be loved."

I told Emilio what I needed to say: I hadn't fully forgiven him for lying to me, but I understood it as well as I ever would. He had begged me not to quit loving him and I never did. But now I had to. I explained that I was using his money to help right a wrong, and I thanked him for that opportunity.

288

I told him, from my heart, the honest truth that I wouldn't have told anyone else: "I would do it all again if only for the chance to put my face against your chest."

My father had a death grip on my hand as we approached the door of the main house at Rancho Rodriguez. There was a group of young children playing in the yard.

"Who are you?" they asked with the unmasked curiosity of children.

"I'm Zeke and this is Margarita. Who are you?"

"I'm Tomas Rodriguez and this is my sister, Elizabeth, and these are my cousins, Jaime, Freddy, and Julia. Do you have children we can play with?"

"This is my baby," Zeke said, and the little boy's look was incredulous.

"I grew up," I said and tousled his hair.

We continued to the house.

When we knocked, a woman came to the door. "Buenas tardes."

We greeted her and said we were looking for members of the Rodriguez family.

"We are the Rodriguez family, and this is our ranch." She invited us to come in before we said who we were.

When I said I was Margarita Ricos, that meant nothing, but when Zeke said, "I'm Zeke Pacheco," her smile faded and her mouth opened. "Zeke Pacheco? You're…" She was speechless a moment and stepped closer to him. "You're?"

"I'm Zeke Pacheco, the son of Lucia and Max Pacheco."

"Oh Dios mío!" Her hands went to her face and then to her heart. She began to cry and laugh and hug Zeke. "We looked for you for so long. I'm Lupita, Lucia's youngest sister. I'm your tía!"

When Zeke extricated himself from her, he introduced me as his daughter. She fell apart double. It was amazing enough that baby Zeke had survived, but that he had a child was just too much. She hugged me and her exclamations became mostly only sounds and more and more excited.

"Tomas!" she yelled a few times. "He's nearly deaf. I'll have to go get him."

She disappeared. Zeke looked at me and shrugged.

In a few moments, she was back bringing a man who looked like her. "This is your tío, Tomas, my brother and Lucia's."

We went through more hugging and exclamations of wonder and disbelief. Their excitement brought everyone into the room. There were more introductions as we met cousins, second cousins, and a few third cousins.

"We've always loved you," Lupita said to Zeke. "We prayed you were alive. It was so hard on us to not know what happened to you. When Lucia died, we had to accept that, but we couldn't accept that we had lost you, too."

We talked for a while about Lucia, and Zeke explained that he never knew his parents names until a few weeks ago.

Lupita said the priest came and told the family he had taken a confession from someone local who knew about their grandson. She had admitted that she and her husband had sold him to rich people in Fort Worth. She claimed to be heartbroken over what she had done. He would never give them her name because she had told him during confession.

Then Lucia's friend, Claudia, came to them several months after Lucia died and admitted what she and her husband had done. Her husband had forced her to do it. He had been involved in drugs and was heavily addicted. Since then he'd died in a drug deal gone wrong. She hadn't even gotten the names of the people she'd sold the baby to. Lupita sobbed at the memory.

When she recovered, she started to say something about Max and then she cried out, "Max! Have you spoken with Max?"

Zeke and I stared at her and then at each other.

"Your father! Have you seen him yet?"

"My father is alive?" Zeke had sprung to his feet.

"Yes; he lives at the next ranch. You haven't seen him."

"I was told he died in prison."

"We thought so too at first. Zeke, Max's father, went to claim his body and it wasn't him. There was a big mix-up at the prison. Max came home while his father was off trying to claim his body. Imagine our relief and happiness."

She jumped up. "My God! Max will be so happy. He looked for you for so many years. He still talks about you, Zeke. You must go to him right now. He never gave up hope that he would find you somehow. Instead, you have found him."

"Just go about a mile down the road," explained one of the cousins, "and you'll come to his house. It's the first one on the left. You can't miss it. The rest of us will come over after a while."

We went back to the rental car, but Zeke just sat there.

"Are you all right, Zeke?"

"My father is alive." His eyes were sparkling. "I am going to meet my father," he said slowly, as if trying out the feel of the words. "I. Zeke Pacheco. Have. A. Father. I can't believe it!"

"I'm so happy for you Zeke. And I have a grandfather!" It seemed unreal to me that I would get to meet Max, a man I had chased for days and felt I already knew.

At last, Zeke started the car and we proceeded down the unpaved road to the Pacheco Ranch. There was a sign before we reached the house: Hermanos Pacheco or in English, Pacheco Brothers.

Zeke took a deep breath and opened the car door. My heart was thumping against walls on the other side of the country.

An energetic man came down the steps. He looked younger than I imagined, but it was Max. I waved and he waved, but he didn't know who we were yet.

Zeke took my hand and we walked towards him.

Max's eyes and mouth grew wide. "You can only be my son."

"I am your son."

Tears stood in his clear brown eyes. "You look exactly like your mother."

The two embraced and Max tried to speak but couldn't. Sometimes there are no words.

Zeke sobbed against his father's shoulder. It was heart wrenching and also the happiest, most incredible, astounding thing I ever witnessed.

Max reached out his arm and drew me into the huddle. We stood there crying and holding each other.

Max said, "I looked for you a long, long time. I was limited by finances, documents, and lack of English. My father let me mortgage his ranch for the money to hire an attorney to search for you. He didn't have any better luck than I did."

Zeke opened his mouth but nothing came out.

Max's hair was still dark. I calculated that he must be about sixty-four years of age, but he seemed younger. He was not an especially tall man, but he was regal in bearing. Though not handsome in the way of his son, he had character and it shone from within. He struck me as being the best possible kind of man.

"Oh how I wish my parents had lived to see this day, Zeke. How proud and happy they would be."

Then Max turned his crystal eyes on me. "You must be Zeke's daughter."

"Yes. I'm Margarita."

He held me close to his heart and then kissed me on the cheek.

Zeke wiped his eyes. "We thought you died in prison."

"Everyone thought that until I came home. I was so happy to get out of that place and excited to go back to you and your mother. My whole world fell apart in a few days, but enough of that. Someday I'll tell you my story."

He motioned towards the house. "Please come inside and tell me everything. I want to know every small detail about you. I love you so much, Son. I never let myself believe you were dead."

That day we learned that Max had remarried after almost six years and built a new life for himself. Through hard work, he and his brothers had made their ranch prosper. He and his wife, Elsa, had raised two daughters. Zeke had sisters living in Chihuahua. He seemed stunned by that news, but I thought he was excited.

When we met Elsa, it was evident she and Max were in love. She treated Zeke as if she had been waiting all her life to meet him, and she melted over me. She touched my face, exclaimed over my beauty, caressed my cheek, and spoke soft words of love. You bet I fell in love with her. She was exactly the abuela (grandmother) I had longed for.

Later, when we were alone with Max and he spoke of Lucia, it was with great emotion. He never forgot her, he said, and carries her in his heart.

"I wish I could have known her," Zeke said.

"You knew her, Son. You think you don't remember, but there is a part of you that does. She lives in you. You even look like her. When you walked towards me earlier, my first thought was *Lucia*."

I was so interested in Max I hadn't noticed Zeke watching me.

When he caught my eye, I mouthed, "I love you, Zeke."

He smiled the most beautiful, love-filled smile I had ever seen on his face.

Though she is no longer in this world, Lucia's love is still here.

AFTERWORDS

A few words about Max and Lucia:

The story of Max and Lucia is all too real for many people coming to this country. The things that happened to them in this novel have happened to people I know, and many of the things were experienced by one person I know well.

The United States offers a glittering promise of a better life, and we offer jobs for men and women willing to work hard. To lure our neighbors here with our promises and then mistreat, demonize, and even kill them is immoral. My prayer is that we will quit doing it. I speak out every chance I have. Will you?

This is a work of fiction, but Max and Lucia are real.

About Deputy Margarita Ricos

Margarita Ricos is a 26 year old sheriff's deputy in Brewster county West Texas. She's smart. She's courageous. She has a lot of heart. She's a *Chicana* with attitude who grew up on the edge of the United States. There, the peoples and cultures of two countries are blended, more than separated, by the once-fierce Rio Grande.

Terlingua is an unincorporated settlement built around a mer-Cury-mining ghost town of the same name. It lies in the southern part of Brewster County, the largest county in the largest state in the lower forty-eight. It has more square miles than inhabitants and more mountains than you can count: tall, short, wide, narrow, jagged, rounded, naked, stunning mountains.

Margarita and her partner, Deputy Barney George, are entrusted with preserving the peace and upholding the law in a land where the flowers and people grow wild.

Because Margarita was raised on the edge of the United States, she has a broad perspective of "the border," its people, and its issues. In spite of its problems, she chooses to remain in the vast land of mountains and desert, a muddy, winding river, fiery sunsets, unique dangers, and indescribable beauty.

Margarita is an advocate of justice and fairness in a world that is neither. She takes comfort in the steadfastness of the scenery she adores and her love for and commitment to her community.

Made in the USA
Columbia, SC
25 May 2020